the WIZARD'S promise

Part 1 – *The Doomspell*

'High fantasy, richly imagined and refreshingly well-written … an excellent novel.'
Sunday Times

'a great new voice in writing for children … an incredible world in which the reader will become totally absorbed.'
The Bookseller

'gripping … racy … [children] have been fighting to borrow it.'
The Guardian

'a vivid world of magical possibilities.'
The Times

Part 2 – *The Scent of Magic*

'McNish tells a rattling good tale, and his well-plotted narrative races through some excellent twists and turns to a spectacular climax.'
The Daily Telegraph

'The language used is rich and evocative, full of visual and sensory imagery …'
School Librarian

'carried off with a verve, pace and sheer passion for pure storytelling … compulsive.'
Amazon

'This is a children's book full of inventive touches … great ideas, evocative descriptions, and page-turning pace.'
Vector

'a spellbinding read full of excitement and suspense. A brilliant sequel to *The Doomspell*.'
Cool Reads

Part 3 – *The Wizard's Promise*

'A fast-paced, gripping read.'
Times Educational Supplement

'this is breathtaking, swashbuckling stuff …'
Birmingham Post

the
WIZARD'S
PROMISE

Cliff McNish

Dolphin Paperbacks

For my mother – there for us all

Find out more about Cliff McNish and the world of *The Doomspell* at
www.cliffmcnish.com

First published in Great Britain in 2002
by Orion Children's Books
This paperback edition first published 2003
by Dolphin paperbacks
a division of the Orion Publishing Group Ltd
Orion House
5 Upper St Martin's Lane
London   WC2H 9EA

A catalogue record for this book is
available from the British Library

Printed in Great Britain by
Clays Ltd, St Ives plc

ISBN 1 85881 844 3

contents

1

schools without children

As Rachel awoke, her information spells automatically swept the house for threats. They probed into each room, an extra set of senses watching out for her.

Nothing out of the ordinary, they reported. Mum lay in her usual morning bath. Dad was in the study, trying to touch his toes. The information spells delved further out. In the garden, two froglets were wondering whether to make a break for it across the dangerous lawn. Next door's dog hid behind a shed, thinking no one else knew about his juicy bone.

Rachel smiled, peering out of her bedroom window. A flock of geese passed by, and, just for a moment, as she gazed up at those birds, and listened to the familiar sounds of home and garden, it was as if nothing had changed in the world.

Then a group of under-fives cut across the sky.

The youngsters flew in tight formation, led by a boy. Rachel guessed he might be three years old, probably less. The group travelled with arms pinned neatly to their sides, little heads thrust proudly ahead. Their eyes all shone some tint of blue, the distinctive colour of flying spells.

The slower geese scattered nervously when the children crossed their path.

Getting up, Rachel brushed out her long dark hair and strolled downstairs to the kitchen. Her younger brother, Eric, sat at the dining table. A bowl of cornflakes crackled satisfyingly in front of him.

'You know, if I had magic,' he said, tucking in, 'I wouldn't bother with flying or the other stuff. I'd just use a spell to keep the taste of cornflakes in my mouth forever.'

'You'd soon get sick of it,' Rachel answered.

'No,' Eric said earnestly. 'I wouldn't.' He waved his spoon at the departing toddlers. 'Those little 'uns are probably long-distance racers. Must be, practising like that. They're so *serious*. At their age I was still happy just chucking things at you.'

'Mm.' Rachel glanced round, expecting to see the prapsies. The prapsies were a mischievous pair of creatures – feathered body of a crow, topped with a baby's face – that had once served a Witch on another world. Usually Eric put them up to some prank when Rachel first came down in the morning.

'Where are the boys then?' she asked warily.

'I let them out early for a change,' Eric said. 'Told them to find me a gift, something interesting.'

'Did you send them far?'

'China.'

'Good.'

Rachel stared up at the rooftops of the town. It was a typical morning, with children all over the sky. A few were up high and alone, practising dead-stops in the tricky April winds. Most children had simply gathered in their usual groups in the clouds, friends laughing and joking together. A few houses down Rachel saw a boy cooing. As he did so a pair of doves, tempted from some thicket, rose to his hand. Further away a girl drifted casually across the sky, plucking cats from gardens. The cats trailed in a long line behind her, complaining mightily.

'Hey look!' Eric cried. 'Lightning-finders!'

Six teenagers were heading purposefully south, their arms raised like spikes.

'It's a brand new game started up by the thrill-seekers,' Eric said. 'You search for heavy weather, find the storms and dodge the lightning forks. Most competitions are held in the Tropics, where the really big storms are. I bet that's where those kids are off to.' He gazed wistfully after the teenagers, who had already disappeared over the horizon.

'What happens if they get hit by the lightning?'

'Bad things, I suppose,' Eric said. 'It's risky, but that's the whole point. Wouldn't be exciting otherwise, would it?'

Rachel shrugged. The new magical games didn't interest her much. She was more interested in those children stationed in the air, watching the skies for Witches.

Nearly a year had passed since the baby boy, Yemi, had released the magic of all the children on Earth. In that first glorious Awakening, there had been a superabundance of magic – enough for the Wizard leader, Larpskendya, to transport every child and adult on Earth to Trin.

When Rachel thought of that purple-skied, plant-filled world, it still hurt. The plants of Trin had a language of leaves so rich that even the Wizards could only guess the meaning of their graceful movements. But the plants were dying. The Witches had poisoned them. On a whim, they had contaminated Trin's soils. And slowly, as their magic drained away, the Trin plants were losing their minds. Each year the great leaves waved ever more frantically in the breezes as they struggled to hear each other.

It was not possible to stay on Trin for long. The special blossoming of magic following the Awakening soon faded, and the adults and children had to return home. But everyone understood: if the Witches could do this amount of damage to Trin, a world that meant nothing to them, what would happen if they returned to Earth? So everyone had prepared. For months children practised their defensive spells. Night and day they patrolled the skies, anticipating a massed attack of Witches that never came.

Meanwhile, Ool – the Witch home world – wrapped itself in hush. A battle, the Wizards knew, was taking place: a battle for control, between the High Witches Rachel and other children had fought before, and the more ferocious warrior-breed, the terrifying Griddas. For a long time Ool had been silent.

Larpskendya had no doubt the Griddas had won. It worried him because the Wizards knew so little about them. The Griddas had been bred by the High Witches, bred to be savage warriors, and kept underground. But the former High Witch leader, Heebra, had made the mistake of releasing them.

And, having tasted freedom, the Griddas had turned on their makers.

As Rachel gazed up at the sky, her slim freckled face perched on her hands, she wondered how ready the people of Earth were to face the Griddas. She also missed a friend. 'I wonder,' she said, half to herself, 'how Morpeth's doing? I miss him.'

'He's only been gone a few days,' Eric protested.

'I *still* miss him.'

'Actually, so do I, but it's his only visit back to Ithrea in ages. Larpskendya's picking him up in a few weeks.'

While Rachel thought fondly about Morpeth, three girls landed beside the garden pond. They walked across the lawn, waving hopefully through the glass doors of the patio.

'Oh no, part of your fan club,' groaned Eric. 'Do they never leave off?'

A few children always loitered near the house, curious to get a glimpse of Rachel. Her reputation drew them, and the sheer quality of her magic. Every child on Earth wanted to be closer to it.

'I've seen those three before,' Eric muttered. 'Two nights ago. It was raining, pouring down, but did they care? Barmy nutters.' He pulled a face, attempting to scare the girls away. 'Clear off!' he yelled. The girls smiled sweetly back. 'They never flipping listen to me,' Eric said. 'Why don't you give them a shock, Rach? You know, send them to the Arctic or something. It'll take them at least an hour to fly back.'

Two of the girls nudged each other forward, trying to get Rachel's attention. The other one looked steadily at Eric.

A little ruffled, he self-consciously smoothed out his baggy pyjamas.

Rachel laughed. 'I'm not the only one with admirers.'

'Can't you get rid of them?'

'Oh, I think we should let that pretty-looking girl in,' Rachel said. 'I can tell she wants to talk to you.'

'Don't you dare!'

The girls stood outside, hoping for a conversation. Rachel, however, had entertained too many admirers lately. She turned away from their stares, feeling a desire to get out of the house.

'Come on,' she said. 'We'll go for a walk.'

'You're joking, aren't you?' Eric said. 'There's no chance of slipping out quietly. The sky's thick with kids.'

'I'll shift us, then.'

'Where to?'

'Let's find the prapsies. Creep up on them, give 'em a scare.'

'Hey, nice idea. Just let me get dressed.'

'*I* could dress you.'

'No way,' Eric snorted. 'I'm not having your spells fiddling with my pyjamas.'

He thumped up the stairs, colliding with Mum.

'Careful,' Mum groaned. Pinning back her wet hair, she smiled at Rachel. 'Going out, love?'

'Yep.'

'You'll need a disguise from the fans, then.' She inspected her daughter critically. 'How about an older look? Add three years on and lose the freckles. Blonde and fifteen?'

Rachel smirked. 'Blonde's out, Mum. Hair fashion's changing.'

'What's in vogue these days?'

'Silver for boys, long and slicked back. With the girls, anything crazy.'

Mum shrugged. Children regularly used magic to alter their appearance now. Nothing surprised her any more.

'You want to come along with us, Mum? I'll take you wherever you like.'

'No, you go off and enjoy yourselves. I'll potter about here.'

Eric reappeared, wearing jeans and his woolly parka coat.

'Ready?' Rachel asked.

'I was born ready.' Hoiking up his collar, Eric noticed her new round-cheeked face. 'Good disguise,' he said. 'You look dumb. That's realistic. Better hide your magic scent, too.'

Rachel did so, kissed Mum lightly on the cheek – and *shifted*.

Immediately, without any sensation of flight, she and Eric had travelled a few miles from the house. Rachel was one of the few children in the world who possessed this skill – the ability to move instantaneously from one place to another.

They stood on the outskirts of town. Above them a boy flew by on some errand or other, his dad perched on his back. Rachel heard their laughter. Magic did not survive the passage to adulthood, but adults who wanted to fly could still enjoy that special thrill through children.

Rachel and Eric tramped up a long path. It brought them to Rachel's old nursery school.

'Oh, it's closed,' Eric said. 'I hadn't heard.'

A thick chain on the school gate barred the way inside. No notice of explanation was provided, or needed.

'Same everywhere,' Rachel said. 'This was the last one. Closed last week. You know what little kids are like – just want to be out playing.'

7

At first it had seemed an ominous development when children stopped turning up for school. But if you could fly, why sit in a classroom? The best teachers soon realized that traditional schooling offered nothing that could rival the fascination of magic. Why bother with textbook geography, with the world at your disposal? Children now went all over the world for their education, and teachers not afraid of flying in the arms of their students went with them.

'It's funny,' Eric noted, as they walked away. 'A couple of kids from my old school took the Head of Maths out flying yesterday. Did I tell you? Wanted to know about vectors and something called thrust quotations. Reckoned it might help them manoeuvre better in high winds.'

'Was he able to help them?'

'Yeah. They were practising with him last night,' Eric said.

'What? They took him out in the dark?'

'Sure. Why not. He was game for it, apparently. A true test for his theories, and all that. They say he enjoyed it, but it was a while before he could talk normally afterwards.'

A couple of sprinters swerved around Rachel. They flew close to the ground, the wind from their passage messing her hair. Eric laughed – knowing they were deliberately trying to goad Rachel into following them.

Flying games were the most popular new sports – fiercely competitive, fast and visible, with rules that were usually easy to master. Rachel could have won them all, and local teams were always trying to get her attention, but such displays didn't interest her. She led Eric from the nursery lane into an adjoining field. There were some rusty swings here and a dilapidated rocking horse. It was the sort of desultory old-style playground only a few children still used.

'Feebles,' Eric said, seeing two children there.

'Don't call them that,' Rachel snapped angrily. 'I *hate* that word.'

'It's what they're being called, Rach, whether you like it or not.'

A young boy and girl, seven or eight years old, sat on the wooden horse. The boy wore shorts and a wind-cheater, and looked cold. The girl had a long white skirt. She had hitched it up over her knees to help her clamber onto the frame. They sat astride the horse, rocking each other back and forth as best they could.

Eric sighed, glancing at Rachel. 'You're going to play with them, aren't you?'

'Just for a bit.'

'That's what you always say. Then it becomes hours.'

Rachel grinned. 'I like being with them. Anyway, these are new. I'm going to introduce myself. And don't call them feebles.'

The children on the rocking horse were the least talented children. Spell-gifts were not evenly distributed. After the initial rush of magic following the Awakening, it was discovered that a few children in each country had little magic – so little that it went virtually unnoticed. In a world where many children could fly effortlessly, others could still only dream of flying. None of these children could take part in the spell-games sprouting up all around, so Rachel had instead set up a programme where the most magical children spent time with them.

In the clouds above a boy the same age as the little girl

sped by, way out of her reach. She longingly followed him until he passed over some hills.

'Hey, who are you two?' Rachel asked, rushing over and putting the brother and sister at ease. The girl lifted her arms, wanting to be picked up. The boy hung back shyly.

'Get on,' Rachel said to them both, lowering her back so they could climb aboard. Then, gently, she rose skyward.

'I'm not scared,' the boy said fiercely.

Rachel laughed. 'I can see that!'

'Up! Up!' the little girl told her. 'Go faster!' As Rachel increased velocity, the girl cried out, 'I'm falling. I'm falling off!'

'No, you're not,' Rachel whispered into her ear. 'I'll never let you fall off!'

The girl gripped her neck, so happy to be paid attention by a child with magic.

For a while Rachel took directions from the brother and sister about what to do. They wanted to transform, so Rachel shifted halfway across the world. Soon the little girl and her brother were disguised in Asia, creeping in tangled forests, sneaking up on tiger cubs.

Finally, after Rachel had exhausted them with many kinds of magic, she took them back home. 'I'll come here tomorrow, if you like,' she said.

The girl sucked her thumb. 'Will you?'

'Promise.' Rachel fixed a time.

She left them with a wave and shifted back to the nursery, where she found Eric scowling. 'Hey, what's going on?' he said. 'I'm stuck out here, left like a twit by the kiddy swings. You said we were going to find the prapsies!'

'We are, we are. Stop moaning and climb on.' As Eric scrambled onto her back some of Rachel's favourite spells, her shifters, eased forward into her mind. She felt her whole body supercharging with exhilaration as they loosened up all their tremendous power.

Eric saw her eyes light up: a thousand glistening shades of blue.

'Get ready,' she told him, balancing on her toes.

'Oh-oh,' Eric said. 'A big trip, then. Where are you dragging us off to?'

'Wouldn't be a surprise if I gave it away.'

'How far? Come on. Just tell me.'

'Everest!'

'Oh no, not the flipping Himalayas again!' He seized her collar.

'Are you ready or not?'

'Yeah, yeah, I suppose.' Eric took a deep breath and half-shut his eyes. 'But you'd better keep me warm. I'm warning you, Rach. Last time we went there you nearly froze off my –'

Rachel launched into the chilly sky.

2

GRIÐÐAS

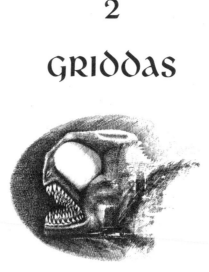

Gultrathaca, pack-leader of the Griddas, entered the eye-chamber.

She was accompanied, as always, by her watchers. The watchers were spiders that lived inside pits criss-crossing her face. As Gultrathaca walked across the chamber floor, they flowed down her body, searching for traps. Some skittered over to the emerald green eye-window. Others lurked in Gultrathaca's footfall, or waited at the doorway.

At fourteen feet tall, Gultrathaca was twice the size of a High Witch. Her imposing orange head was rectangular and all bone, bone impenetrable where it protected the brain. Like all Griddas she had no exposed nose or lips, no yielding part for an enemy to exploit. Nothing protruded from her face except five jaws. Four of these pointed forward. The fifth jaw was clamped to the back of her skull. Her eyes were vast, covering over half her face, and entirely solid – like shaped stone.

As Gultrathaca squeezed her body into the chamber, she said, 'What are you waiting for? Join me.' Seeing there was no danger, her watcher spiders swarmed happily onto her face.

Gultrathaca opened the eye-window – and gazed out in triumph.

Beneath her Thûn, greatest city of the Highs, lay in ruins. For thousands of centuries the High Witches had imprisoned the Griddas underground, while they built their eye-towers in the freedom of the skies. The first action the Griddas had taken after defeating the High Witches was to smash all those eye-towers. Knowing how much the High Witches loved them, the Griddas took each of the stones into their massive claws and crushed them.

Only one object remained intact to mark the reign of the Highs: this place, Heebra's old home, the Great Tower itself.

The last of the fighting Highs lay at its base. In the end, when all the other towers had been taken, the surviving Witches had come here to make a final stand. For several days, incredibly, they had held Heebra's tower against all the power and frenzy of the Griddas. Their bravery was soon forgotten. The eternally-falling grey snow of Ool covered up the High Witches. It settled over their intricate black dresses; it smothered their lifeless red faces and beloved soul-snakes. As Gultrathaca looked down now, only one High Witch remained, poking above her sisters. Piled atop them, she stared up as if in defiance of every-thing. Then her dead eyes too filled with snow, hiding the tattoos forever.

Gultrathaca intended to destroy the last of the towers. First, though, she wanted to walk amongst Heebra's old possessions, her personal items, clawing them. And – there was another reason.

'Come closer,' she said. 'Are you afraid?'

Jarius, a junior member of Gultrathaca's pack, hung back from the eye-window. Having spent most of her life in tunnels, she had never been so far up. 'How can you bear it?' she asked, trembling.

'We need to reach higher still to leave this world,' Gultrathaca told her. 'You can be trained to bear it, as I was.'

Jarius edged hesitantly forward. Like Gultrathaca, her body was all raw heaviness. Bony extensions erupted from her chest and shoulders. Her thick brown fur was untearable. Under it bunched layer upon layer of muscle. Each muscle was constantly gorged with blood – continually battle-ready, even in sleep. Such excess of power was of little benefit to mere survival in the tunnels under the cities, but there was a reason for it: the High Witches had deliberately bred the Griddas this way. In the event of an invasion of Ool, the Highs had always planned to retreat underground, where the Griddas would keep them safe. From birth that was all the Griddas were ever intended for. They could not recall a time when they had not lived, bred and died in the tunnels, waiting for the call to protect.

Jarius forced herself to step nearer the window. Outside it was dark, virtually black, but for her it was still too bright. Lowering her eye-shields, she looked across the sky. She did not look down; not even her own watcher spiders could bear to look down.

'This is an unnatural place,' she gasped, clutching Gultrathaca. 'I – I am frightened.'

'I know. Step closer.'

'Do not make me do this.'

'I must,' said Gultrathaca. 'We cannot stay in the home-tunnels if we wish to confront Larpskendya.'

Jarius shuffled up to the eye-window. For several minutes she stared outward. She could endure it, but only because she knew Gultrathaca would not allow her to step away.

'Now put your head out,' ordered Gultrathaca.

'No!' Jarius attempted to draw back, but Gultrathaca caught her face and bent it towards the ground. When Jarius tried to clamp her eye-shields shut, Gultrathaca held them open. In Jarius's panic, new spiders gushed from her mouths: soldiers. The soldiers ran onto Gultrathaca's claw, trying to loosen the grip. To oppose them, Gultrathaca unleashed her own soldiers; soldier against soldier, the same number – a stalemate.

Gultrathaca made her stare down the tower walls for a long time. When she was finally released, Jarius threw herself to the back of the eye-chamber. She squeezed into an unlit corner, needing to feel safe. The soldiers disengaged. Both groups of spiders studied each other warily, professionally. Then they returned to their owner's jaws.

'It was necessary,' said Gultrathaca.

'Why!'

'To show you what can be achieved. Look below. It is possible, now.'

Calming herself, Jarius approached the window again. She gazed at the faraway ground – only briefly, but she could do it. 'Is this the treatment we can all expect?' she demanded.

'There will be worse to endure than this,' Gultrathaca

told her. 'Knowing how dangerous we are, do you think the Wizards will allow us to live quietly in our tunnels? No. We are loose now, they know that. They will endeavour to destroy us immediately, while we are all still on Ool, contained in one place. That is why we must leave as soon as possible.'

'And go where?'

'Anywhere. Everywhere. I have seen the sun-fed creatures of other worlds, Jarius. You have no idea what strength we have compared to them.'

Jarius remained beside the eye-window. She knew it was important for her to impress Gultrathaca. She had already disgraced herself by being the last of the pack to leave the home tunnels. Worse, it had taken her countless attempts before she dared go onto the surface during daylight hours. Snow terrified her. When it first struck their bodies, the other pack-members had not screamed – but Jarius had.

I've been brought here as a test, she realized. If I perform badly this time the pack will desert me altogether.

Encouraged by her soldiers, Jarius thrust her face boldly out of the window. She made herself peer down.

'There,' said Gultrathaca. 'It is not impossible, after all.'

'No, I am used to it now.'

'Are you?'

'Yes,' Jarius said firmly. To show how steady her nerve had become, she put her head further out. All her spiders deliberately took up relaxed postures, trying to show Gultrathaca that they were completely unconcerned.

Gultrathaca was not fooled by the spiders. She understood exactly how Jarius felt. Only a year earlier, a High Witch had come to drag her out of her own tunnel. How she had implored for mercy! Like the meekest of infants she had begged, rather than face that horror of light!

Yet Gultrathaca adapted – swiftly. Within a day she was helping the other pack-leaders adjust to the snow. And within a week she could fly, not well, not with the elegance of a High Witch, but even so. And finally the moment arrived when punishments were no longer required to make her leave the ground. The time came when Gultrathaca could open her eyes and actually enjoy it. That special morning Heebra herself had travelled alongside her. Like pack-sisters on a jaunt, they had circled the city.

Jarius, however, understood none of this. She pressed her face into the air, wincing at the touch of snowflakes.

Gultrathaca did nothing to put her at ease. All the other pack-sisters had been made to prove themselves. If Jarius could not cope with the eye-tower, she did not belong in the pack. There could be no compassion for those Griddas too frightened to leave the safety of the tunnels – not even for blood-relatives.

Jarius tried not to shiver. Her soldiers finally persuaded her to open her eye-shields a little more. While staring out, she said, 'What was it really like? What was it like to be amongst the first Griddas to leave Ool and fight the Wizards?'

'It was exhilarating.' Gultrathaca laughed. 'And terrifying.'

She recalled the moment. At the brink of the clouds, she and the other hand-picked Griddas had waited for Heebra's command to move out into the emptiness of space. It was to have been a last decisive offensive against the Wizards. To support it the Griddas, for the first time, had been released from the tunnels of Ool to spread as much havoc as possible.

'We weren't meant for such places,' Jarius said, waving in disgust at the sky. 'We were intended for stone floors and ceilings, not this.'

'That is what you think now,' said Gultrathaca. 'That is what the High Witches wanted you to believe. But you are more impressive than they ever knew.'

'I will never fly. Not willingly.'

'No,' Gultrathaca said. 'That is obvious.'

A few healer spiders fussed over Jarius's eye-shields. They were checking for any damage Gultrathaca might have caused earlier. Finding none, they polished the hard eye surfaces.

'I hear Calen, the new High Witch leader, hasn't been found yet,' Jarius said.

'Leave Calen to me,' Gultrathaca replied. 'She is not the threat her mother Heebra once represented.'

'But surely while Calen is still alive the imprisoned Highs will always be a threat. I don't understand why you haven't just killed all those left in the cells.'

'That would be too easy,' Gultrathaca said.

'Too easy?'

'You have no idea what the Highs denied us.'

Jarius regarded her blankly.

'Tell me,' Gultrathaca said, 'what is the most repulsive aspect of a High Witch?'

'Her soul-snake,' Jarius replied at once.

'You think so? At one time we possessed our own soul-snakes. We knew their friendship. Our ancestors were High Witches.'

Jarius stared at her in disbelief.

'When I left the tunnels I learned a great deal,'

Gultrathaca said. 'The Griddas were an experiment. The High Witches wanted something better adapted to the tunnels. So they took a few of their own Witches and put them into the dark to see what would happen. Our soul-snakes joined us underground. But after hundreds of generations we became so altered that the snakes could no longer bear the taste of our skin. They left us. Nor was this musculature' – Gultrathaca raised her hugely swollen arms – 'and the constant desire to use it, to fight, originally part of us. The Highs designed us this way.'

Jarius shook her head, not quite able to believe this. The senior pack members did not bother to share such information with her, given her low status.

'We also mature far more quickly,' said Gultrathaca. 'The Highs wanted that, too; fast-breeders, capable like them of fertilizing our own eggs. That way they could produce a Gridda army whenever they needed it. Of course, we could never be allowed to grow in numbers that might threaten the High Witches. Imagine if we had wanted to share their food or their precious skies! But they found a solution for that. They culled us.'

'Culled?'

'Killed us off,' Gultrathaca said. 'We didn't question why our pack-members never returned from the wars. Why should we have done? Weren't they dying in glorious battles? The truth was that the Highs didn't want us in their wars. They simply killed a certain amount of us from time to time. That kept our numbers in check. For the Highs it was the easiest solution.'

Jarius stepped away from the window. To die in such a manner filled her with such shame that she was unable to speak.

'Now you see why I keep some High Witches in the worst of the tunnels,' said Gultrathaca. 'Let them fester. I'll never release them.'

Jarius lowered her head, preoccupied with what she had learned.

'The High Witches always despised our kind,' Gultrathaca said, 'but their reign is over. There will be no more culling. From now on the Griddas will breed in numbers even the Highs could not imagine.'

'Won't we fill the tunnels?' Jarius asked. 'They are already crowded.'

'That doesn't matter. You will soon learn to think beyond tunnel boundaries. You must, if we are to leave this world.'

'How far can we get,' Jarius said, 'if the Wizards stand in our way?'

'Not far, perhaps. We need to find Orin Fen, the Wizard home world, and kill them there. Until we do, Larpskendya and his kind will always be safe – and we will not.'

'The Highs never managed to find their home world.'

'Perhaps they searched in the wrong way,' Gultrathaca said. 'Perhaps they needed the help of an infant.'

'An infant?'

'Heebra did not die at the hands of a Wizard, Jarius. A human child was responsible. The returning Highs spoke of talents they had never seen before in the Yemi boy. I believe he may have the skills we need to find Orin Fen. Or perhaps he has other gifts we can use.' Gultrathaca joined Jarius by the eye-window. 'You have been gazing down for many minutes, without needing to look away,' she said. 'Had you noticed?'

'No,' Jarius admitted. 'Is that so?' She realized many of her watchers had genuinely forgotten their earlier fears. They now stared with simple curiosity at the snow pulsing against the stone and glass. Springing back and forth from the window, Jarius found that she was able to look out without flinching. There was still fear, but she could master it.

Jarius is ready, Gultrathaca thought. Or as ready as she could ever be.

'Our youngsters will adapt better than us,' she said. 'They will barely know the tunnels at all, Jarius. It will be so much easier for them.' She sniffed, picking out the distinctive aroma of Gridda infants. As she had requested, one pack had been driven to the surface. 'I wanted you to be here for this,' she told Jarius. 'For the first time Griddas are due to be brought directly from the birthing chambers to see the world. Let's observe how they behave.'

A pack of recently hatched Griddas showed at a tunnel entrance near the base of the eye-tower. The first one to emerge howled when the daylight touched her eyes. She would not have come further except that her sisters shoved her from beneath. Finally all twenty-four blood-related sisters were on the surface. They huddled together, beating at the falling snow as if it was trying to strike them. A searing wind blew into their faces. The sensation of that wind was so unusual and so appalling to the young Griddas that all their spiders acted as though they were being attacked. They formed hopeless little shields around their owners' faces, trying to use their bodies to fend off the winds.

As Jarius watched the youngsters, it seemed that they might have stayed in their crouched position forever if they had been allowed. But an adult Gridda prodded them forward. Awkwardly, trying to fend off the adult, the infants were hurried towards the entrance of Heebra's tower. Their spiders hurried after them, not wanting to be left behind. Bounding in long leaps, the infants bent their backs low, tunnel-fashion. It never occurred to them to check how high the eye-tower was. In the tunnels there was rarely any reason to look up.

The last of the infants were pushed inside the tower entrance. The pounding of their bodies reverberated through the stone as they made their way up the enormous stairway.

'What are you going to do with them?' Jarius asked.

'I am going to test them, of course,' answered Gultrathaca.

Jarius glanced across. 'Test them how?'

'I want to see how quickly newborns can be made to adjust. I intend to bring them to the eye-window and throw them out.'

'What? But they can't fly. They don't know how yet!'

The infants were closer. Jarius could hear their fearful, confused chatter. The first watcher spiders, baby-sized like the infants they belonged to, preceded their arrival. They called back, warning their owners about the strange green light of the window.

'It is unfair to ask them so soon,' Jarius protested.

Gultrathaca shattered the eye-window. Shards of glass and ice showered the chamber, blown back by the wind. 'I agree,' she said. 'That is why I have prepared you, Jarius. I want you to show them how it can be done. I want you to jump first.'

3

COUNTRIES
WITHOUT BORDERS

'Rachel, skip the tourist run and do some proper flying,' Eric complained.

'Why don't you just relax? Take it easy. Enjoy the sights.'

'I've *seen* the sights.'

'Speed,' she groaned. 'Is that all you get excited about?'

'What else is there?'

With Eric loosely hitched on her back, Rachel cruised over the Himalayas. Below them some of Earth's tallest mountains offered alluring views of their frozen tips: K2, Nanga Parbat, the majestic precipices of the Annapurna range. Rachel breathed in the coldness, cherishing the winds gusting through her hair.

Above Makalu, the Earth's fifth highest summit, she found children plunging feet first. As their bodies impacted the north face, a great sheet of snow broke away. Gleefully they rode the avalanche, racing each other down the slopes.

'I think we can match that,' Rachel said. 'Ready for a dare?'

'Yeah. Why not!'

Rachel immediately dived towards the nearest ridge. As her trajectory spells took charge Eric attempted to keep his cool. 'OK, tell me when,' Rachel said. 'Don't mess up, now.'

Eric tried to calculate how long before they hit the ridge – but they were travelling too swiftly.

'I can't … slow down … *now!*' he bawled, screwing up his eyes.

Rachel deliberately waited. At the last possible second her manoeuvring spells kicked in. She dragged her shoes against the slope, showering Eric with ice particles.

'Very funny,' he muttered.

'Too fast for you, eh?'

'I wasn't scared a bit,' Eric said stiffly, wiping the ice and snow from the hood of his parka. 'Do it again if you like. See if I care.'

'Later, maybe. Let's check out what's going on at the other peaks first.'

Rachel returned eastwards, swooping over the Everest region. The fittest of adults had failed to climb a handful of these mountains, but children had conquered them all. As Rachel flew by Everest itself, there were hundreds circling the summit. Some carried adult relatives or helped friends whose magic was not strong enough to reach this altitude on their own. Many of the world's best flyers were here on this day of near-perfect visibility. One was a teenage girl. She plunged and rose at will in the thin air, and then returned to a crèche of toddlers to show them, more slowly, how she had done so.

'What about the prapsies?' asked Eric, seeing no one he recognized. 'I thought you were taking us to see the boys.'

'Let's stop off for a tan first.'

Eric shrugged. 'Where? The Caribbean?'

'Maybe.'

Rachel changed direction and gave control to her shifting spells, heading west.

'Florida Bay,' she announced, as they arrived.

They were a long way from shore, perhaps four miles. A few adults were dotted about, churning the surface in their pleasure boats, but they were outnumbered. In these warm latitudes the waters abounded with children. They did not require boats. Their magic allowed them to swim directly with the life of the sea. As Rachel looked on, she saw boys following dolphins, half in and half out of the surf. Two girls were arching their backs, shadowing a group of hunting barracuda.

'Hey, what's *he* doing?' Eric called out.

A slim boy was out alone amongst the waves. With smooth underwater kicks he followed a broken fishing line. The line led to a marlin, twisting on a barb. The boy caught the thrashing head of the marlin, held it steady and wrenched out the hook. Eric gave him a salute. Seeing this, the boy saluted back, then broke from the waters and headed further out to sea.

Rachel followed him for a while. There were fewer children this far from shore, but an exclusive few specialized in underwater spells. They were able to dive down to the pits and trenches at the bottom of the world.

'Deepers!' Rachel called out, craning her neck. 'Way down! Right under us!'

Over a mile below, the deepers were holding onto the

flukes of sperm whales, hoping to witness an encounter with giant squid. Rachel's information spells reported that among the diving children was a magical signature she knew. It belonged to a little French boy whose rainbow she had once spoiled on a hot summer's day.

She smiled, shifting back over land.

Amongst the steaming sawgrasses of the Florida Everglades, they passed over a baby petting the crusty hide of an alligator. Nearby some brothers were chasing raccoons up a tree, giving the animals a head start.

Typical sights.

There were youngsters here from all parts of the world. The national borderlines between countries had never meant much to children, and now they meant nothing at all.

Eric laughed, seeing a small girl. 'How would you like to try that, Rach?'

The girl was hunkered down in the dry dirt next to a diamondback rattlesnake. The snake had been minding its own business, but the girl wanted to play. Planting her elbows on the ground, she nudged the snake's slatted mouth with her nose – daring it to strike.

'Too easy,' Rachel replied.

'You're joking!'

'Only one snake, and not especially poisonous.' She glanced around for a new direction to take.

'Let's move on,' Eric said, and, as he guided her around Florida, Rachel soon knew why.

A thin boy in shorts and a dirty long-sleeved shirt stood in the shallows of the Okeechobee river.

'A spectrum.' Eric whispered the name in awe.

Rachel alighted in the muddy waters and walked over to the boy. As they approached the boy took no notice of them. He kept so still, so perfectly still, that his ankles made no ripples whatsoever.

'They're so rare,' Rachel said. 'I've never been this close to a spectrum before.'

'It's their leader,' Eric remarked. 'It's Albertus Robertson himself.'

'Is it? Are you sure?'

'I know them all.'

'How? They all look similar to me.'

Eric shook his head. 'No, Rachel, they don't.'

Albertus Robertson was a sensitive-looking boy, around ten years old, with light brown eyes. His hair was a long, straggly mess, clearly not brushed for weeks. Like all spectrums, he was slightly short for his age, with the usual abstracted gaze. In all other ways Albertus resembled any other child, except for one extraordinary feature: his ears. They were unnaturally wide and thin, several sizes too large, almost comical. Hinged on a specialized joint no child had ever possessed before, the ear could turn flexibly in all directions. As Rachel watched Albertus Robertson, she perceived a tiny rotation; his head moved. The motion was so small that only her spells detected it, not her eyes. It was a precise movement – a single degree of arc – as he scanned a pre-selected segment of the sky.

Rachel murmured, 'Seems as if Albertus hasn't bothered to wash or take care of himself lately.'

'He's probably got better things to do.'

'Like what?' Rachel hoped Albertus could not hear her. 'What's he looking for out here?'

'I don't know, Rach. Albertus doesn't either. That's what's so interesting about the spectrums. None of them has a clue what they're doing it for. There're dozens of them around the world, just gazing all day at the sky.'

For a while Rachel watched Albertus Robertson, but there was no change in his unnerving stillness. Even in a world now filled with unusual children, the spectrums were different. They were the only ones who had changed physically. Before the Awakening they had looked and behaved like anyone else. Following it, their ears developed within days, along with their silence and lack of movement.

'They can't fly or do the simplest spells,' Eric told Rachel.

'I've heard they don't even talk.'

'I think you're wrong about that. Everyone is. They might not talk to us, but they talk to each other – or they're going to.'

Rachel glanced sharply at Eric. 'How do you know that?'

'I'm not sure, it's just a hunch.' He could hardly take his eyes off Albertus Robertson.

'A hunch? No, there's something else going on between you and the spectrums,' Rachel said. 'You're always noticing things about them no one else does. Albertus has never been identified as their leader. How can you know he is?'

Eric shrugged.

'The spectrums don't even meet,' Rachel said. 'Surely they don't have a leader. They're all loners.'

'They don't meet *yet*, Rach. I think that's going to change as well.'

As Eric said this Albertus Robertson cocked his head. He stared at Eric, intrigued. A spectrum had not been known to do this before. They never reacted to another human presence. For a moment Albertus's placid brown eyes lingered on Eric, then his head whisked back to its former position.

Deeply affected by what had just happened, Eric said, 'There's something else about the spectrums, too. Thrill-seekers like to hang around them.'

'Thrill-seekers! Are you serious?' Thrill-seeker was the general term given to the most reckless children, always pushing their magic to dangerous extremes. To Rachel, the contrast between those daredevils of magic and the passive spectrums was ludicrous.

Eric said, 'Surprising, eh? I can't imagine what they've got in common, but something's going on. I'll bet there's a thrill-seeker round here somewhere. In fact, I know there is.'

Now that Eric had mentioned it, Rachel could detect another magical presence nearby, though keeping out of sight.

'Anyway, let's leave Albertus in peace,' Eric said, dragging his gaze away. 'He enjoys his peace and quiet, old Albertus.'

'How do you know that?' Rachel demanded, exasperated.

'Dunno, just do.' He prodded her. 'What about the prapsies? You promised! Have you forgotten again?'

Rachel said, 'No, I've just been putting it off. For as long as possible.'

'Ah, you know you love the boys really, Rach!'

'Mmm.' With a final glance at Albertus Robertson, she shifted.

They reappeared over southern Italy. Local children were plunging in and out of the Vesuvius volcano, but Rachel's destination was different. She alighted in bustling Naples. Eric was happy to be on the ground and, for a time, on foot, both of them simply explored the narrow twisting roads of the city. They passed a chic jewellery shop, extremely expensive.

'Look at that,' Eric said.

The heavy steel doors of the shop had been destroyed. Only bent edges remained to show where they had once been. Three children were placed at the entrance to guard the shop instead. They stood outside, looking casually menacing.

'Must be a lot of thievers about,' Eric noted. 'I wouldn't have expected that here. Not during the day, anyhow.'

Rachel nodded bleakly. Fences, walls, locks, reinforced concrete, barbed-wire – traditional defences like these could not keep out the really gifted children. 'I've seen worse,' she said. 'In Africa, especially. Cairo. Nairobi. Lagos. Terrible things are still going on.'

The emergence of magic had brought new problems as well as joys. The thiever gangs had started up in the poorest countries. After the Awakening millions of children who had never had enough to eat did not wait. They simply took what they needed. On the world of Ithrea, in one special room Rachel had created food seemingly from magic alone – but that was only the trick of a Witch. Even the most magical children could not conjure food out of nothing.

Typically the thievers came at night, raiding crops, stealing cattle. An experienced gang could take what they wanted before an adult could even spot them. For a hefty price kids might hire themselves out as anti-thievers to help guard a valuable property or chase down an attacker, but hardly any children could be bothered with such dull work unless it was their own family possessions they were protecting. And, supposing a thiever was caught, who dared punish the offender? Adults were no match physically for most children any longer. In a few countries desperate to keep some control over the thieves, children themselves had been sworn into the security forces, given special powers by the courts. But it made little difference. Children escaped detention; they evaded jail. Even if less talented children could be safely locked away, friends would soon use their magic to free them.

A sudden fluttering of wings, though, made Eric and Rachel forget altogether about thieves.

'Whoa! Here they come!' he said. 'Here come the boys!'

Hurrying into an alley where they would be less easily seen, he watched the prapsies flap jubilantly towards him. They headed directly for Eric, in perfectly straight lines, and incredibly swiftly. Not even the most agile child could catch a prapsy – though many had tried.

Devoted to Eric, the child-birds had recently taken to flying far and wide to find him gifts, each trying to outdo the other. Eric clicked his fingers – and the prapsies landed, at exactly the same time, on his head. Their rosy cheeks perspired in the spring air, dripping sweat on his scalp. Eric didn't care.

'Hey boys, what you got?'

One prapsy carried a broken comb in its toothless mouth. Without waiting for Eric's opinion, the child-bird attempted to tidy his blond curly hair. 'Oh, this will make you handsome,' the prapsy promised, ineffectually dragging the comb against his ear.

'Where did it find that comb?' Rachel asked. 'It's filthy.'

Eric shrugged. 'Who cares? I'll wash my hair later. You worry too much, Rach.' He turned to the other prapsy. 'And what've you got for me, then?'

The second prapsy held a knob of chewing gum in one claw. It offered this to Eric.

'Er,' said Eric. 'Where'd you find that? Did you nick it from someone's mouth?'

'Oh, no! No, Eric!' wailed the prapsy. 'I wouldn't give you second-hands. It's fresh. Only my gums.'

'Well, that's all right, then.' Eric opened his mouth and the prapsy dropped the thoroughly chewed gum inside.

'Go on,' the prapsy said expectantly. 'Chew it.'

Eric chewed away. 'No taste,' he said. 'I suppose it's been in your gob a while, eh?'

Rachel said, 'I think the question you should be asking is where it found the gum.'

'On a fence,' answered the prapsy cheerfully. 'There was dirt on it, and a fly, and some stink – but I licked that off.'

Eric spat the gum out. 'Blimey, boys,' he spluttered. 'What are you trying to do? Kill me?'

'Not good? You don't want my present?' The prapsy sniffed. Its face wobbled as it held back a tear. 'I'm sorry, Eric. Did you want the dirt and fly on it? I didn't think so.' It turned angrily to its companion. 'Your fault! You told me to suck the dirt off, you stupid pigeon.'

The other prapsy smiled smugly, saying nothing.

'Off you go!' Eric shooed them away. 'Find me a *proper* treat. Something really good!'

Immediately both prapsies hovered side by side, trembling with excitement.

'Whaddaya want? Whaddaya want, Eric?' they squealed.

'Something nice and *tasty*. Without stink!'

The prapsies sped off, spitting at each other. Rachel could still hear them when they were well out of sight, bickering and swearing.

4

tokyo

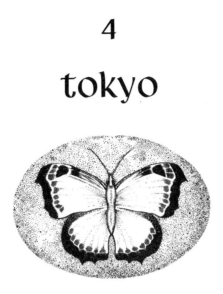

Rachel flicked away the comb still protruding from Eric's hair. 'Let's go,' she said. 'I still want to do some shopping.'

'Do we have to?'

'Yes.'

'Where, then? New York?'

'Japan!'

Rachel shifted them to the Far East, following the sun as it dipped down the sky: sunset in Tokyo. For a while she soared over the glass and steel skyscrapers of Shinjuko district, in the western part of the city. Rachel loved this area, especially the massive twin forty-eight-storey towers of the Metropolitan Government Building. By day thirteen thousand city bureaucrats still worked in the offices, but at night the structure belonged to the children.

'Check out the gangs,' Eric said. 'They weren't here last time we came.'

Several rival groups of children surveyed each other

from the roofs of the skyscrapers. Each group was distinctly dressed, so there could be no mistaking where their allegiances lay.

'See the no-go zones?' Eric indicated the gaps between the buildings, the invisible places where no children flew. The atmosphere was uneasy, with few adults about. As Eric watched, a baby – flying solo – cut across the various invisible territories. The gangs jeered as he passed, mocking the baby's jerky progress across the sky.

Eric blew on his forefinger. As if it was a smoking gun he pointed it at the gang children, smiling thinly. 'Zap, zap,' he said, under his breath. 'Want me to teach those gang kids a lesson, Rach? Knock them right out of the sky?'

Rachel glanced at him as he lowered his finger resignedly. 'Are you tempted?'

'I'm *always* tempted. Especially with kids like these.'

Eric's special gift was that of a destroyer of spells. The Wizard leader, Larpskendya, had himself been puzzled by this ability. In all the Wizards' experience across many worlds they had never come across a similar gift. After the Awakening, Larpskendya had expected other children on Earth like Eric to emerge. That had not happened.

Eric was unique.

Rachel understood how much he wanted to practise his anti-magic, but how could he? Each time Eric focused on a child's spell it killed that particular spell forever. It could never be used again. Spells were precious; even the most modest had its worth and value. No child would willingly give one up.

'It doesn't matter,' Eric said, then added in an undertone, 'I'm improving anyway. Even without practising, I'm getting better all the time.'

'Better at what?'

'I can detect distant spells. I mean really faint spells, out a long way.'

'How far away?'

'Do you know where the prapsies are?'

The magical scent of the prapsies was always hard to follow because they flew so swiftly. At last, more than a thousand miles to the north-west, Rachel's information spells tracked them down. 'They're over the Gobi desert,' she said. 'Flying south.'

'How close together are they?'

Rachel stared blankly at Eric. 'I can't tell that from this distance. I can barely trace them at all.'

'No?' Eric raised his eyebrows. 'Then I'll tell you. They're very close, no more than a foot apart. And one is flying slightly above the other, piggy-back style. They're cold, too. They must be because their speed's six percent down on normal. And,' he added jauntily, 'they're flying at over twelve thousand feet. They like being way up high like that. It reminds them of all those centuries they spent in the skies of Ithrea.'

Rachel gazed at him, shocked. 'Eric, how long have you been able to detect so accurately? You've never mentioned it before.'

He shrugged. 'It's been happening gradually.'

'We need to tell Larpskendya straightaway.'

'Sure, I suppose.'

'Eric, you can't just keep something this important to yourself. You know that. If –'

'All right, lay off, will you? I *was* going to tell Larpskendya tomorrow, actually, when he takes us to visit Yemi. And – er – talking of Yemi,' Eric said, 'here come his little Beauties.'

A shadow had spread over the Tokyo skyline. It was composed entirely of yellow Camberwell Beauty butter-flies. There were billions of them, the flock so enormous that for several minutes it entirely hid the early stars as it steadily moved across the city. The sight was such a famil-iar occurrence that most of the children did not even bother to look up.

'I still don't understand why Yemi sends them everywhere,' Eric said.

'I think I do.' Rachel pictured Yemi, the two-year-old Nigerian boy, and smiled. Even her remarkable spells were in awe of Yemi's magic. Like her, he could shift and trans-form his shape, but he could do much more. And his magic was maturing all the time. No one had any idea what its limits might be.

As Rachel stared up, she said, 'These lovely butterflies. They're a gift. Yemi's trying to bring a bit of extra happi-ness to the world. But there's more to it than that. The animals – have you seen how interested they become when the butterflies are overhead? I've no idea what's going on, but their behaviour definitely changes.'

'It's their magic,' Eric said.

'What – the animals?'

'Yeah. They're not like us, but they've got a trace. It responds to Yemi and his butterflies.'

'Are you sure?'

'Dead sure.'

The Camberwell Beauties gradually passed beyond the city. There were hundreds of such flocks, wheeling in great endless migrations. By day and night they flew, their wings ceaselessly charting paths that would take them over every part of the world.

'Let's get away from the gangs,' Rachel said as the last of the butterflies melted inside the sunset glow. 'I still want to shop. Fancy anywhere in particular?'

'Not really, but I'm hungry.'

'Me, too.'

She shifted them to one of the world's premier shopping districts: Tokyo's Ginza-chrome crossroads. For a while, with Rachel disguising them as typical Japanese children, they strolled amongst the neon-splashed bars and sushi stalls. There was an even mixture of adults and children here running the entertainment centres and food outlets. Rachel and Eric bought some yakitari chicken and ice cream and sauntered up the wide streets. As they turned up the Chou-dori road, Eric whispered, 'Stop.'

'A holding spell,' Rachel said.

'Yeah. And whoever it's being used on isn't fighting back.'

'Must be an adult, then.'

'Do you want me to destroy the spell?'

'No,' Rachel said. 'Let's check it out, first.' She picked Eric up and flew along a network of side-streets until they reached a murky alley. Half-concealed by some bins a girl around seven years old stood over an old man. Without being touched the man's body was being held down, while the girl used a searching spell to check his pockets for money, or whatever she was after.

'Stop it!' Rachel shouted in Japanese – and then realized the girl was not Japanese at all. She switched to English. 'Leave him alone!' When the girl still showed no comprehension, Rachel's linguistic spells stated the same message in various languages.

Finally the girl understood. She spat on the ground near Rachel, defiant.

'She'll fight you if she can,' Eric said. 'She's preparing to.'

'I don't think so,' Rachel answered. 'She knows she's outmatched. This one's smart.'

'Who he?' the girl asked, in laboured English. She pressed her toe against the man's chest. 'Your dada? Your da?'

'No,' Rachel said. 'Of course not.'

'Then … why you help?' The girl seemed genuinely puzzled.

'I –' Rachel halted. If this girl couldn't understand that it was wrong to terrorize an adult, what could she say to persuade her?

The girl turned away. Calling a mangy cat from the shadows, she cradled it in her arms and swaggered to the back of the alley, her head held high.

The old man got up shakily, shuffling off in the opposite direction.

'Wait,' Rachel said to him. 'Are you all right? Are you hurt?'

The man clearly wanted to get away from her. Rachel was a child, and he was alone, and afraid of her even though she had helped him. He clung to the wall, edging past Rachel and Eric, bowing several times, but not lifting his eyes.

'You don't usually find adults on their own at night these days in the big cities,' Eric said. 'I can't believe he hasn't got his kids with him in a busy place like this.'

'Not everyone has children of their own,' Rachel said. 'Does that mean they have to stay indoors? Never go out?'

'Either that or accept the risk. You know the rule in the cities: adults indoors by ten p.m., or take the consequences.'

'That's a gang rule,' Rachel said angrily. 'You sound like one of them.'

Eric shrugged. 'Parents made up enough of their own rules before, Rach.'

'So it's time to even things up, is that what you're saying?'

'No, I'm not saying that. I don't like it any more than you, but adults have to be careful, don't they? Stay inside unless they know they've got a child escort, and —'

'That man could be *our* dad,' Rachel said.

Eric looked alarmed. 'Have you protected our house?'

'Of course. The point is that some adults haven't got any special protection. They shouldn't need it.'

She gazed up. The slot of sky between the alley walls teemed with children. To Rachel they suddenly appeared mildly sinister. The old man was still running down the alley, trying to reach safety. He seemed to belong to a different world. She kept an eye on him until he reached a side door. His hands shook as he fumbled with the lock. Perhaps he would be safe inside, perhaps not. Rachel knew that while most parts of the world were safe for adults, juveniles were taking control in the largest cities. Street gangs had always existed, but now they were armed with magic. Generally adults could go about their business freely, but in certain areas after dark menacing children strutted around, behaving unpredictably. A few specialized in taunting grown-ups just for the hell of it.

The old man's hands were shaking so much he could not undo the lock. He kept glancing at Rachel as if she might be about to do horrible things to him. Rachel could have used a spell to disengage the lock, but she knew that would only frighten the old man more. To make him feel less threatened, she moved down the alley — though staying close enough to make sure he got inside safely.

The whole world's turned upside down, she thought.

Nearly all of the changes were for the better. Parents rarely had to go to work any longer, unless they wished to. Their children, using magic, could perform routine chores, freeing most adults for the first time ever from drudgery. But it was still difficult for the adults, and not just because of the child gangs. Many parents had always judged their worth by how they brought up their children, by how much their children needed them. Children didn't need taking care of in quite the same way any longer. By and large they still shared the same loving relationships, but many children now spent more time exploring their magic than with their parents. And, of course, there was also jealousy. Some parents were envious of their own children. Why should only children have magic? Adults wanted to be masters of their own trajectories. They wanted to be able to fly, too ...

The old man had at last dealt with the door lock. He slipped inside. Rachel wondered what kind of life he led. He seemed so frail. I hope he's not alone, she thought. Alone in a city of child gangs. What could be worse? Overhead a baby chuckled, pursuing a night bird across the sky. Where is your mother? Rachel found herself silently asking. Where is she? How does she feel about you being so far from her?

Suddenly Rachel wanted to return home and make sure Mum and Dad were safe.

The Griddas are out there somewhere, she thought. Since the High Witches know where our world is, the Griddas must know as well. And I bet they don't waste time on games or joining stupid gangs, or fleecing adults. When the Griddas finally decide to come, she thought, how are we ever going to be ready?

'Let's get back, Eric,' she said. 'Let's go home.'

5

fire
without heat

'He's late,' Rachel said.

Mum squeezed her hand. 'He won't be much longer now, I'm sure.'

Rachel nodded tensely and hugged her knees, rocking back and forth on one of the kitchen chairs. A few sandwiches lay untouched on a plate next to her. She could never eat before she saw Larpskendya. She was too filled with anticipation.

Eric was more relaxed. He lounged nearby, flipping through a comic. The prapsies were in a tree a few gardens down, arguing with a family of crows.

'What are the boys up to?' Mum asked Eric, not really caring.

'They're telling the crows to stop messing about and grow some proper faces.'

As Mum rolled her eyes, Rachel whispered to her, 'Are *you* nervous? You know, when Larpskendya comes, do you feel like' – she pressed her heart – 'like this as well?'

'Yes, every time,' Mum replied. 'Oh, but it's a nice kind of nervous, isn't it?'

They grinned at one another.

A few minutes passed. Rachel smoothed out her skirt. Mum made some tea and nobody drank it except Eric. Bored with the crows the prapsies squashed their noses against the window, wanting to be back inside. Mum automatically checked they weren't carrying anything disgusting before letting them fly over to Eric.

'How'd you get on, boys?' he asked, as they alighted on his shoulders.

'They won't listen,' one prapsy said forlornly. 'They won't grow faces.'

'Did you tell them off?'

'We did, Eric. They just flew away. They always do.'

Eric leaned towards the prapsies. 'I'll tell you why they do that, boys. It's because they're ashamed. They're only crows, after all. You two can fly like geniuses, talk, everything. When you're beside them, the crows are embarrassed. They know they're nowhere near as good as either of you.'

Both prapsies beamed happily. This explanation had never occurred to them.

The patio door opened and Dad came in from the garage, wiping car grease from his hands. He was a tall, rangy man with greying hair.

'Nearly done it,' he said with satisfaction, going over to the sink to clean up. 'Almost fixed that engine. A couple more hours' work, that's all.'

Rachel could have fixed the car, but she knew better. Dad liked doing it.

Dad stood with his hands under the tap, methodically removing traces of oil. Then he came to sit near everyone else on one of the kitchen chairs, and in a hoarse voice said, 'He's overdue, isn't he?'

Mum nodded. No one needed to say who he meant. Dad sat forward to pour himself a cup of tea, then stopped. He forgot about the tea. Everyone in the room broke out into the same broad smile as they sensed it: a thrill in the sky, an ache. The clouds seemed to know; eagles halted their flight.

Rachel whispered, 'He's coming. He's coming.'

Dad straightened up to steady himself. The prapsies bounced up and down on the radiator. Eric, forgetting his cool, rushed into the living room, hoping to catch a glimpse of the Wizard bursting through the clouds.

But he was too late – Larpskendya had already shifted into the hallway.

The prapsies were there first. Searching for a gift, they found a bit of dirt on the carpet. After Larpskendya accepted this graciously, he turned to the girl dashing along the hall – and she did not need to ask his permission. He opened out his arms and Rachel ran into them. She pressed her face against his chest and held him.

'Oh, Larpskendya!' she cried out.

Her spells rushed crazily into her eyes, all wanting to see him first. Larpskendya threw back his head and laughed, kissing her and Eric and both parents in a completely informal way.

Dad, as always, was unable to take his gaze off the

Wizard. What was it about him? Not the Wizard's features – they were like those of any impressive man. It was the eyes: human-shaped, but more vibrantly passionate than any man's.

Rachel clung to Larpskendya's cream robe as she told him about recent magical developments. As usual he seemed to know already, though he did not interrupt her. Finally, after speaking with Mum and Dad in private, Larpskendya held hands with Rachel and Eric. The prapsies buzzed around his head like flies, knowing something was about to happen. With a movement too swift to see, Larpskendya caught them and tucked each prapsy inside Eric's shirt.

'Keep them close to you today,' Larpskendya advised Eric.

'Why?'

'In the place we're visiting, they might lose their hearts to another. Yemi has changed since the last time you saw him.' Eric shared a quizzical look with Rachel. 'Are you ready?' Larpskendya said. Eric did up the buttons of his jacket, pressing the heads of the prapsies down.

'Where's Larpy taking us?' one prapsy asked.

'Shush. Don't call him that,' Eric said.

'Why not, Eric?'

'It's just not a good idea, that's all.'

'Oh, I have been called worse names,' Larpskendya remarked. He laughed – and shifted. There was no sensation of flight or movement. Rachel's own spells could never grasp the silky ease with which Larpskendya shifted. The next instant – and thousands of miles – later, Rachel and Eric found themselves letting go of his hands, blinking in semi-darkness.

They were underground, in a cave. Once it might have

been an ordinary cave, but Yemi's magic had transformed it. Inside there were no windows, but endless views. To Rachel's right a fire raged, without heat. Over Eric's head a waterfall cascaded, without wetting him. Howler monkeys appeared from nowhere, screeched, vanished – and reappeared. And all around were the sights, sounds and fragrances Yemi treasured most, those of his old African home, Fiditi. And that meant warmth; it meant humidity; it meant smells of good home cooking, burning fuel and the noise of lonely night birds calling. One sound dominated all the others: the murmur of rainforest leaves.

That sound, beautifully rich, was everywhere.

'This is only one of Yemi's residences,' Larpskendya said, leading them further in. 'He creates new ones wherever he goes, an infinite number.'

They turned a corner, into the main part of the cave and there – bursting with life – was a small boy.

'Yemi!' Rachel cried, rushing over to him.

As soon as he heard her Yemi shifted into Rachel's arms. For a while he simply lay there, gazing at her in a way that asked nothing and everything. It had been three months since Rachel last visited him, and in outward appearance Yemi had hardly changed at all – still a toddler, with short-cropped curly hair, ebony skin and soft brown eyes. Characteristically, he chose for himself the least fussy clothes, a pair of wrinkled blue shorts and a plain orange T-shirt. But Rachel did not even notice what he wore. What she noticed were the animals. Dozens surrounded him, every kind of creature: mice, dogs, a marmoset, an elk, and cats, big cats – fully-grown Siberian tigers.

'We're not certain how Yemi brings them, or why,' Larpskendya said. 'Yet it seems no animal can resist him.'

Eric glanced at the prapsies, still inside his shirt. They stared back reassuringly.

Rachel rocked Yemi against her chest. While she did so a gibbon monkey jumped on her shoulder. It started preening her hair. She laughed at the tickling sensation and bent forward to kiss Yemi on the mouth.

He pulled back. He shouted at her. Shoving Rachel away, he flew to another part of the cave.

'Sorry,' said a voice from the shadows. 'I should have warned you.'

Yemi's sister, Fola, stepped forward. She was about Rachel's age, but taller, with braided hair and full lips that smiled readily. After greeting Rachel and Eric she knelt down and ruffled Yemi's hair. 'He no go let anyone near his mouth. He never does, not for long time.'

Yemi tottered over to his big cats for comfort. The Siberian tigers sat either side of him, their heads platforms for his hands. When his little temper ended, Yemi returned to Rachel, clearly wanting her forgiveness. As she pulled him close, she said, 'I think I know why he doesn't accept kisses. It's because of Heebra. She put her death spell into his mouth that way. He's scared, that's all.'

Yemi wriggled to be put down, then clapped loudly for everyone's attention.

'Flipping heck!' Eric gasped.

The animals they had already seen were not the only ones in the cave. The rest now arrived from the leafy areas. Mice hopped alongside cats; a cobra clung to the neck of a swan; a hawk settled near a chick, with no thought to snap it up.

With a splash, another animal emerged from a small pool. It was only a baby. Fat with blubber, it hauled itself forward. On five-clawed foreflippers it made its way across to Eric and gazed up at him.

'A Weddell seal,' Larpskendya said. 'From the Antarctic. The animals come from everywhere, drawn to Yemi wherever he goes.' He picked up the seal cub. 'This one was blue with cold when it arrived. It must have travelled over many nights across half an ocean just to be with Yemi. Can you imagine that?'

Eric stared in awe. 'How many make it to him?'

'Not many. Yemi is restless, always shifting off somewhere else. Only the most determined animals have a chance to catch him before he leaves.'

Eric bent down to one of the hawks. The prapsies took the opportunity to escape from his shirt. 'Hey, come back!' he yelled – but they were out, scrambling onto his shoulders.

Seeing them, Yemi jumped with excitement. He held out his arms. When the prapsies did not immediately fly across to him, Yemi was astonished. 'Come, come,' he said in a sing-song voice. 'Want.'

'I can see that,' Eric said stonily.

'Want.'

'I don't care what you want. You can't have.'

'Please.' Yemi tried smiling.

Placing both prapsies on the floor, Eric said, 'Free choice, boys. Go with Yemi if you like. I won't stop you.'

The prapsies flew straight back to Eric's shoulders.

'We know where we want to be,' one said.

Eric peered at Yemi. 'I think the boys have made their choice, don't you?'

Yemi had no idea how to react. This had never happened to him before. He tried everything to get the prapsies to change their minds. He frowned, stamped his feet, shook his fists. He implored them. When they continued to refuse, he finally burst into tears. One of his Siberian tigers came across, nuzzling him.

Larpskendya said, 'Eric, I want you to tell me exactly how you did that. I've never seen Yemi refused by any creature.'

'I didn't do anything,' Eric said. 'Nothing at all.'

'That's not true. Yemi hasn't been denied that way before, I'm certain.'

'Well,' Eric said coolly, 'I'm not sure it's right for little kids to get what they want all the time. It's not good for them, is it?'

He stared at Yemi and Yemi stared back – a meeting of eyes. For a moment Rachel knew the two boys were measuring each other in ways she could not understand.

'There, there,' Fola said, hugging Yemi. 'See, look at that! You cannot have everything!'

Yemi remained sorrowful until one of the Siberian tigers licked his face, making him laugh. His usual cheerfulness returned immediately. He jumped onto the tiger's back, slapping its flanks for a ride.

'Yemi's not really an ordinary child any more, is he?' Rachel said. 'He's more than that.'

'He is many things,' Larpskendya answered. 'But most of the time he still behaves typically for a child his age. He enjoys sweets and toys, and the usual kinds of games, especially hide-and-seek.'

'Oh yes!' added Fola. 'He no like if the animals hide for too long. But the animals must never find *him* when he hide, oh no! He's just a baby still, a *pikin*. He like this –' she took him from the tiger's back and bumped him up and down on her knee, sending Yemi into fits of laughter – 'and he has such moods, and must get his way! Crying for nothing!'

Rachel glanced across at the Siberian tigers. The behaviour of one of them had started to concern her. It was no common tiger, she was certain of that. Its movements were too precise, too calculated, almost too affectionate. Each time she studied it the tiger stopped what it was doing and gazed thoughtfully at her – an almost human gesture.

At one point Yemi spoke to the tiger. In response the tiger buried its wet nose in his ear and whispered something back. Rachel distinctly heard words.

'That's not an animal!' she shouted.

6

serpantha

Raising all her defensive spells, Rachel drew Eric behind her.

'Do not be alarmed,' said the tiger, transforming.

Rachel expected a Witch, but it was a Wizard who rose before her. Wearing a simple aquamarine robe, he was approximately seven feet high, equally tall as Larpskendya, with the same wild, unreadable eyes. Rachel found she could only look at him for a moment. She glanced at Eric and saw he felt the same way.

'I am Serpantha,' the Wizard said. His voice was rich and light and seemed to come from a noticeably younger age than that of Larpskendya. Was he younger? Not for the first time, Rachel wondered how old the wizards were. Bowing low to Rachel and Eric, Serpantha said, 'It is an honour to meet you at last, though I feel I already know you well. Larpskendya is right. There is a strength in both of you that will not be easily challenged on this world, or beyond it.'

Yemi tugged at Serpantha's sleeve, clearly wanting to play.

'You and Larpskendya are brothers,' Rachel said. 'I'm right, aren't I?'

Larpskendya said, 'I told you she would know. It is difficult to keep any secrets from this one.'

'But you are ... older than Larpskendya,' Eric said. 'You sound younger, but you're much older. I can sense it in your magic.'

Serpantha gave Eric a look that was almost fearful. 'How can you tell? That should not be possible.'

'Your spells are so tired, that's how,' Eric said. His eyes moistened as he felt Serpantha's spells calling desperately out to him. 'They've been fighting so long. It's hard for them to continue. Oh, and they don't want to, they don't want to.'

Serpantha reached out. With trembling hands he held Eric. 'Yes,' he said. 'I have asked too much of them these last years – and then I have asked more, and more again. The war – there has been no rest for myself or Larpskendya.' He lowered his gaze, then said, with a crooked smile, 'Can you tell how much strength my spells have left, Eric? It is difficult for me to be certain. They lie to me, you know.'

'They won't fail you soon,' Eric rasped.

'That is good to hear,' Serpantha said, his voice lightening again. He picked Yemi up, placing him on his broad shoulders. 'I have been here for a while with this little one.'

'Are you here to protect him from the Griddas?' Rachel asked.

'Partly. A typical Gridda would try to destroy Yemi at once – unless she thought she could use him. But actually

Yemi needs watching for other reasons as well. It is not that he is bad – of course not – it is just that an idle or misguided thought of his could accidentally destroy many things of value on your world.' Serpantha kissed Yemi, then whispered to him, 'Even your happiest thoughts can be dangerous, you wonder…'

Rachel recalled the incident with the bears. On his second birthday Fola had given Yemi a brown bear cub. Yemi could not contain his joy at this surprise. He wanted each person to share it. The next morning everyone – every child *and* adult on Earth – woke to find a pretty cub cuddled up beside them.

'The same problems,' Serpantha said, 'beset all gifted youngsters.' He glanced knowingly at Larpskendya, who laughed. 'But Yemi's skills exceed anything I've seen before, even in a Wizard. I have been attempting to teach him the hardest thing of all – to realize that he cannot always have everything he wants. With great difficulty he's beginning to accept such things. And he has a beautiful, resourceful sister to help him do so.' Serpantha reached out and pulled Fola into his wide embrace. She smiled shyly, looking up at him. 'Fola cannot be the ever-adapting play companion I have been,' Serpantha said to Rachel, 'but with your help I am sure I will not be missed. And it is just as well, for I must leave.'

'Leave?' Rachel wanted to weep, but she did not know why.

'An opportunity has arisen,' Serpantha said. 'One we never expected. The High Witches have requested a meeting between us.'

'I… I thought the Griddas had killed them all.'

'No, some are imprisoned, and a few survive in the

tunnels. One of these managed to escape from Ool and deliver a message, though she died afterwards of wounds even Larpskendya could not repair. The message was from Calen.'

'Calen? That's Heebra's daughter!' Rachel said. 'Her mother died here. How can you trust Calen? She must hate us.'

'Yes, she must,' Serpantha said, 'and normally I would not trust her at all. And who is to say I can now? I have spent many of your lifetimes distrusting the High Witches. It is difficult for me to change, too, though I must.' He tickled Yemi, making him giggle, then stared solemnly at Rachel. 'You have no idea what a pitiful state the High Witches are in. They are truly desperate, I've no doubt of that. I will meet with them.'

'Alone?' Rachel asked.

'If it is a trap,' Serpantha said, 'ten Wizards will probably be no better than one. I –'

'Don't go,' Eric said. 'Please don't.'

'Why, Eric?'

'I don't know. Just don't. I don't want you to.'

There was silence in the cave.

'I must go, Eric,' Serpantha said. 'Our war with the Witches has been an endless one. I would not wish the same on you. This may be the only opportunity to end it. The Griddas are a different species. I do not think their leader, Gultrathaca, will be so eager to negotiate. And there is something else you should know. The Griddas have nearly found Ithrea. We've tried to obscure it, but our concealments will not hold them off for long.'

Morpeth, Rachel thought, her heart leaping.

'So you see,' Serpantha said, 'there is more than the

welfare of your own world wrapped up in these matters. I know the risk I am taking, and though I'm cautioned against it, I will travel alone.' He turned sadly to Larpskendya. 'Well, brother, it is time for my leaving. Yemi is not happy, but he is being brave about it, as you must.'

Larpskendya said nothing. He could not meet his brother's eyes as they held each other.

'I wish I had the opportunity to spend more time with you,' Serpantha said to Eric and Rachel. 'However, I am confident this will not be the last time we meet.' He took Yemi's hand, leading the party in silence from the cave to the surface. The air was warm. The sun shone down on a field dappled with poppies and cornflowers. Rachel did not notice. She hardly saw the field at all. Something inside her wanted to keep Serpantha close.

'You can't leave,' she said. 'Who will protect Yemi if you go?'

'Fola – and there is another I have been training,' Serpantha said. 'I believe you know her well.'

He motioned to the sky. A girl arrived from it. She had pure blond hair, and eyes so light blue that those first meeting her could notice nothing else.

'Heiki!' Rachel cried out.

Heiki alighted next to Rachel, and they kissed like the true friends they had become.

Serpantha watched them interact, saw how easy the girls were with each other. 'Once, you two battled as if nothing else had any meaning except that battle,' he reminded them. 'But that has changed. We must all be prepared to change now.'

Heiki exchanged a few words with Eric and Rachel,

then took her place beside Yemi. Already her eyes scanned the sky, alert for danger to him.

'Brother, are you ready?' Serpantha asked. 'I need your strength now.'

The Wizards placed their heads together. Rachel sensed the beginnings of a shift so potent that she could not begin to comprehend it.

Yemi gazed adoringly at Serpantha. For once his animals had stayed behind, knowing he wanted to be on his own with Serpantha for as long as possible. Seeing that Serpantha was about to leave, he forgot his promise to be brave. He clasped Serpantha's leg and hung determinedly on.

With infinite care Serpantha loosened Yemi's fingers. He took a final look over the field and the undulating green hills beyond.

'I love this world,' he said to Eric and Rachel. 'And I love your race; the most magical of you give so much. It is not always so.' He embraced them – and they couldn't stand it. It was as if they were losing something they had longed for their whole lives. Fola clumsily touched Serpantha's face.

Eric stepped up. 'I wish I knew you better,' he blurted. 'I wish I did.'

'You will,' Serpantha told him firmly.

And shifted.

7

passion

Serpantha made his way cautiously along the tunnels.

For some time he had been travelling downwards, following the magical scent of High Witches. That scent was overwhelmingly strong now – the Witches so close he could hear their stifled whisperings. The tunnels of Ool were covered in tiny luminous life-forms that emitted a murky beige light. That meant Serpantha could see, but his nails were not designed to clutch rock. Unable to find any grip at all on the smooth walls, he flew where the tunnels were steepest. At last the tunnels flattened out to become the entrance to a large cave.

Serpantha stood upright and walked boldly inside.

The Witches were waiting. There were ten of them, ten mature High Witches. Seeing Serpantha, each responded differently. Most retreated in fear to the back of the cave, their soul-snakes hissing. A few Witches held their ground, clamping their jaws to prevent them lashing out.

Serpantha had expected these reactions. Not wishing to invite an attack, he deliberately kept a discreet distance – and waited.

At first the Witches dared not approach. Then, in a swift flurry, they jumped on Serpantha and dragged him out of the cave.

Serpantha was not surprised at the roughness of the treatment. He did nothing to retaliate, though the stone cut his skin. The Witches hauled him along several corridors before throwing their burden at the feet of another Witch. If this Witch dreaded the appearance of Serpantha as much as the others, she hid it well. Her yellow soul-snake examined him with frank curiosity.

'Welcome, Serpantha,' she said.

'Welcome, Calen.'

For a considerable time Calen and Serpantha simply gazed at one another. This was the first occasion in more than two hundred thousand years that a High Witch and a Wizard had met outside of a battleground. Finally Serpantha bowed. In the nearly forgotten manner he held out his arms, offering to bond with Calen in the formal style.

Nylo, Calen's soul-snake, wanted no contact with the Wizard, but she made him fleetingly entwine with Serpantha's wrists. Neither Serpantha nor Calen expected it, but the touch sent deep surges of loss through them. Feelings arose that they had difficulty speaking through, and for a moment the original purpose of their meeting was forgotten. Raising their eyes, they looked intently at one another, saying nothing, not knowing what to say.

For much of her life Calen had wondered what it might

be like to match herself against the legendary Serpantha. Now that he stood before her, she knew how foolish that notion had been. A single glance at him showed the plenitude of his power. Even her mother, Heebra, had never possessed such ardent, lucid intelligence. His eyes held her: solemn, candid, beautiful. Beautiful? Calen caught herself. How could his eyes be beautiful? Nylo stared and stared at the Wizard, disregarding her silent command to stop. In embarrassment, Calen stepped away. She had never felt the way she felt now – unmade by the steady slow gaze of a Wizard.

Serpantha felt the same bewildering emotions. He tried to gather himself. Brushing cave dirt from his shoulder, he said bluntly, 'I expected a warmer greeting than this.'

'No doubt you did!' Calen replied. 'Check the rest of the tunnels,' she snapped at her Witches. 'Make sure there are no more Wizards.'

'I came alone,' Serpantha assured her.

'Surely you don't expect me to accept your word on that?' Calen motioned for scouts to sniff up the connecting tunnels. While waiting, she attempted to contain her emotions. What was she feeling? This was ridiculous! She had prepared so long for this negotiation. The lives of all her Witches depended on its outcome! When her scouts returned Calen, composing herself, faced Serpantha again.

'It gives me no pleasure to be here,' she said. 'Can you talk for all your kind?'

'Each Wizard speaks for all others. Always.'

'If this is some kind of Wizard trick…'

'You requested the meeting, not I.'

Calen half-smiled. 'Heebra taught me that conversation with Wizards is pointless.'

'Did she?' Serpantha said. 'How could she have known? Heebra never asked for a meeting, though we invited her. What was your mother so afraid of?'

Calen tried to think clearly. Her attention was being diverted by Serpantha's eyes. They were smaller than hers, only slightly larger than human eyes. Absurdly, she had a strong temptation to explore the delicate brows above them. She resisted it.

Serpantha wondered: did she even know? Or had so much time passed that all memory amongst the Witches had been forgotten or removed?

'Do you realize,' he said, 'that Wizards and Witches came originally from the same world?' He watched for a reaction. 'We were once a single race, sharing all things.'

Calen's mind reeled. 'I don't believe that!' She retreated from him, staring fiercely at his body. Could it be true? Serpantha's jaws were far tinier than her own, the teeth delicate. 'We never had jaws like yours,' she said.

'No,' Serpantha replied. 'Your original jaws were smaller than ours. You altered them.'

'You're lying!'

'Am I? What advantage would I gain from it?'

While Calen absorbed this, Serpantha appraised the other Witches. Normally Highs took immense pride in their appearance. Even battle-weary Highs used magic to hide their injuries for as long as they could. These Witches were all filthy and thin, their black dresses in shreds; some had slackening jaws where the muscles no longer had the strength to support the heavy teeth.

It meant they were close to death.

Or, Serpantha realized, it could mean the Witches were pretending to be injured.

His information spells automatically performed another sweep of the Witches. Their injuries were genuine. Serpantha trusted the judgement of his spells. Not once in his ancient life had they misled him in a matter of such importance. He stroked the damaged arm of the closest Witch – a tenderness she withdrew from only slowly.

'You have suffered terribly,' he murmured. 'I see how much.'

'We are still to be feared!' Calen shouted.

'I have no doubt of that.'

Keeping Nylo close, Calen tried to determine what to do next. Instinctively she knew Serpantha was telling the truth about their origins. It both disgusted and excited her to know this, but why should it change anything between them? She could not afford to make a mistake. Already several of her Witches were lowering their guard, drawing closer to Serpantha, their fear less than it had been. One reached out to him – and Calen surprised herself by slapping the claw away herself. Strong feelings welled inside her again.

Serpantha counted the Witches in the cave. 'Is this ... all that is left of the Highs?' he asked.

'No. There are remnants hiding in other tunnels. Some are in locations I know nothing about – in case I am caught. I lead a few, where I am able.'

Serpantha nodded. 'As the daughter of Heebra, the Griddas must have a considerable bounty on your head.'

Calen laughed grimly. 'I hope so! I would be disappointed if that were not the case!'

'How have you managed to avoid them?'

'We don't avoid them,' Calen said. 'If we can smell the Griddas in time, we flee. Where that is not possible, we fight. As you can see, we have fought…many times. In any case, now that they have won the main battle, the Gridda leaders have less interest in us than you think. They are more intrigued by something else – the human child, Yemi.'

Serpantha tried to hide his concern. 'You told them about the boy?'

'Under torture even a High Witch can be made to talk, Wizard. The Griddas were curious to know why over five hundred of Heebra's best fighters returned in defeat from Earth, speaking of the spell Yemi released.'

'What do the Griddas know about him?'

'Everything we know. His scent, his skills. His innocence.' She eyed him. 'Your guard must be slacking, Serpantha. Gridda scouts study all Wizard movements to and from Earth. I am surprised you have not stationed more Wizards there to protect the boy.'

'Two are enough,' Serpantha said. 'More would have drawn greater attention.'

'Only two? Thank you,' said a new voice.

From the shadows, watcher and soldier spiders suddenly appeared. Like a tide, they swarmed from all directions across the floor of the cave. Griddas followed behind.

Serpantha reacted at once. He had never been so completely surprised by an ambush, but now was not the time to dwell on the reason. A nest of spells, some of the deadliest any creature had ever summoned, sprang to defend him. The first cluster he sent to seal off any further entrances. A second, to deflect attacks, sought to alter his body shape, scent and chemical structure. The third cluster was a battery of fast assault spells – to distract his opponents while he escaped.

But none of Serpantha's spells worked.

They lay uselessly in his mind, screaming in fear for him.

The Griddas, two full packs, ranged themselves about the Wizard. When they were in position a final Gridda dropped her bulk down from the ceiling.

She bounded across and raised herself to her full height. 'I am Gultrathaca,' she said.

'I know who you are.'

'Do you know what I am going to do to you?'

Serpantha knew. He tried to shift, but his spells could not fix the transfer points.

'An inhibiting spell,' Gultrathaca explained. 'Effective only in contact with skin. In this case, Nylo's skin. Of course, how could you have known? No High Witch ever used such a spell. When we used it on them, they were equally surprised!'

'Do as you wish,' said Serpantha, facing her. 'I will tell you nothing.'

'We shall see.'

Several Griddas trussed his arms and legs with spell-thread.

Serpantha turned to Calen. 'What have you done?' he said, his voice shuddering with regret and pity. 'Oh, Calen, what bargain do you think the Griddas will ever honour?'

With difficulty, Calen ignored him. Facing Gultrathaca, she said, 'I did what you asked. Now fulfil *your* promise. Release my High Witches.'

Gultrathaca lifted an arm and struck Calen's face. Two of her jaws were shattered. From the floor, Calen screamed, 'But ... you promised! We bonded, snake and spiders! The agreement cannot be broken!'

'Do you think the niceties of your bonds and promises mean anything to me?' said Gultrathaca. She stared at Calen with contempt. 'You have betrayed all your Witches.'

Calen struggled to get up. 'But we let you maim us! We allowed it. To convince the Wizard we let you …' Her face hardened. 'You won't find us all,' she yelled. 'There are more of us than you realize!'

'You fool,' Gultrathaca said. 'We know where all the High Witches are. Your kind make so much noise any Gridda infant can hear you approaching.'

As she was led away, Calen looked at Serpantha. A fundamental change had occurred in him. His face was blank, his eyes glazed over. All the warmth had begun to drain from his skin.

'What's happening?' asked a Gridda, prodding at Serpantha's cheek.

'It is not our doing,' Gultrathaca said. 'The Wizard is retreating inside some private realm. He thinks we cannot reach him there, but he is wrong. Eventually, he'll tell us everything we need to know about Yemi. Perhaps he'll even lead us to Larpskendya himself.'

Serpantha lay quietly in the arms of the Griddas. He no longer moved. A serene expression had spread across his features. His eyes were closed, at peace. Forcing open the lids, Gultrathaca gazed into them. The colours, once so bright, had started to fade. The Gridda pack hauled the body of Serpantha from the cave to the interrogation levels.

'Hurry!' Gultrathaca shrieked.

8

floating koalas, and other pretties

Eric strode purposefully along a winding path.

He was in an isolated wood, hundreds of miles from home. The prapsies accompanied him, taking short flights to keep up. So far they had managed not to annoy too many of the woodland animals, and normally Eric would have rewarded them by playing a game. Not today. He had a special reason for asking Rachel to bring him here.

Eric was seeking an explanation from Albertus Robertson.

Since Larpskendya left Earth to investigate Serpantha's failure to return from Ool, the behaviour of all the spectrums had altered. Until then they had been content to stay entirely still for days. Suddenly spectrums worldwide were on the move. And they were not alone. The thrill-seekers had joined them. They no longer hung back, out

of sight. They had openly united with the spectrums –
flying them wherever they wished to go.

Eric left the path, picking his way between scattered
beech trees.

'Are we nearly there, boys?' one prapsy asked.

'Shush,' Eric replied. 'Don't want to scare him off, do
we?' He tiptoed around a bush.

And there, in a small clearing, stood Albertus Robertson.

He was balanced on one bent leg. His other leg was off
the ground, as though something had caught Albertus's
interest in mid-step. No child in the world other than a
spectrum could have held such an unnatural position for
more than a few seconds. For a while Eric just hung
around, trying to disentangle his feelings. What drew him
to the spectrums? The things other children found creepy
about them, fascinated him...

Albertus paid Eric no attention. His narrow shoulders
and thin neck did not seem quite strong enough to hold
his heavy head – as if, Eric thought, on a windy day an
unexpected gust might snap it off.

He wanted to start a conversation with Albertus, but
was put off by the presence of the thrill-seekers. There
were two of them, two teenage girls. That in itself was
unusual – Eric did not know of any spectrum with more
than one thrill-seeker. Both girls were only inches from
Albertus. Their arms were stretched out towards him,
ready to lift him up at a moment's notice. One of them
clearly did not welcome Eric's arrival. She glanced briefly,
angrily, in his direction.

'Hi,' Eric said, feeling awkward. When there was no
reply one of the prapsies screeched, 'Wake up when Eric is
speaking to you!'

'It's all right, boys,' Eric said. 'Let it go.'

One of the thrill-seeker girls rotated fractionally towards him. 'Please don't interfere,' she said. 'Go away. Leave us in solitude.'

'I'm not going to bother you. I just want to ask a few questions.'

'We don't want to answer them.'

'Why?'

'If we speak to you, then some of our mindfulness will wander.'

'Wander?' Eric hesitated. 'You mean – from Albertus?'

'Of course. Please leave. You are distracting him, and there is danger.'

'What danger?' Eric stepped closer, forcing the closest girl to pay him attention. She immediately took up a defensive stance. Eric felt her attack spells being readied. At the same time the other thrill-seeker held Albertus Robertson's waist, preparing to lift him to safety.

'I'm not a danger to you!' Eric said. 'Surely you know that.'

'Go away!' the girl demanded.

The prapsies flew around her head, shouting insults she ignored.

In frustration, Eric gazed directly at Albertus Robertson. A falling leaf had come to rest on one of his upturned ears. With extraordinary speed the nearest of his thrill-seekers ripped the leaf away.

'Look, talk to me,' Eric said to Albertus. 'I'm close to Rachel and others who have our safety in mind. I sense you're part of that somehow, but you must explain your-selves. What are you all looking for? Why are you all on the move? What –'

Albertus Robertson flinched. At first Eric thought he was responding to him, but it soon became apparent that the spectrum's conduct had nothing to do with Eric. His head cocked skyward. With panic in his eyes, Albertus silently opened and closed his mouth, desperate to say something. Glancing at one another, his thrill-seekers picked him up. They flew above the trees and away.

'What is it?' Eric called after them. 'What's –'

Suddenly he gasped and fell back, understanding.

The prapsies stared at Eric. They touched the tips of their wings against his face, as they always did when they were frightened.

'Eric, what's wrong? Eric!'

'Find Rachel,' he rasped. 'Oh, boys, find her fast!'

Nine Gridda packs descended into the mild-weathered skies of Earth.

Using her spies, Gultrathaca had chosen a time when she was certain Larpskendya was absent, and there was a brief gap in the network of children patrolling the skies. The task should have been easier, but Serpantha had given Gultrathaca nothing. Throughout the interrogations he had stayed silent. Gultrathaca could hardly believe his resistance. How could he hold out for so long against the unrelenting battery of spells the packs breathed inside him? Even causing Serpantha true pain had eluded her. He had entered some kind of tranquil region where her Griddas could not reach him...

Gultrathaca countered Serpantha's silence with numbers. On their last visit to Earth, the High Witches had helpfully left boosters to improve speeds between the two worlds. Gultrathaca used them and hundreds of

Griddas – all those who had learned to shift – streamed across the continents of Earth.

In the absence of better information, they sniffed for an individual child whose magical signature was more remarkable than all others. They should never have succeeded. Before he left Larpskendya had created a spell to camouflage Yemi's magical scent. But Yemi himself, not understanding its importance, had merely seen the spell as a challenge – and broken it.

The pack of Griddas who came across him were fortunate in another way. Heiki, charged with protecting him, had not allowed Yemi outside in recent days. This morning Yemi, in his boredom, had mischievously shifted to a summer meadow. Heiki could not persuade him back underground, and the Griddas found him in bright sunshine, playing with his animal friends.

Heiki saw the Griddas first – a sight that baffled her. She had been prepared for outstretched claws and teeth, not these oddities. Confused, she called sharply to Fola, who was talking with her brother.

'What is it?' Fola asked.

'Say the safety words to Yemi.'

'What's wrong?'

'Just say them!'

Fola turned to look. If the Griddas had come in their true form she would have known at once to whisper in Yemi's ear the words she had practised with him over and over – words Yemi had been taught meant danger, to get away.

But Gultrathaca had planned for this.

Her first instinct had been to use the tactics of terror: to scare Yemi by threatening him and those he loved. However, she had heard how easily Yemi had disposed of

Witches in the past, and sensed her Griddas would not be able to *force* this particular human child to join them.

So – to entice him instead – the Griddas came in other guises.

Having questioned the High Witches they knew what young children liked, and they came in that fashion. They came as the playthings of children. They came disguised as animals: as furry dogs and oversized kittens, floating koalas, and other pretties. They came as dolphins with merrily flicking tails. And they came as made-up things – things that were warm, that smiled at Yemi, that reached out their arms for him, that were soft and downy and pleasant to look upon. They came in bright, noisy, chuckling shapes that swept down from the clouds.

Fola reacted too slowly to Heiki's warning. Before she could open her mouth a Gridda spell sealed her lips. She tried to make Yemi understand as the Griddas closed in, but he was too mesmerized to notice.

Yemi knew that the things approaching with open paws and crazily wagging tails were not real, but that only excited him. Serpantha had assumed many animal guises when they played together; and while Yemi knew these new creatures were not disguised Wizards, they were certainly magical, powerfully so. It did not worry him that they were not real. He had himself made many objects that were not real, and those had never harmed him, after all.

Heiki seized one Gridda as it passed by. Briefly, as she fought it, the manufactured kitten-smile masking the true face of the Gridda faded. But it was too powerful for Heiki to deal with on her own. It cuffed her with a hairy blow. The blow was calculated to disable Heiki without killing her – in case Yemi noticed.

Heiki was left dazed amongst the grass and small flowers of a field.

The Griddas drifted to the ground. All Yemi's animals were joined by the new brightly-glowing companions, each given its own to play with – there were welcoming Gridda arms for them all.

An impossibly floppy puppy plucked Yemi off the ground. As the other Griddas hastily surrounded him, he did not notice that his true animal friends were left behind.

On a tide of chattering, mirth-filled magic he was carried beyond the skies of Earth.

Eric and Rachel arrived too late.

They found Heiki in the flowered field, her cheeks burning with anguish. Animals surrounded her, searching vainly in the grass for Yemi. Eric could faintly detect Yemi's dwindling scent; then even that faint smell was snuffed out as the Griddas erased it.

Rachel placed a distress call to Larpskendya while she tended to Heiki's injuries. Too distraught to speak, Heiki sat gazing at the clouds, as if they themselves had betrayed her.

Other children arrived at last from the sky, stunned by the speed of the kidnap.

For a while all Yemi's special animal friends crawled, walked or flew around the fields, searching. A few dug at the soil, thinking Yemi might be under it. Then, at the same moment, each animal stopped. They sat quite still, faces all tilted up expectantly.

'Hey, what's going on?' Eric asked. 'What are they doing?'

Rachel's information spells scanned the local area. 'I can't tell. I don't detect anything.'

'It's Yemi's butterflies,' Heiki said. 'Normally this is the time they fly overhead here.'

The skies were empty.

Rachel and Eric scanned the rest of the world. Everywhere, the flocks of yellow Camberwell Beauties had vanished – and animals all over the world were beginning to pine for them.

'At least,' Eric said huskily, 'Yemi has his sister. They took Fola, too. I wonder why they did that? She's not got much magic.'

Rachel exchanged a glance with Heiki.

'To help control him,' Heiki said.

Rachel nodded. 'Until the Griddas learn how to do it themselves.'

9

the spectrums

News of Yemi's abduction changed the world.

Virtually overnight the game-playing of older children came to a stop as Heiki, filled with an almost insane energy, turned all their talents to more serious ends. Thereafter, day and night across the Earth, children honed their defensive spells. They toiled until they were so tired they nearly dropped out of the skies.

Animals everywhere were devastated by Yemi's loss. Many refused to accept the missing butterflies. They searched everywhere: on the land, in the deep seas. Birds of many species came together in swarms so dense that their bodies blackened the skies. Those animals who had been privileged enough to have had personal contact with Yemi lost all interest in the normal rhythms of life. They ignored their food and stopped caring for themselves.

But the most dramatic reaction came from the spectrums.

Shortly after Yemi was taken they travelled from all countries to the equator. Once there, they spread out at equal intervals, forming a line to encompass the world. The thrill-seekers came with them. No longer just trans-porters of the spectrums, the thrill-seekers started attend-ing to all of their needs. They clothed and fed the spectrums. They bathed them. When their throats were dry, they quenched them.

The spectrums themselves offered no explanation for any of this. They merely watched, keeping up their precise geometrical sweep of the skies. Then, one evening, there was another development: all the spectrums began to radiate pulses of energy. Some pulses they sent out into space in measured intervals; others passed between them. They were talking – a din and cross-chatter of high-speed communication that disturbed the workings of almost every item of electromagnetic equipment on the globe.

Rachel and Eric followed all these developments, but they were more concerned about the wellbeing of Larpskendya and Serpantha. Weeks passed without any further news. Eric's skill of pinpointing magic at long range outstripped that of anyone else, so every day, for hours at a stretch, Rachel carried him into the upper atmosphere, hopeful of finding the magical scent of Wizards.

Across the Earth, new defences were installed by Heiki. They were far tighter than any before; that, at least, was a lesson the Griddas had taught them all. Everyone waited. And then, one afternoon while Rachel sat at home talking quietly with Mum and Dad, Eric's face sprang to life.

'It's Larpskendya!' he cried. Then Rachel saw his face crumple.

'What's the matter, Eric?'

'Something's wrong with his flying.'

As soon as the Wizard came into range of Rachel's own information spells, she knew. 'He's hurt.'

'How badly?' Dad asked.

'Terribly.'

'Larpskendya's not even shifting,' Eric said. 'He can barely fly at all.'

All four of them stood up, rushing to the windows. Normally it was impossible to catch Larpskendya's arrival, but on this occasion there was plenty of time to see him. He flew towards the house with such difficulty that Rachel, running into the garden, had to catch him as he landed. Larpskendya's knees folded under him. He picked himself up, stumbled, tried to smile, to reassure them. Rachel placed her shoulder under the Wizard's arm and, with Dad's and Eric's help, half-dragged his large frame through the door.

'Don't let go,' Larpskendya told Rachel hoarsely.

'I won't.'

For a moment Larpskendya's whole weight leaned against her. She held out her arm to steady him. As she did so, Rachel knew that Larpskendya needed it; in that instant only a single human arm held him upright. Sensing that, her world turned upside down. It took all her self-control not to scream and scream.

'Shush, now,' Larpskendya murmured. 'There's no need for that.'

'But you're frightening me.'

'Don't be frightened. Not you. I couldn't bear that.'

Rachel's information spells found injuries everywhere. No part of Larpskendya was undamaged. He should have een dead from Gridda attacks already; only the Wizard's magic, his extraordinary spells, kept his body together.

Larpskendya tried to disentangle himself from Rachel's embrace, but she would not let him. Together they dropped down on the floor. They lay there, saying nothing, while Larpskendya recovered. At last he told them all, 'Yemi has been taken to Ool.'

Rachel's chest tightened. 'What … what will they do to him?'

Larpskendya shook his head. 'He is probably safe for now. The Griddas went to great lengths to get him. I doubt they will harm Yemi, at least not immediately. I am more concerned for Serpantha.'

Eric hardly dared ask, 'Is he alive?'

'Yes, but if the Griddas have him, it would be better if that were not so.' Larpskendya trembled, not from his wounds. 'I should have gone myself to Ool,' he said. 'Serpantha would not allow it. He was always … protecting me … He –' Suddenly Larpskendya's entire body convulsed. 'Oh my brother,' he burst out. 'What have they done to you? What are they doing now?'

Rachel reached out to touch him, and when she did Larpskendya wept.

He wept uncontrollably. Rachel and Eric were so affected that they burst out with tears of their own, without clearly understanding why. It was because Larpskendya wept, that was reason enough. They made a pile that held onto Larpskendya in the middle of the carpet. The prapsies joined them, nuzzling the Wizard's face.

Larpskendya's body was wracked by tears. Then he roused himself and stood up to his full height. 'Well,' he said solemnly, 'now it has come to this, I think it is time to explain all. I have not lied, but I have not told you everything.' He looked at Rachel.

'Larpskendya, what is it?' she asked, still holding his robe.

'The creatures you know as High Witches,' Larpskendya said, 'are not as different from Wizards as you believe. In fact, there was once almost no difference between us at all.'

Rachel let go of his robe, confused. Then she fell back as she noticed his eyes. Larpskendya no longer camouflaged the truth: tattoos, the same tattoos that had stared so mercilessly from the sockets of Dragwena and Heebra and Calen, stared out of them. Seeing Rachel's reaction, Larpskendya moved forward to console her. He stopped when she screamed.

'I know,' he said. 'It is too much.' He wanted to approach Rachel, but knew she could not accept it. 'At one time we belonged to the same species,' he explained. 'The females you know as High Witches were like us, or as similar as your own men and women are to each other, or your children. I am sorry to have concealed this truth from you, of all people, Rachel. Try to forgive me. It was not what I wanted.'

Rachel felt too appalled to answer. She felt betrayed.

While she clutched Mum and retreated, Eric gathered up the frightened prapsies. He did not recoil from the Wizard as Rachel had done.

Larpskendya stared at him. 'Did you know, Eric?'

'Not really, but I sensed something. You've occasionally used similar-patterned spells to the Witches. I wondered why. I see now.'

'Tell us the rest,' Dad demanded.

'Our species,' Larpskendya said, 'was possibly the first in which magic evolved. We discovered that we could fly, as you have done. We explored our world. We explored ourselves in ways you are only beginning to consider. And we ventured to other worlds. We travelled.' Larpskendya paused. Again, he looked at Rachel, but she was not ready to meet his eyes. 'For many ages,' Larpskendya continued, 'Witches and Wizards worked together. But as our magic developed, disputes started to arise about how to use it. A sect of powerful females decided they no longer wanted to be restricted by the jurisdiction of our magical laws. They left, and for many generations nothing was heard from them. But finally they began to leave their mark on the civilizations of other worlds, and it was always destructive. They would not reconsider or stop. The endless war began at that time.'

Dad cleared his throat. 'Why...why do the High Witches look so different from you now?'

'Partly because they simply no longer wanted to look like us,' Larpskendya answered. 'And another reason: to suit their new aggressiveness.'

'Were you there at the start?' Eric asked. 'When the war began?'

'No. I am old, but I have only been alive for a fraction of the war. It is all I have known, Eric: war, or preparations for it, or fear of it; and fear for those drawn in, such as yourselves.'

Rachel spluttered, suddenly finding her voice, 'Why didn't...why didn't you tell us, tell *me*, about this before? I could have accepted it! Why didn't you trust me?'

'I wanted to,' Larpskendya said. 'I wanted to so much. But the fate of many other worlds, perhaps all worlds, depended on this one. I was frightened, Rachel, of a second failure.'

'A second?'

'We – the Wizards – came to your Earth ages ago, but we made a mistake. The Witch Dragwena had dominated your world for a long time before we arrived. She implanted a fear of us deep within children. I didn't dare stir up that ancient memory.' He sighed. 'Try to understand. I could not risk telling you the truth because I knew there would be times when I needed to have your absolute trust.'

'You had it!' Rachel said. 'Of course you did!'

'Did I?' As he moved towards her, Rachel shrank back. 'You can barely accept the truth now, Rachel, as well as you know me. If you had known the Wizards were so closely related to the Witches, would you have really believed in me that time at the North Pole? When I said Heebra could take your life and that of Eric, would you have continued to believe in me? When I needed you to look into my eyes then – these tattooed eyes – and completely trust me with all your heart, would you have done so?'

Rachel searched herself. 'No, yes, I…I don't know! I might not have done. But' – her body shook with emotion – 'it's too much, too much. Truths and lies…how do I know you're telling the truth now?' She glared at him. 'You sent Serpantha to Ool. Why? You sent a Wizard who knew all about Yemi and the defences about him. If you've been fighting a war for so long, how could you make such a stupid mistake?'

'I cannot tell you that. I may never be able to do so.'

'More secrets?' Rachel blasted. 'How many others are there?'

Larpskendya was silent. Eric could sense his immense weariness.

'I could *force* you to believe anything I want,' Larpskendya said at last. 'I have a spell for that. I will not use it, but I am tempted to do so because more depends on me now than I can convey.' He passed his fingers over his face and robe. 'This is what I am like,' he said. 'I have come back to Earth, leaving those I care deeply about, to discuss what can be done to rescue Yemi. If –'

'Wait,' Eric said. 'Something's heading this way. Griddas.'

'I'm aware of them,' Larpskendya said calmly. 'A few only, near your moon, probably the remnants of those who ambushed me on my way here.'

'No, not those ones. There are several more packs, much further out – between Saturn and Jupiter.'

Larpskendya glanced up, startled. 'Even my spells can't detect that far. Are you sure, Eric?'

'Yes. Absolutely.'

'Then I must leave at once.'

Rachel half-lurched towards him. 'Larpskendya, what are you saying? You can't do that! I've measured your strength. You can still shift, but in your weakened state if you meet any Griddas...'

'If I stay I will endanger you all,' Larpskendya said. He touched her arm. 'I won't do that.'

Through his fingertips, Rachel felt something reaching out to her. It was Larpskendya's spells, half-insane with weariness, trying to hold the Wizard together. They needed more rest; it was too soon; they had not recovered enough. As Rachel tried to comfort them, they begged her to stay with Larpskendya and help strengthen him.

Rachel forgot all her uncertainty and rushed the short space into Larpskendya's arms. 'You can't leave,' she said, trying to think. 'You *mustn't* leave. I'll contact Heiki and the kids she's training. We'll protect you here. We'll all protect you.'

'No,' he replied firmly. 'You are not yet ready to confront the Griddas. If I die I may yet serve a purpose in giving you more time to prepare for them.' Rachel pleaded for him to reconsider, but Larpskendya would not be moved. Then, as he was about to depart, a sound filtered through the windows.

It was a rising note, a sound of urgency and terror.

'What – what's happening?' Mum put her hands over her ears.

Rachel's information spells radiated out of the house. All around, she sensed children everywhere listening.

'It's the spectrums,' Eric murmured. 'They're speaking.'

Across the world the spectrums had risen skyward. Carried by their thrill-seekers they scattered, taking up positions where every child would be able to hear their message. The message was not composed of syllables or words, but it was a message nevertheless – a clear and articulate call. The voices of the spectrums swelled, rising to an almost unbearable pitch. Each one sang until he or she had no breath left, but there was always one left to sustain the note, so at no point was there an end to it.

No child had ever heard such a message before – but their magic instantly understood. In the living room only Dad and Mum did not understand. They gazed helplessly at Eric.

'Our world is in jeopardy,' Eric told them. 'It's a warning, the first of the spectrums: *There is danger. Stay alert and defend your homes.* That's all it says.' He and Rachel listened as the note altered slightly.

Rachel looked wildly at Larpskendya. 'It's you,' she said. '*You* are in danger!'

Larpskendya nodded. 'Do you understand what the spectrums are now?'

Rachel had no doubt; nor, suddenly, with that first utterance, did any other child on Earth. 'They're protectors of some kind, aren't they?'

'A special type,' replied Larpskendya. 'I have seen their kind develop only once before. They are *species protectors*. With the emergence of magic in children, they've evolved to serve you all. You will find that their own safety or comfort are irrelevant to them. Their purpose is to listen, to warn, to raise a call to arms, to advise brilliantly, to fight if they must; to do anything in their power to safeguard the children of Earth.' Larpskendya paused. 'It seems the danger to me has brought them out. They believe your world will be in peril if I am killed. We shall see. Whatever happens, I am grateful to have witnessed the coming of age of the spectrums. That gives me more hope than I had for you. Well, there is no more time ...'

Gathering himself, Larpskendya hurriedly said his goodbyes to them all.

Rachel could not bear it. Events were happening too fast.

Larpskendya held her hands.

'Find Yemi,' he told her. 'Find him.'

'How can I?' Rachel asked. 'Without you ...'

'Don't you know how strong you are?' Larpskendya almost shouted at her. 'I have never seen a child face a Witch with more courage than you!' He held her tightly and she shook in his embrace. 'You must understand, I may not be able to return,' he said. 'I have cheated the Griddas on enough occasions, but this time... Listen: Yemi's magic is beyond anything the Wizards have ever known. He's so young... the Griddas might be able to influence him. You *must* get to Yemi somehow. Find a way.' Releasing Rachel, Larpskendya turned to Eric. 'Eric, more may now depend on your decisions than in the past. Everything may do so. Everything. Trust your instinct. You have powers beyond comprehension within you.'

Kissing them all, fighting a vast weariness, Larpskendya took a last look round. The prapsies stared up at him. Rachel tried to find some words to express how she felt, but her mind was in pieces. Larpskendya smiled at her. 'Who will comfort my spells now?' he whispered.

Closing his eyes, the Wizard called on his exhausted magic for one last great effort – and shifted.

10

the gratitude
of spiders

Soon after Yemi's arrival on Ool, Gultrathaca ordered
Jarius to visit her.

Jarius did not want to go. She had already disgraced
herself again by refusing to jump out of Heebra's eye-
window. Gultrathaca had been forced to push her. How
humiliating! Even the fearful newborns had been amused
by that!

This time Gultrathaca had invited her to an even worse
location: the Assessment Chamber. It was an appalling
place. The spell-quality of all Griddas was ruthlessly tested
within the Chamber from time to time. Jarius had only
just survived her last trial inside.

How could a human baby, she wondered, survive there?

As she travelled towards it, Jarius noticed an unusual
number of tunnel creatures heading the same way. There

were rodents, skittering insects, even shy burrowers normally far too timid to come near a Gridda tunnel. All the creatures seemed heedless of her – as if there was something below they could not bear to miss.

The traps caught them, of course. They snapped into life, passing the scampering creatures into the food processors. Little mouths waited for them: infants. Jarius heard a wail of anticipation through the walls of her tunnel.

Vast numbers of new Griddas were being raised now. If Jarius listened closely she could hear the distant sound of a newborn biting through her egg, followed by her first scream of hunger. Like all Griddas she arrived starving, desperate to inflate her muscles to a size that would impress her pack.

Jarius resumed the journey. At the Assessment Chamber entrance she quieted all her spiders. The soldiers were especially tense. They perched in the corners of her mouths, readying themselves. Scratching at the seals of the doorway, her watchers tried to peep inside without opening it.

'Welcome,' came Gultrathaca's voice from within.

Jarius warily opened the door a crack.

Instead of the usual dimness, the Chamber was flooded in brilliant sunshine – an intensity of light Jarius had not experienced before. 'No!' she wailed, withdrawing.

Gultrathaca caught her arm, pulling her inside the Chamber. 'Bear it! Bear it!' she raged.

Jarius tried to construct a darkening spell, but she had never needed one before, and she was too frightened to think. If her eye-shields had not automatically clamped shut she would have been blinded. But her loyal watcher spiders had no shields to cover their eyes. The light scorched them. Despite this, believing that Jarius was under attack, they kept scanning the Chamber, shouting out what they saw.

The bright light faded to gloom.

Jarius partially re-opened her eye-shields. 'What … what happened?'

'Yemi responded to your fear,' Gultrathaca told her, 'and to that of your spiders.'

Jarius looked anxiously up at the child. Her pack had told her of the smallness of human children, but she was still unprepared for the size of Yemi. He appeared so frail, so vulnerable, no larger than a newborn Gridda – like a thing she might accidentally fracture.

Yemi held out his arms to her, his face full of complex worry.

Jarius backed away. 'What is he doing?'

'Apologizing. For wounding you.'

'Apologizing?' Jarius blinked in astonishment. 'Doesn't the boy realize what this place is? What harm we can do to him here?'

'No. Let him approach you.'

Yemi toddled over to Jarius. His shorts and shirt brushed against her skin. Not naked, Jarius realized. This was clothing – like the dresses of the Highs. He smiled at her, showing his teeth. Curious, Jarius ran a claw over the edges, searching for sharpness. Yemi laughed, seeing the puzzled expression on her face. Then he made his way up her torso, babbling amiably. Mountaineer-style he scrambled over one jaw, planted his toe on another and reached around to get a purchase on her bony cheeks. Swaying slightly, he pursed his lips and kissed each of her eyes.

A delicious balm settled over them.

'Oh!' Jarius glanced at him. She could not read Yemi's

expression – the architecture of his face was too different – but there was no mistaking his good intentions. His magical greeting showed that he hoped to become her friend. It was shocking: a genuine offer.

When Jarius did not respond Yemi patted her arm reassuringly, as if used to such confusion in the Griddas he met. Shimmying back down her body, he wandered to the rear of the Chamber. Jarius noticed another of his species there, reaching out a hand.

'Fola,' Yemi announced proudly.

Jarius saw an older, larger human: presumably the female. It had more hair, and a long red garment covering all the flesh down from the neck.

Fola gazed in dismay at Jarius. 'Another one!' she groaned. 'Always another one is coming! You want to be hurt like the others? Is that what you want?' She pointed at Gultrathaca. 'While she watches!'

Jarius could not understand Fola's words, but she sensed the anger. It helped her relax. This was behaviour Jarius could better understand. 'The human girl is wary at least,' she said with satisfaction to Gultrathaca. 'She fears us, I see. What does the boy fear?'

Gultrathaca smiled. 'The dark.'

This concept was too perverse for Jarius to understand.

'Humans crave light,' Gultrathaca explained. 'They need it.'

'Then – then why did he remove it when I entered?'

'Yemi wants you to be happy, Jarius,' Gultrathaca said, without amusement. 'He wants you to be his friend. He wants to play with you.'

'But – he's our prisoner! Doesn't he understand that?'

Gultrathaca laughed grimly. 'No, he doesn't. He

doesn't understand at all.' She walked over to Jarius and examined her eyes. 'What little damage was done, Yemi has repaired with his kiss. You are luckier than the first Griddas. When they entered the Chamber, Yemi thought there was something wrong with their eyes. He created a spell to redesign them. It took the shrieks of several Griddas to make him realize his error.'

'But he looks so ... so harmless.'

'Yes, doesn't he,' Gultrathaca agreed. 'Perhaps that is the reason Heebra underestimated him. I will not make the same mistake.'

Jarius studied Fola, fascinated by the way she held Yemi, the way she ran her clawless fingers through his hair. Yemi giggled, half-fighting Fola off. 'I don't understand their gestures,' Jarius said, 'but clearly the female possesses little magic. Does Yemi keep her as live food?'

'No. They share a kind of pack-relationship. He protects her.'

'But she is so weak!'

'Nevertheless, he cares for her. And she cares for him. That is the meaning of the clutching motions.'

Staring at Fola, Jarius felt disgust. It dismayed her to see attention lavished on a puny creature of any species. Enfeebled Griddas were strangled at birth. It was simply the way, and she had never questioned it. How else could the pack be kept strong?

'Don't underestimate the girl,' Gultrathaca told her. 'I started off by thinking she would be easy to manipulate, but she has never co-operated, and made it far more difficult for me to obtain Yemi's trust.'

'If Fola hinders us, why not kill her and work directly on the boy?'

'We tried that. Yemi's reaction was intriguing. When we attacked Fola, for the first time he became angry.'

'Did he retaliate?'

'Yes. And that was even more intriguing. He punished not only the Gridda who attacked Fola. He punished her pack-members as well. Over the three cities they were scattered, thousands of miles apart, yet somehow his spell found them all. They felt only a fraction of the agony intended for Fola, but I believe it was a real warning that he will not tolerate any harm against his sister.'

'Then – what progress has been made?'

'None,' Gultrathaca muttered, frustration edging her voice. 'By now I had hoped to have Yemi's trust, or at least get him to perform spells that might be useful to us. But he does not react in any of the usual ways. When I threaten him he treats it as an amusement. He does what he likes.'

'What he *likes*? Something must affect him!'

'If so, I've yet to find it.'

Yemi was staring at Jarius's feet. He chuckled, crooked his fingers, beckoning.

The next moment Jarius's spiders began to desert her.

She shrieked in terror because this only happened to dying Griddas. Until death arrived a Gridda's spiders, who had cherished her through all dramas, would stay with her. Only when the healer spiders confirmed that her last breath had expired did they leave. If their owner had been killed by another Gridda, the spiders would offer themselves to the newcomer, hoping she might take a few. But if their owner died by accident, or was killed by a tunnel predator, the spiders were held equally responsible for that failure. Those spiders were never taken by other Griddas.

Left alone in the tunnels to fend for themselves, they could not survive long. There were plenty of creatures adapted specifically to hunt them down.

As her spiders ran from her to Yemi, Jarius could not speak. She explored her limbs for unknown injuries, frantically questioned her healers. Was she dying?

'No!' she pleaded, staring wildly at Gultrathaca. 'Look at me! I am healthy! Young!'

Her spiders continued to leave. Only the oldest soldiers, those whose loyalty was absolute and who would stay guarding her body even after her death, held back. The rest crept from her mouths and face-pits, hurrying across the floor to be with Yemi.

He giggled, welcoming them.

'You are not dying,' Gultrathaca told Jarius. 'My spiders also sneak off to him.'

'But – why?'

'I'm not certain,' Gultrathaca said. 'They're attracted by the boy's magic, but it's more than that.' She glanced at Jarius. 'I doubt you noticed, but several of your watchers were blinded when you entered the Chamber. Yemi is repairing them.'

'Repairing? You mean he actually cares for them?' The idea of looking after her spiders had never occurred to Jarius. Spiders were constantly being born inside her body to replace those old or ill.

Yemi attended diligently to all the injured watchers, cooling and reconstructing their eyes. The other spiders clustered on his knees. When the watchers were fixed, Yemi sent all the spiders back to Jarius. They did not want to leave him, but he insisted, sweeping them along the floor with the flat of his hand.

'They like him,' said Gultrathaca. 'And they are not the only ones.' She indicated dozens of other creatures that had started to emerge as soon as the spiders left. From the shadows they wriggled, swarmed and oozed around Yemi's feet. Jarius recognized animals and insects from all parts of Ool. There were even a few brainless slime mosses that lived in the deep silence below the Gridda caves. How could they be here? She watched as the mosses found a snug place along the pocket-linings of Yemi's shorts.

And then, in their silent way, came a pair of huraks.

Involuntarily Jarius shrank back, preparing to defend herself.

Of all the native animals that dwelled in the tunnels under the world of Ool, only this one was truly feared by the Griddas. The hurak was a huge animal, the same size as Jarius herself, feline-shaped, but with a heavy jaw capable of severing even Gridda skull-bone. What made a hurak really dangerous, however, was that its breath contained an anaesthetic to lull the watcher spiders. It could approach a Gridda completely undetected.

The two huraks settled in front of Yemi and Fola. They allowed Yemi to stroke their dark blue fur.

With a trace of awe in her tone, Gultrathaca said, 'Yemi draws them somehow, keeps them docile. If any Gridda approaches him too quickly they also guard him. These two arrived this morning.'

'From where?'

'I don't know.'

Jarius stared at Yemi. He smiled back. 'Does he ever try to get out of the Chamber?' she asked.

'All the time. He obviously wants to leave, and it is becoming harder to stop him. He keeps breaking through the holding spells. Over a dozen Griddas encircle the Chamber at all times, devising new ones just to keep him imprisoned.'

'There has to be a way to threaten him, Gultrathaca!'

'No. He is happy.'

'Happy? Happy *here*, in the Chamber? What tests have you tried?'

'Every kind. He enjoys them, like a game. I have yet to find a test he cannot pass with ease. In fact, he's becoming bored. I can't devise them fast enough for him.'

'I find that hard to believe.'

'Do you?' Gultrathaca stepped away from Jarius, and said lightly, 'The Chamber is yours to use against the boy as you wish. Perhaps you will have more success than those who tried previously.'

Fola saw what was about to happen. She had seen it many times before with the other Griddas Gultrathaca invited. '*Iro!* No!' she warned Jarius. 'Don't attack Yemi, you must not!' But, of course, it was pointless. All the Griddas who came here were too afraid of Gultrathaca to disobey her. 'Yemi will hurt you!' she shouted at Jarius. 'He no mean to, but he will! Don't make him!'

Jarius listened to the sounds of the ranting girl – and glanced warily at Gultrathaca. She had moved away, entirely across the Chamber. Not for the first time Jarius wondered why she had been called here. There were higher-ranking members of her pack who had not yet seen Yemi. Why had Gultrathaca requested her?

Because she was expendable?

Yes, Jarius thought, unable to think of another reason. This was obviously a final chance to prove her pack-worthiness. There would be no opportunity to refuse this time. Gliding shakily across the Chamber, she located the area where the main attack spells were hidden. The spells could be triggered singly or in clusters. The main advantage of the Chamber was that far more could be launched simultaneously than a single Gridda could summon on her own. When Yemi saw which way Jarius was heading he started jumping up and down.

'*Sere! Sere! Sere!*' he called out excitedly.

'I believe it is his word for play,' said Gultrathaca.

Yemi clapped his hands over and over. He could not wait to start.

Jarius twisted away, trying to hide her nervousness. How could she possibly intimidate the boy if Gultrathaca had failed? There was one chance, perhaps – a speciality spell she had made her own: a panic spell. It was intended to disable an opponent, unseat its mind, before the real attack. In one so young as Yemi it might be effective... She composed herself and faced him. Yemi backed away dramatically. He put his hands over his eyes.

He *is* frightened, Jarius thought in triumph. Then she saw him peeping between his fingers. Pretending to be frightened, she realized – to make the game more entertaining.

She glanced once more at Gultrathaca – and knew that she would kill her if there was any hesitation.

Opening her jaws, Jarius unleashed the panic.

In the fraction of a second it took the spell to reach him, Yemi reacted. He plucked the spell out of the air. He examined it. Gultrathaca bent forward avidly to watch. Eventually Yemi blew on the spell, offering it back to Jarius.

'Better!' he told her.

Jarius reached out a claw.

'No!' yelled Fola. 'Don't take it!'

Too late. As soon as Jarius's old spell made contact with her skin it gripped her heart. It was not the same panic spell she knew so well. Yemi had improved it. An immeasurable terror blazed across her mind. She collapsed on the floor. She curled up, stuffing her claws into her mouths to stifle the screams.

Seeing this, Yemi ran across to her, understanding his mistake. He removed the spell and hastily ordered all Jarius's spiders to console her.

Gultrathaca sighed. She stepped over Jarius, ignoring her agony.

Another failure, she thought. Another lost Gridda – and a member of her own pack this time. Well, there were many brighter stars than Jarius ... She stared at Fola, who stared back with unsuppressed fury. 'Why did you do that? Why?' Fola shouted.

Gultrathaca disregarded her. She walked to another part of the Chamber where Jarius's unseemly writhing would not be a distraction. What else could she do to affect the boy? Hadn't she tried everything to influence him? Every spell, threat, enticement or attempt at persuasion led to nothing! These human children as a whole, Gultrathaca thought. What are they really like? A few High Witches knew their language and customs well, those who had returned from Earth as part of Heebra's failed army. When questioned, they had called Yemi an aberration: a remarkable child, tantalizing but untypical. Fola was more typical; less magical than many children, but capable of being frightened.

I've persisted too long with my challenges on the boy, Gultrathaca realized. I need a new approach. The longer Yemi withstands the Assessment Chamber the more wary the Griddas become. If a baby human can do this, what of the older children? Every day he makes me appear weaker...

While Gultrathaca made her way to the prison levels to question the remaining High Witches, Jarius lay shuddering on the Chamber floor. When she did not respond to his kind words, Yemi wanted to help her more, but he hesitated. He was frightened to put his lips near her jaws, though it was the only way he knew. He knelt beside her. He bent across her face. Placing his lips gently against her mouths, he sent soothing spells inside.

Jarius's panic ceased instantly. It was replaced by a new feeling, one she had never experienced. An indescribable peacefulness worked its way through, gathering into her heart. Jarius forgot where she was. There was no panic. There was only the breath of Yemi.

She allowed him to put his arms half-round her massive head, and rock it.

11

invitation

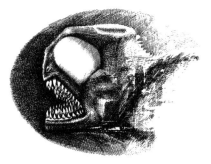

Rachel sat in the garden, staring at the empty skies. It had been three weeks since they last saw Larpskendya.

'I don't like it,' she said to Eric. 'No kids about. This exclusion zone of Heiki's feels wrong.'

'I think it's great,' Eric said. 'Peace and quiet for a flipping change. Plus Heiki's right to protect you.' He eyed her meaningfully. 'Before Yemi, the last time a Witch came to Earth was to get you, Rach.'

Heiki's surveillance teams were positioned around the house and nearby streets. They were efficient, the best available. Only the most determined fans still tried to sneak through the cordon; they never got close.

Rachel squinted up, where Albertus Robertson, as usual, hovered near the chimney. He had appeared the moment Larpskendya left. A fixture over the roof of the house ever since, he rarely moved. Rachel welcomed his presence. She trusted him without truly understanding why. It was a feeling about the spectrums all children now shared.

'Brilliant, isn't he,' Eric said. 'I could watch Albertus all day.'

'You usually *do*,' Rachel said, grinning. 'I've been out here all morning, and I swear Albertus hasn't moved. Not an eyelash.'

'Why should he?' Eric replied. 'He will, if something interests him. Those ears of his are amazing, you know. They don't just hear things; they can also pick up x-rays, gamma rays, radio emissions, all the wavelengths.'

'Mmm, but why doesn't he tell us what he's *thinking*? It's unnerving, the way the spectrums are so quiet all the time. We've heard nothing since their first message.'

'When we need their advice, they'll tell us soon enough,' Eric said.

Clinging to Albertus were his two female thrill-seekers. They took turns to hold him aloft. On windy days they held his hair to keep it out of his eyes. Occasionally they bathed his ears, keeping the surfaces free from dust or other particles.

'I wonder,' Rachel mused, 'why a spectrum's companion is always a thrill-seeker?'

'Don't you know?' Eric said. 'I thought you understood. It's because of the danger. Only the thrill-seekers are crazy enough to take the spectrums to the places they expect to go, Rach.' He gazed earnestly at her. 'Threats and more threats. The spectrums expect them; they're thinking about them all the time. That's why they're so hopeless about ordinary stuff like eating. They can't spare a second for humdrum things like that.'

Rachel realized that this was not just a guess. Eric knew. 'Are you … are you in communication with them?'

'Yes.' Eric's voice trembled. 'Only glimpses. But I'll tell you something. The spectrums care deeply about us. They're all that way, afraid all the time. They can't bear the thought of harm coming to any of us. But Albertus – well, he cares especially about you, Rach.'

'Me?'

'Yes. You personally.'

Rachel glanced up, astonished. 'Really? Why?'

'I don't know, Rach. I've no idea, but I can feel his concern.'

As Rachel gazed up at Albertus, a group of children passed over his head. It was a routine fly-over by a team of sentinels. The sentinel units were Heiki's special new guardians, the most magical children. Within a few weeks she had succeeded in turning them into a force of considerable resolve. They trained chiefly at night, knowing that the tunnel-dwelling Griddas were more likely to attack then.

Rachel stared at them, filled with doubts. 'The sentinels,' she said. 'I don't care how disciplined or brave they are. Do you think children, any children, stand a chance against Griddas? We've seen what they did to Larpskendya – *Larpskendya*, Eric, a Wizard. I don't –'

'Shush a minute.'

Above them Albertus Robertson had moved. His thrill-seekers spun him in tight circles, a frenzied motion. Eric pressed his hands to his head as communications between spectrums worldwide reached an instantly feverish level. The nearest sentinel unit changed course. It descended to surround Rachel and Eric. From another part of the world Heiki arrived, shifting crazily. She hurtled towards them, her face terrified.

Eric looked at Rachel. 'It's the Griddas.'

'I know,' she said. 'They're here.'

Heiki flew straight to Rachel. 'This is it,' she murmured. 'Oh, Rachel, this is it.'

Rachel steadied her. 'Come on, now. The sentinels need you. Remember all that training? You'll be fine. I'm with you. I'm here.'

Heiki nodded, regaining her poise sufficiently to instruct the sentinel unit. The sentinels adopted tactical positions best suited to a surprise raid. Albertus Robertson stayed aloft. His head shook as he was bombarded by dozens of frantic messages from spectrums around the world.

Eric sighed – a gloriously relieved sigh. 'Three! Only three Griddas!'

'Are you sure?' Rachel asked. 'There aren't more further out?'

'I'm sure.'

'I can't believe it's an attack, then. Not if there's so few.'

Eric called the prapsies over, tucking them into the usual place inside his shirt. Heiki deployed the sentinels around Rachel and Eric, then soared off to gather more forces.

'The Griddas are travelling slowly,' Eric said. 'Hey, Rach, *really* slow. Giving us plenty of chance to notice them.'

'Maybe they want us to know they're coming,' Rachel said. She hurried back inside the house to tell Mum and Dad what was happening, imploring them to stay indoors.

When she returned, Eric said, 'The Griddas are coming in this direction.'

'I know. Toward *us*. Let's get away from the house, at least.'

Taking Eric's arm she flew to an area of barren fields several miles south. Four more sentinel units, led by Heiki, joined them on the way. A handful of spectrums also arrived, their thrill-seekers flying at breathtaking speed to make it in time.

'I wonder if the Griddas have come to talk,' Eric said. 'They aren't exactly sneaking up on us.'

'Don't assume that,' said a voice they had never heard before.

It belonged to Albertus Robertson.

He had appeared at Rachel's shoulder, held by both his thrill-seekers. Everyone gazed at him in shock. Rachel had often imagined that if Albertus ever spoke his voice would be flat or mechanical, like his movements. Not so. Albertus spoke as if all his life he had been devoted to her.

'What – what do you mean?' she asked him.

'I –' Albertus's throat dried up from such long disuse, the words becoming a whisper. Furiously his thrill-seekers massaged his windpipe until the sounds were more coherent. When Albertus started speaking again it was in a great stream of words, at breakneck speed. 'If I was a Gridda,' he said, 'and I wanted to invade Earth with minimum loss of life to my own kind, I would start by eliminating the most dangerous children. In priority sequence, given the absence of Yemi, these children are Rachel and Eric, followed by Heiki, followed by all the spectrums, followed by the deepers, the sentinels, the –'

One of the thrill-seekers put her fingers over Albertus's mouth, forcing him to take a breath. She said to Rachel, 'Is he speaking too quickly for you? Tell me.'

'No, it's … it's all right.'

'To kill you,' Albertus continued, 'that is, to kill you, Rachel, and you, Eric, the Griddas have to get close enough. How? How do you put humans at ease? By approaching like these Griddas, not as a large threatening force, but a small group; not hiding, but coming openly; not rapid, but slowly. To seem to be a delegation. To arrive peaceably. To draw you both out.' He took another fast breath.

Rachel said, 'What do you suggest we do?'

'I am seeking strategies.' For a few seconds Albertus's head twitched as he took advice from all the other spectrums. 'Too many unknown factors,' he said. 'The majority view is that the three Griddas are either a murder party or an advance group to test our readiness.'

'Our readiness for what?' Eric asked.

'To defend. To attack. To fight.'

'So we should bring as many kids as possible,' Eric said. 'Show them we're not scared.'

'Not necessarily,' Albertus answered. 'Why big numbers of children against only three Griddas? Will they be impressed? Why bring so many if we are confident?'

'We can't just ignore them!' Heiki argued.

'Actually, we *could* just ignore them,' Albertus said. 'However, the Griddas might regard that as demonstrating weakness. Or they may be insulted. Either reaction might precipitate conflict. We could destroy the Griddas, but being too aggressive might also precipitate conflict. I suggest this,' Albertus went on immediately. 'Eric and Rachel do not meet with the Griddas. I will go, flanked by a minimum of sentinels. That way we will *invite* combat. This will give us more time to determine the Griddas' true intentions. It will also enable us to protect both Eric and Rachel. And it will endanger as few children as possible – in case this is a trap.'

'Do you think everything's a trap?' Eric asked.

'Yes.' Albertus Robertson's expression did not alter. 'Or that it may be.'

Rachel looked around at all the children. 'No,' she said. 'I won't put anyone else in danger to protect me.'

'You must do what is best for us all!' Albertus shouted at her, with sudden ferocity. Then he laid a hand against Rachel's cheek. 'The sentinel children are more steadfast than they realize,' he said. 'Let us do this.'

'Too late,' Heiki said. 'The Griddas have speeded up. We'll meet them in the sky. Sentinels! Stay close to Rachel and Eric.'

There was no time for further debate. Albertus remained by Rachel's shoulder, giving her last-minute advice. 'Say nothing about Serpantha,' he warned. 'The Griddas may know nothing about him.'

'Here they come,' Eric said.

The three Griddas dipped unhurriedly in and out of the cumulus clouds. When their orange heads and brown-furred bodies could be clearly seen, most children reacted with disbelief.

'Flipping heck!' Eric clutched the prapsies.

'Do not react to their appearance,' Albertus Robertson said.

Only the other spectrums were able to follow his advice. The rest of the children quailed at the bulk of the Griddas, their excessive muscularity, the bone-encrusted heads. Like a devil or dragon, Rachel thought. A demon, she decided. There was a vague similarity with the High Witches, but while even Dragwena had possessed some scrap of female-ness, these creatures did not even have a truly identifiable face. They seemed deformed, every part of their skull an angle, tooth or slash of bone. Only the eyes were recogniz-able, and how could such eyes be real? They covered too much of the head for humans to accept.

Rachel squeezed Eric's hand as the Griddas stopped nearby.

For a few moments the children of Earth and the Griddas assessed one another. Then one of the Griddas, the largest, addressed Rachel. 'As leader of all the Gridda packs of Ool, I have the honour. I am Gultrathaca. I greet you.'

Gultrathaca's voice astonished the children. Not the harshness everyone expected from that face, but the oppo-site: a female voice, perfectly modulated, human. All around her Rachel sensed children relaxing slightly.

'It's a lie,' Albertus Robertson said quietly to Rachel. 'No creature of this shape would naturally speak like a woman. There's only one reason for such an imitation: to put us at ease. Stay alert. Allow no physical contact.'

Gultrathaca held out a claw for Rachel to take. 'Shall we?'

A handshake? It was such a disarming gesture, such a human thing to do, that Rachel almost put her hand into Gultrathaca's giant claw. These Griddas already know who I am, she thought. They know all about us, can talk like us. Even the greeting had been appropriate: civil, compli-mentary. What do we know about the Griddas? Rachel asked herself. What had even Larpskendya known? Virtually nothing.

The children furthest away from the Griddas were

becoming visibly less tense. That mustn't happen, Rachel realized. Take control.

'Why did you kidnap Yemi?' she demanded.

'To protect ourselves. What other reason could there be?' Gultrathaca's tone was reserved, quiet. 'We have no doubt that Larpskendya intends to train the boy as a killer. We couldn't allow that.'

'Do you really expect us to believe you?' Rachel said.

'No, I do not. Larpskendya has already influenced you against us. Apparently you believe everything the Wizard says, though he is mistaken about us.'

Rachel hesitated. Gultrathaca was not what she had expected.

'Where is Larpskendya?' Eric asked. 'Is he ...'

'Alive. Is that what you are asking? Yes. He escaped.'

Rachel and the other children did not try to hide their relief.

Gultrathaca said, 'Yes, you love Larpskendya, don't you. He comes making promises that appeal. You believe them because you are actually a relatively simple species that judges largely on appearances. He tells you we Griddas are without conscience, but that is not true. We have honour. We look brutal to you, so you think we must be.'

Rachel was unsure what to say next. She felt Albertus's hand on her shoulder, strengthening her.

'It is we who have taken a risk in coming here,' Gultrathaca continued. 'Do you think it is easy for us to fly to this world, knowing how many of Larpskendya's Wizards protect it?'

'Don't tell her anything about the Wizards, especially numbers,' Albertus murmured in Rachel's ear. 'Neither agree nor disagree.'

'Larpskendya doesn't frighten anyone,' Eric said.

'Doesn't he?' Gultrathaca faced him. 'If you saw a Wizard fight you would think differently! There is nothing to match that ferocity! What do you really know about the Wizards?'

'We know we can trust them!'

'Yes, trust; you place a lot of trust in Larpskendya. But where is he now, when you need him?'

'You chased him off!' Eric said angrily.

'And we had good reason. But let me ask this: why didn't Larpskendya return with other Wizards? There has been time for him to do so. If he truly cared for you, wouldn't he or other Wizards be here now? On Orin Fen there are millions of Wizards, yet none are here. Not one Wizard spared to guard you while Larpskendya goes about his mysterious business. Doesn't that strike you as wrong?'

Rachel glanced at Eric, saw his brow creased thoughtfully.

Gultrathaca wriggled her face. All her spiders, which until now had been hiding inside the pits, crept out. Many children swore, backing away. With difficulty, Rachel held her ground.

'This is what we look like,' Gultrathaca said. 'We were bred to be defenders. That is why we have these appalling features. But now that we have defeated the High Witches, there is no more reason to fight. The war between the Wizards and the Highs was *their* endless war, not ours. The Griddas are ready for peace.' Gultrathaca's enormous eyes stared unblinkingly at Rachel. 'We even want peace with the Wizards, if they will allow it. We are not interested in conquest. We will stay on Ool.' She paused, studying them all. 'I see none of you believe me. You do not believe me because your understanding of the Griddas comes from Larpskendya. Let me tell you: he knows nothing about us. His judgement has been poisoned by centuries of war against the Highs. But I am here, and he is not. I am ready to extend friendship to your world, Rachel. Are you prepared to do the same?'

Rachel glanced at Albertus Robertson.

'Conclude the discussion as soon as possible,' he told her.

'All this peace talk,' Heiki said, 'but you kidnapped Yemi!'

'Yemi is safe,' Gultrathaca replied. 'We haven't harmed him, or his sister. I invite you to come and see for yourself. I invite you to Ool.' She gazed at Rachel. 'Will you come back with us? You will be honoured there, I promise.'

'What proof do we have that you are telling the truth?' Rachel said. 'Why should I believe you?'

'Why shouldn't you?' Gultrathaca replied. 'You trusted the word of Larpskendya, without any proof. What more do you expect from me? I will leave the other Griddas here as your hostages, and send more if you wish. If you travel back with me I will also be revealing the location of Ool itself. Once you know that you could send an army there. I will take that great risk, if you will take a smaller one. I doubt Larpskendya ever offered you that, did he? I'm sure he never offered to take you to Orin Fen.' Gultrathaca studied the children's expressions closely.

'Why not bring Yemi and Fola back to Earth?' Albertus Robertson said. 'If you are sincere in wanting accord, return them.'

'I cannot,' Gultrathaca said. 'I daren't take the risk that the Wizards will snatch Yemi back. And, as you must know, Yemi will not be parted from Fola.'

'If we agree, who goes to Ool?' Eric asked.

'Everyone is invited. Anyone who can shift, that is. The journey is too far otherwise.'

Was that a lie? Rachel wondered. She almost said, 'Only Heiki and I can shift,' but an alarmed look from Albertus Robertson stopped her in time. It was just the sort of accidental slippage that might prove so costly. Staring at Gultrathaca, Rachel had the feeling she never made such elementary mistakes. 'What happens if none of us go back with you?'

'Most Gridda pack-leaders are already convinced you are enslaved by the Wizards,' Gultrathaca answered. 'If no one returns with me, how will I convince them that is not the case? Especially if you, Rachel, do not return. You helped rid us of Heebra. There are Griddas who hold you in awe. I, personally, feel a debt of gratitude towards you.'

Before Rachel could reply, Albertus Robertson said, 'Thank you. We will consider what you have told us.'

'That is all I ask,' Gultrathaca said. Lowering her head, she made an almost perfect bow. For a creature with so many bunched muscles around her chest, it was not easy. She had clearly practised.

12

trust

Leaving most of the sentinels guarding the Griddas, Heiki flew to Rachel's home with Eric and Albertus Robertson to decide what to do.

Dad drew them inside and Mum shut the door, while Rachel explained what had happened. 'Well,' she said at last, taking a deep breath. 'These Griddas – what does everyone think?'

Heiki shook her head. 'Grotesque, aren't they? I liked one thing, though – the way the Griddas can't stand the High Witches. And Gultrathaca – she's interesting. But can we trust her? I don't think so. Forget the words Gultrathaca used. That's no way to tell if she's lying. I was more interested in something else. Rachel, you must have noticed: Gultrathaca talked about peace, but all I felt were her death spells rising and rising.'

'Yes,' Rachel said thoughtfully. 'I did notice. But how many of us were up there threatening her? I'm not sure we should judge the Griddas in the same way as High Witches. They're only distantly related to the Highs.'

'Are you crazy?' Heiki said. 'Witches are Witches. They don't change!'

'Don't they?' Rachel looked at her. '*You* did.'

Heiki cast her eyes down. 'Even so ...'

Rachel crossed the room. 'Look, I know they're frightening, and I don't want to believe them either, but has anyone given the Griddas a chance? Has even Larpskendya? Gultrathaca had a couple of interesting things to say about the Wizards, too ...'

Eric said, 'Hey, I'd sooner wait here to get Larpskendya's answers than run off to Ool.'

'I agree,' Mum said, with finality. 'It would be madness to trust the Griddas. None of you can even think about going.'

'What do the spectrums think?' Rachel asked Albertus Robertson.

For a while Albertus did not speak. The silence in the room was broken only by the noise of his two thrill-seekers breaking up biscuits that had been left on the dining table earlier that day. After making sure the pieces were manageable, the girls softened the biscuit in their mouths before placing it between Albertus's lips. Dad watched with uneasy fascination. Albertus seemed barely aware of the food. That's why they soften it, Dad realized. Otherwise, he might choke.

'We are undecided,' Albertus said. 'During the conversation with Gultrathaca spectrums monitored fluctuations in her temperature, heart rate and respiratory system. Amongst humans it is easy for us to know from these if someone is telling a lie, even a half-lie. But the Griddas can't be read that way. Their bodies are permanently hot, their hearts erratic, racing all the time.'

'That definitely wasn't her real voice, though,' Eric said.

'True,' Albertus replied. 'However, Gultrathaca may have been using a womanly voice for our benefit. Perhaps she did not want to frighten us. Perhaps her natural voice is so different from ours that we could not have understood it at all if she had not changed it.'

Mum restlessly paced the room. 'So we can't be sure of anything. Except the size of those claws, of course. And those teeth!' She pointed at Rachel. 'I've seen that look on your face before. Already made up your mind, haven't you? Well, unmake it; I won't allow you to go. Are you listening to me?'

'Yes, I'm listening, Mum,' Rachel answered. 'I'm also remembering the last thing Larpskendya told us. He said get to Yemi. He said find a way, before the Griddas do something terrible to him. This is the way, the *only* way. We can't help Yemi from here.' As Mum tried to interrupt, Rachel added, 'I won't leave Yemi and Fola on Ool. We didn't know how to find them before. There was no chance to help. Now there is.' She felt all the spells inside her shiver as she made her decision. 'I'll go on my own if I have to.'

'Whoa!' Eric said, as Mum exploded and Dad stood up.

'Now listen,' Dad said. 'I want all of you to calm down. Especially you, Rachel. No one wants any harm to come to Yemi or Fola. Everyone in this room wants to do the right thing by them.'

Rachel nodded. 'Yes … sorry … I know, Dad. Of course they do.'

'All right, then. So the question is how to judge whether to believe Gultrathaca or not. I can't see a way to be sure.'

'There's another thing, Rach,' Eric said. 'Once you're off Earth nobody can protect you. The Griddas probably know that. What's to stop them murdering you quietly in space?'

'Nothing,' Rachel said. 'I know. But why come all this way just to do that? It doesn't make sense.'

Mum came across to Rachel, held her hands, met her eyes. 'Please don't go,' she murmured.

Through her tears, Rachel said, 'I don't *want* to go, Mum! It's just... how can I leave Yemi there? I can't do that! I can't!'

Albertus rose. Without the aid of his thrill-seekers he walked the short distance across to Rachel and knelt beside her. 'I know what you are thinking,' he said. 'There is a picture, Rachel. It is in your head. A picture of Yemi and Fola, and also Serpantha, being mistreated in some awful place with no one to help them. You can't endure it. You're thinking that by charging to Ool you might be able to help. Perhaps you can, perhaps not. But think of this: what if Gultrathaca has come to Earth just to get *you*. Perhaps she can't get Yemi to do what she wants. She intends to get you to help her. Or she needs you for other reasons we could never calculate or guess.'

Mum jumped up and hugged Albertus. 'Exactly, exactly,' she said to Rachel. 'That settles it. I'm prepared to accept the advice of Albertus. Are you?'

Rachel did not want to commit herself.

'Well?' Mum pressed.

Rachel finally assented.

Albertus stared at Mum, his expression grave. 'I think you have misunderstood. The danger to Rachel is real, but there are important reasons why her presence on Ool is required. Our judgement – the combined view of the spectrums – is that Rachel should go.'

Mum flinched, her face blank.

'Here are the major reasons,' Albertus said. 'If you, Rachel, are killed, that loss would be terrible. But the loss of Yemi would be catastrophic for the world, especially if the Griddas find a way to use him against us. Thus, if there is a small chance you can prevent that, the risk to your life is worthwhile. It is difficult for me to say this, because I am your spectrum, and you are precious to me. So long as I live and so long as you live I am devoted to your welfare, but my first priority must be the welfare of all children. By going to Ool, Rachel, you may avoid war. The spectrums' view is that children could not win a war against the Griddas. You *may*, after all, discover that Gultrathaca is telling the truth. Even if she lied, and your visit only delays war, it will have served a purpose. It may give us adequate time to prepare for an invasion, should it come.'

Mum stared bitterly at Albertus Robertson. 'Tell me,' she said, 'what is the likelihood that Rachel will be killed by the Griddas?'

Albertus Robertson looked directly at Rachel, a personal look full of candour. 'It is doubtful you will ever return.'

'But you still think I should go?'

'I would request it, yes.'

'Then I'm going,' Rachel said, rushing across to Mum.

For a while Mum tried desperately to make Rachel change her mind. Eric knew it would hurt too much if he told her his own decision later. He would have to tell her now. 'I'm going, too,' he said.

'What? No, you're not!' Dad blasted. 'You are *not* going, Eric!'

'Dad, Mum, you don't understand. I can actually fight these Griddas. I don't think they've any idea what my anti-magic can do.'

Rachel shook her head. 'No, Eric, I'm not risking you as well.'

'Let Albertus decide,' Eric insisted.

Albertus stared at Eric. His thrill-seekers also stared at Eric. One of the girls' faces, for the first time, betrayed strong emotion.

'You are the fatal gift,' she said, her face white with fear.

'What? What's that supposed to mean?'

'The fatal gift is the name the spectrums have given you, Eric,' Albertus said. 'You have the ability to destroy magic. Our task on Earth is to value and honour the magic of children. You frighten us, because of what you can do. As to whether you should stay on Earth or go with Rachel, I cannot say.'

There was a period of silence while everyone absorbed this.

'The fatal gift ...' Eric said to the girl. 'The way you say it ... it's ... you make me sound like some kind of monster.'

'No,' Albertus replied firmly. 'You are not that, and you must make up your own mind about what to do. You must choose yourself.'

The girl thrill-seeker who had spoken suddenly put her face close to Eric, so close that her long dark hair fell on his knees. No one had ever looked at Eric the way she looked at him now – as if she wanted to kiss him, or to bite him, or both. The other girl pulled her back.

Eric sat still, stroking the prapsies to calm himself down. Then he said, 'Larpskendya suggested more might depend on me than before. He said trust my instinct. My instinct tells me to go.'

Mum's face was ashen. Dad held her, fighting his own dread.

'I'll also go with you,' said Heiki. 'If you –'

'No, please stay, please,' Rachel asked, clutching Heiki's wrist. 'I need someone strong here. I need *you* working with the sentinels.'

Heiki nodded. Everyone gazed at Albertus Robertson.

'I would be of little use to you,' Albertus said matter-of-factly. 'It is the connected intelligence of the spectrums that serves the Earth. Once I am isolated from the others, I will be just like any other child. And remember, I have no magic of my own. Unless I am mistaken – and I am not mistaken – even you, Rachel, will not be able to shift large distances with more than one companion.'

Rachel could not look at Mum or Dad. 'Then it's only us,' she said to Eric.

The Griddas were escorted to a safer location, and Rachel and Eric spent most of the next hours with their parents. The painful run-through of arguments over the decision to leave never quite came to an end, but there were also preparations for Ool to be made. Rachel knew she should be able to fashion whatever clothing they needed with her spells – but what if her magic didn't work on Ool? She decided on practical light-weight body suits, comfortable to move around in but fur-lined, waterproof and well insulated. Eric's suit had extra large pockets because, of course, the prapsies refused to stay behind.

Before she left, Rachel offered a few final words of advice to Albertus Robertson, but they were not needed –

the spectrums had already commenced defensive strategies far more apt than anything Rachel could have devised. She said goodbye to Albertus and he kissed her.

There were other goodbyes, many.

And then there was no more reason to delay.

As Rachel zipped up her white body-suit, Dad slowly re-fastened one of the collar straps. Mum smoothed Eric's hair under his hood. Her children gazed back at her; only their eyes and part of their foreheads were exposed. Everyone was too distraught to speak.

'I'll take care of them,' Heiki whispered to Rachel.

'I know you will.' She looked at Heiki. 'Will you follow us up?'

'Of course.'

They departed into a warm blue morning sky. Rachel could not believe how beautiful that ordinary sky looked to her today. Millions of children had come to see them off. They flew into the air until their magic could take them no higher, then waved and called out their hopes until Rachel and Eric were out of sight.

Some spectrums ordered their thrill-seekers to escort Rachel as far as they could. It was a terrible parting for the thrill-seekers. They were bereft without their spectrums, and Rachel was glad to see them return to the ground as she rose into the stratosphere. Here, in the thinnest air, where no birds could fly, only the most magical children could still follow. Paul and Marshall were amongst them, close friends from another time of impossible decisions. The smiles of the boys were strained as they tried to hearten her. Finally Rachel, wrapping Eric in a protective blanket of warmth and oxygen, outflew even those two special children.

Only one child remained with them now.

'Oh, Rachel,' murmured Heiki. 'Are you doing the right thing? Are you sure?'

Rachel did not reply. Instead she turned away from all she knew, and said to Gultrathaca, 'Which way?' Rachel thought she saw a smile, then. Was it a smile? Even in that busted face of shattered angles, Rachel thought she recognized the expression.

'Follow me,' Gultrathaca said.

13

homage

Rachel had shifted many times before, sometimes stretching it out gloriously for hours, but never for this long – and never through the vacuum of space.

Yet instead of tiring, her shifting spells wanted more. After half a day carrying Eric without rest, they were lean, trimmed and ready for new velocities. Sensing this, Gultrathaca increased the pace. She shifted at greater and greater intervals.

Testing me, Rachel realized. I can test you too, Gultrathaca, she thought. If you've spent most of your life underground, there must be limitations to your flying skills. So each time Gultrathaca accelerated, Rachel nudged the speed on. They flew side by side, studying each other intently: for frailties, for infirmity, for the slightest defect.

Suns streaked by, beautiful constellations, barely noticed by either of them.

The talkative version of Gultrathaca vanished as soon as they left Earth. Throughout the journey she seemed self-absorbed. 'Ool is near,' she repeated distractedly every hour or so. Otherwise she hardly responded to their questions.

Eric said privately to Rachel, 'Where's the charm gone now? I thought Gultrathaca would use this time to tell us more about Ool. She's not bothering. Why?'

'I don't know. What do you reckon to those spiders?'

Gultrathaca's watchers perched on every edge of her face. Not once had they taken their eyes off Rachel.

Eric whispered, 'Do you think Gultrathaca's just going to kill us? Is that why she's so quiet?'

'If that was all Gultrathaca intended, we'd probably be dead already.'

'Maybe she's waiting for help, waiting until we get to Ool.'

Rachel wished she could answer that.

There were no stopping places on the journey. They ate while they flew. Gultrathaca's meals were tucked inside the crevices of her skin: light snacks, small live creatures. It was repulsive to watch her eat, but Rachel made herself do so – there might be far worse to come on Ool. Was Gultrathaca a typical Gridda? she wondered. Were they all so intimidating?

'The prapsies are getting hungry,' Eric complained after a few hours. 'I didn't bring much food because you told us not to bother. How far is there to go?'

'Not far at all.' Allowing all her anxieties to flow away, Gultrathaca said, 'Welcome to Ool. Welcome to the world of the Griddas!'

Ool appeared before them suddenly. It was a shade of

red, though so deep it was almost black. Rachel tried to pick out details on the surface, but there were none. A sun shone adamantly down, but gigantic cloud-formations gathered against it, like a fortress against the warmth and brightness.

Before Rachel's information spells could investigate further, Gultrathaca pointed below. 'Here come the youngsters,' she said.

Countless Gridda infants rose in long thrashing lines from the surface of Ool. Flight was awkward for them, but with jerky, frog-like kicks of their legs they clawed at the space ahead. They bit their own pack-members, desperate to be the first to arrive.

Dread trickled through Rachel. Was this a welcome? How could it be? More likely a killing party. Would it end here, before they even knew if Yemi was alive or dead?

The prapsies were frantic under Eric's body-suit. With an effort he kept them inside. 'Better get ready to defend ourselves,' he said to Rachel.

Too many, and too late for that, she thought.

Gultrathaca seemed confused by Eric's reaction. 'The infants will not intentionally damage you,' she assured him. 'Let them feel your bodies. Touch is the way they learn to identify each another in the birthing tunnels.'

Rachel tried not to flinch as the first infants arrived.

Exploratory claws reached out, almost shyly at first. Rachel's lack of angularity intrigued the infants. They circled her, looking for edges. Such woeful eyes, such claw-lessness! And where were her jaws? Marvelling at her pale skin, they wanted to taste her hair, confused by its long loose texture. Eric closed his eyes as the infants sniffed up and down his body. Where were his spiders hiding? they wondered. They poked his clothes – as if the strange garments might poke back.

'Get away!' Eric warned, as one infant reached for a prapsy.

Hearing Eric's raised voice the nearest infants backed off – only to be pushed aside by others. Once it was obvious they would not be harmed, more infants braved an approach. They brushed up against Rachel and Eric: jabbering, rubbing up against them, insatiable.

One dropped a batch of spiders onto Rachel's legs.

'A gift,' Gultrathaca told her. 'From an admirer.'

'An admirer?' Rachel gazed at the infant in bewilderment, striving to see beyond the bony face to the expressions beneath.

'Get them off now!' Eric screamed, suddenly no longer able to bear it. 'Get them off! Get them off!'

Gultrathaca uttered a guttural click, and all the infants started kicking back to the surface of Ool. The one who had offered her spiders to Rachel sucked them back into her mouths, reluctantly leaving with the other infants.

Rachel tried to steady herself as Gultrathaca led them down towards the planet. How big was Ool? Her information spells measured its circumference: over thirty times the size of Earth.

They entered the atmosphere – and a sky the colour of dull metal.

For dozens of miles, Gultrathaca guided them through snow-clouds. Even on Ithrea, Rachel had never seen snow-fall so heavy. At another time she might have thought the flakes had a beauty all of their own, but she was too conscious of danger. The snows themselves felt dangerous. They were not light and scattered, with gaps to see the world through. These snows were so dense it was like the weight of a person pressed on all parts of her. She drew Eric close, wiping the flakes from his eyes. The prapsies huddled against his breast, where they could watch his face and feel the reassuring thump of his heart.

At last the clouds thinned, and they burst through into clearer air.

'The Detaclyver,' Gultrathaca said tonelessly, pointing below. 'The place of death. No Gridda survives for long here.'

Rachel gasped as she saw mountains: a colossal range. Peak after peak extended over the entire southern and western continents of Ool.

'It's moving!' Eric cried out. 'Rachel, it's ... living!'

The Detaclyver's body was like a vast buckling and heaving tide, trying to extend over the world. At its northerly extremity, the peaks were not turned towards the sky. They were sharper, modified for ramming into the ground ahead.

'Do you recognize what's holding it back?' Rachel called out. 'Storm-whirls!'

On Ithrea the Witch Dragwena had used her magic to create similar immense hurricanes. Those lifeless objects, however, bore no resemblance to the true sentient storm-whirls of Ool. Hundreds of them stood massively between ground and sky. Rooted against the outer border of the Detaclyver, they kept it in check.

'A ceaseless, patient battle,' Gultrathaca explained. 'Both species were part of Ool long before Witches came. The High Witches could never control the Detaclyver, but eventually were able to gain a hold on the minds of the storm-whirls. Now they obey us.'

'I don't understand,' Rachel said. 'Why do you need the storm-whirls?'

'To keep our homes safe from the Detaclyver,' Gultrathaca answered. 'The Detaclyver tries to destroy the cities. Naturally it does. It hates us.'

As they flew over the summits of the Detaclyver, Rachel looked between her feet. It seemed that nothing should be able to live among the desolate peaks but she was wrong. Her information spells discovered life and spells. Creatures were everywhere below her, in the endlessly falling snow itself, or under it, within the flesh of the Detaclyver. Amongst them were magical signatures that throbbed as powerfully as any Witch, though the creatures were not Witches – or anything like them.

While Rachel pondered this, Eric murmured to her, 'Yemi's here. Still a long way off and deep underground. Fola's with him, too.' He grinned. 'She's alive. They both are!'

Gultrathaca gazed at Eric, shocked. 'You can detect Fola's minute scent from this distance? What else can you detect?'

'Nothing,' growled Eric. He peered down at the prap-sies. They peered back, fearful for him. So quiet, Eric thought. They hadn't said a thing since they arrived on Ool. He stroked their heads, feeling them shiver.

'Eric,' one said nervously. 'Look out for the snow.'

'I know,' Eric said. 'It's everywhere. Just keep your heads down, boys. I'll watch out for you.'

'No, Eric. The snow's wrong. It's going the wrong way.'

Great plumes of snow had burst from the Detaclyver's peaks. They rose, then changed direction, sweeping towards Gultrathaca. This was no ordinary snow, Rachel saw. The flakes were not blown by the wind. They were *fighting* the wind to get to her.

The snow was alive.

'What are they?' Rachel cried.

'Essa,' Gultrathaca said. 'Servants of the Detaclyver. Protect yourselves.'

Rachel held Eric close and raised her defensive spells.

Gultrathaca moved upward into fiercer winds. The Essa followed, millions of tons of tiny life wheeling in a great arc to cut her off.

'What – what should I do?' Eric asked. 'Use my anti-magic on them?'

'No, not yet,' Rachel whispered.

'But they're coming!'

'Wait, Eric!'

A small number of the Essa reached her. They hovered, quivering with interest. Who was she? Rachel felt them in her mind, all hope and expectation, their thoughts chasing into her.

They meant her no harm. Rachel knew that at once. Their target was Gultrathaca.

Gultrathaca raced through the thickest clouds, trying to throw the Essa off. But they caught her. Landing on her jaws, they overpowered the soldier spiders, and crept inside her throat. For a while Gultrathaca was slowed down; then she coughed the Essa from her body. She flew on, crossing the boundary of the Detaclyver.

A few Essa remained with Rachel. They were as light and insubstantial as the snow itself. Briefly their warm bodies clung to her face, curious and full of questions. Then they had no choice; they departed, returning to their homes in the summits of the Detaclyver. Rachel held out her hands, not wishing them to go.

'I see the Essa have taken a liking to you,' Gultrathaca said, amused. She guided Eric and Rachel northwards, leaving the Detaclyver behind. They reached the storm-whirls. When Gultrathaca ordered one to move aside, it did so at once.

Behind the storm-whirls was an area of smooth ice. 'The Prag Sea,' Gultrathaca informed them. 'Good hunting grounds for the brave.' Rachel sent her information spells under the frozen waters. There was life here, fish in their millions. Each was armoured, their blood kept at boiling temperatures to burn a path through the solid ice.

Finally they traversed the Prag Sea and entered a vast region of featureless snow plains. At their margin mountains rose starkly, and Rachel saw a line of smashed eye-towers that had once marked the edge of a city.

Eric bent towards Rachel. 'There are High Witches under us. Not many.'

'The others are dead,' Gultrathaca told him. 'We keep a few to entertain the infants.' As they soared over the remains of the towers, Rachel tried to take in the scale of the devastation. 'Thûn,' Gultrathaca declared. 'The ruined city. During Heebra's reign the greatest Highs lived here, though Gaffilex and Tamretis are larger. We tore those cities down as well.'

There were no eye-towers left standing, but as they dropped lower Eric saw that the Gridda infants occupied the ruins. Some lurked amidst the debris of stones. Others dived in and out of underground entrances, yelling with fear or excitement – Eric couldn't tell which. Many flew – with greater or lesser ability – about the sky.

At the heart of Thûn a single storm-whirl turned. It was smaller than the others Rachel had seen. 'A juvenile whirl,' Gultrathaca told her. 'It makes a playground for our infants.' She indicated the base, where the winds were light and infants vaulted and tumbled. 'A place they can learn how to fly without fear,' Gultrathaca said.

Higher up in the whirl Rachel spotted older Griddas. They fought in small groups, supervised by trainers. Occasionally one would fall, to be caught by the infants below, gathering around and howling their scorn.

'The true battles take place at the top, where the winds are hardest,' Gultrathaca said. Rachel saw one of the Griddas in the upper whirl fall. As she hit the ground her spiders were scattered across the snow. Before she could gather them up, the infants trampled them.

Rachel tried to keep her voice steady. 'Why did they do that?'

'Why not? Poor quality magic must be punished.' Gultrathaca gazed at Rachel, genuinely puzzled by her reaction.

Such casual cruelty means nothing here, Rachel realized. She thought of Yemi and Fola, wondering what the Griddas might have done to them.

From the edge of the juvenile whirl a group of young Griddas emerged. One flew over to Gultrathaca and said something.

Gultrathaca laughed – Rachel could half-recognize such expressions now.

'These ones are in awe of you, defeater of Heebra,' Gultrathaca told Rachel. 'They have waited a long time for this privilege.'

The eyes of the youngsters lingered over every detail of

Rachel's body. Then they bowed to her. There was no doubting the sincerity of the gesture. After a last look, each of the youngsters flew eastwards, calling noisily to others.

'Please take us to see Yemi now,' Rachel said.

'One thing first.' Gultrathaca halted in the sky. Several adult Griddas, considerably larger than the infants, approached Rachel and Eric. They arrived in an elegant line, unhurried. Rachel noticed that Gultrathaca acknowledged each of them individually – these Griddas were obviously important. The adults stared in an uninhibited way at Rachel. Then each in turn, starting with Gultrathaca, lowered their head. They exposed the entire length of their necks.

What did it mean? This is a warrior race, Rachel's information spells told her. They are exposing their most vulnerable areas as a way of honouring you.

The Gridda pack-leaders left their necks laid bare a long while. Finally they raised their heads and Gultrathaca said, sincerely, 'We hope you enjoyed the affections of the infants. That was why we asked them to greet you. The Griddas alongside me are the highest ranking leaders of the packs of Ool. They have gathered to acclaim you both. We esteem you, Rachel, and you, Eric. The death of Heebra means more to us than you can know.' All the pack-leaders bowed. The members of their packs close enough to witness also bowed, enormous swells of movement crossing the city.

Rachel could not believe this. A genuine tribute. Not killed in space, she thought. Not killed on arrival. Her spells jumped into her eyes, filled with hope.

'And now it is the turn of the youngsters to honour you in their own fashion,' said Gultrathaca. She led the way towards the easternmost perimeter of Thûn. Ool's pack-leaders fell in deferentially behind. As they flew remnants of the eye-towers flashed past, fewer and fewer until they left the city altogether. Infant Griddas followed. Most flew. Those not yet able to fly bounded or trampled over each other in the same direction.

Beyond the city the snows flattened out. Gultrathaca slowed down and all the Griddas became utterly silent, even the infants.

Rachel saw it before she understood: a great oval structure on the surface. It was hundreds of feet high and wide. The group of youngsters who had earlier studied Rachel were fussing over it, finishing just as she arrived.

'Oh, my –' Rachel started.

It was her face: a snow sculpture.

There was a thoughtful expression on the sculpture – a measured look, the same one Rachel had given the youngsters, captured perfectly. A strand of hair fell over one eye. Her nostrils were caves large enough to hibernate inside. Scuffed snow formed the eyebrows. A spider, tiny, sat in one of them.

Rachel lifted her hand to her real face. The spider was there, motionless. She flicked it off.

For a moment there was quiet as all the Griddas humbly waited to see whether Rachel approved of their efforts. Then Rachel heard the voices. She had heard nothing like it. Gultrathaca had arranged for all the Griddas of the city to be here. They filled the sky and ground, as numerous as the falling snow.

While Rachel and Eric stared, all the Griddas opened their jaws and roared their homage.

14

PARTING

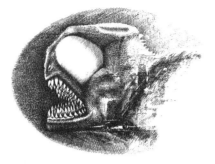

The homage of the Griddas was so deafening that Rachel and Eric had to cover their ears until it subsided. Each time that happened, Gultrathaca renewed it. Finally the pack-leaders raised their claws and there was silence.

Gultrathaca turned her attention back to Rachel. 'Now we will honour you in another way,' she said. 'Every Gridda wishes to be the first to fight you. Choose a suitable contestant.'

'Fight ... me?'

'Of course. What did you expect?'

'I don't understand. We don't need to fight. We came here for ... for peace.'

Gultrathaca regarded her contemptuously. 'Did you really believe I wanted peace?'

'But I don't ... want to fight,' Rachel said.

A look of disgust passed across the faces of the pack-leaders. Gultrathaca, with difficulty, calmed them. 'Don't dishonour yourself, Rachel,' she said menacingly.

'I *won't* fight!'

'You have no choice. There is no going back now.'

Rachel glanced in dismay at Eric, preparing to shift evasively.

Gultrathaca's eyes shone. 'Yes, why not try? By now, however, you must realize that you can never shift fast enough to escape from me if you're carrying Eric. Discard him. Give yourself a chance...'

'We should have killed you on Earth!' Eric thundered.

'That was a mistake,' Gultrathaca agreed. 'I realized you were weak, then. But how to convince my Griddas? They know you faced down Heebra, Rachel. You make them anxious. I must cut you down to size. When they see how readily you can be dispatched, the invasion of your world will be more easily accomplished.'

'Please,' Rachel began, then stopped. She knew, seeing Gultrathaca's expression, that no argument would change her mind. 'What about Eric?' she said. 'If I co-operate, agree to fight, will you –'

'Spare him? No. I plan to give him to the infants as entertainment.'

'You mustn't... I –'

'Don't plead,' Gultrathaca said. She gestured for Eric to be removed. Eric freed his hands, prepared to use his spell-killing. The prapsies sprang onto his shoulders.

'Wait,' Rachel said to Gultrathaca. 'Leave Eric. I'll... I'll do it. I'll entertain the infants for you instead of him.'

'Very well,' Gultrathaca said indifferently. 'I promised the youngsters something, after all. In that case, the first contest for you will start tomorrow.' While Rachel tried to take in what this might mean, Gultrathaca added, 'Make your parting. This is the last time you will see Eric.'

'No!' Rachel reached out for him, but her arm was knocked away.

'Quick! Should I use my anti-spells?' Eric asked. 'Should I use them now?'

Rachel agonized. 'Yes. No – not yet, Eric.'

Gultrathaca separated them. Before Rachel had time to say anything else two young Griddas flew across the sky. Knocking the prapsies off, they clasped Eric's shoulders in their foot-claws and headed out over the city. The prapsies followed, shrieking insults at them.

'Please –' Rachel begged, as she was dragged away. 'Let me –'

'You are a warrior,' Gultrathaca said. 'There is no need for goodbyes.'

'No. I –' Rachel craned her head, trying to see what was happening to Eric.

'Pathetic!' Gultrathaca hissed. 'Hold your head erect!'

'Let me talk to Eric!'

'No.'

Eric was carried southwards across the darkening skies, already too far for his voice or that of the prapsies to reach her.

As Gultrathaca picked her up, Rachel tried to shift. It did not work.

'At least you've tried something!' Gultrathaca sneered.

Rachel felt all her spells quail inside her. She trembled. 'What have you done to me?'

'I've used a skin-contact spell,' Gultrathaca said. 'It reduces your abilities. I must give the infants a chance against you tonight, after all. You cannot shift. You cannot fly. Oh, and you will not be able to shape-change either. None of your other spells are affected.'

'You've left me nothing!'

'Nothing? Hardly nothing. Your death spells are still intact. You will need your deaths tonight.'

Rachel shuddered. The deaths had always been part of her magic – the part she hid from, ignored, detested – yet they were there. Grasping her arm, Gultrathaca flew to a western part of Thûn Rachel had not seen. Here Heebra's eye-tower still stood, piercing the sky. 'A fitting place for you to stay,' Gultrathaca said. 'If you were a High Witch there could have been no greater glory – to rest in Heebra's tower, above all others! You see, I honour you still.'

'I don't care about your code of honour!'

'Do you care what happens to the children of your world?'

'Of course!'

'In that case kill yourself now. A Gridda would, the least of them. The longer you are alive, the more we'll learn from you. We'll see your spells, recognize how to counter them. We'll know what to expect when we face the children of Earth. Is that what you want?'

Rachel had no reply. 'What will you do to Eric?' she asked shakily.

'Whatever I like.' Gultrathaca flew Rachel through the cracked eye-window, depositing her on the chamber floor. 'Actually, there may be a use for Eric. I'd heard from the High Witches how he could destroy spells, but perhaps they missed something more important.' Gultrathaca left. Outside, in the gathering dark, Rachel saw the silhouettes of infants.

They scrambled over the snow, heading for the tower.

15

the long night of ool

Rachel stood next to the shattered eye-window, watching the infants.

While daylight lasted they remained at the base of Heebra's tower, content to observe her with half-shut eyes. The arrival of night changed everything. There was no dusk, no gentle sunset. One moment there was enough meagre light by which to see; the next there was nothing. Instinctively, Rachel strained to find the last of the sun. Like someone who would perish without light, who was starved and whose only food was light, she sought the disappearing patch low in the east. Ool's sun made a final stand against the dark. Then it was extinguished – and a vast shadow came hurtling across the world.

And then there was no light at all.

There was only the unbelievable cold and the sound of

breathing – Rachel's own ragged breaths mixed with new ones, the noise of infants labouring up the walls of the tower.

Rachel blinked over and over, assuming her eyes would adjust. But they did not adjust. Her pupils enlarged to feed on what light they could find, but there was nothing to find. Ool had no moon. Stars had never winked through the clouds. Rachel was so frightened that she would have welcomed even the emerald-green light that once shone from Heebra's tower – but the Griddas had forever removed that colour from the world.

Her magic came to her aid at once. First it created a candle-brightness. Seeing the Griddas outside the window cower, Rachel intensified the light, driving them back. If she could not fly, if she could not leave the eye-tower, where was the safest place to be? She chose the middle of the floor – close enough to see what might come in through the window, and close enough to react to what might enter from the doorway. In the darkness her night eyes opened, a brilliant silver.

The night of Ool had never known such gleams.

Despite this, the braver infants edged forward. Soon they became used to the glare of Rachel's eyes, and after that they did not give her any peace at all. Stimulated by her strange looks, and the stories they had heard, and daring each other, they gathered wherever there was a space: in the eye-chamber, in the stairway leading up to it, in the snows outside. They clung to the steeps of the eye-tower walls; they peered in from the darkness.

The first infants were too frightened to enter the eye-chamber. But they soon forgot their fears when Rachel made the mistake of not punishing those who came nearest. They wanted a closer look at her. She was so deformed. Why hadn't she been killed at birth?

Rachel didn't dare take her eyes off them for a second. She was hungry, thirsty, cold, needing to think, needing to rest, to sleep, most of all to sleep – but there was no opportunity for that. All through the night her spells built dams and shields and small illusions to confuse the infants. She had never needed to call on her magic so continuously before.

But the Griddas had their eye-shields, and there was plenty of time. They started finding ways around Rachel's barriers. Unable to fly away or shape-change, Rachel had to constantly rebuild and repair her defences. And, she knew, this was just a few curious infants. Her first real trial hadn't even started...

As the hours passed Rachel believed that dawn would never come. The dark deepened; the infants seemed tireless. Then, in the middle of the night, one of them punctured her shield. When that happened Rachel did something she had promised herself she would never do: she summoned her death spells. For the first time in her life Rachel invited the deaths forward, and momentarily her eyes turned black with their power.

The deaths were something the infants understood, feared. For a while they left Rachel in peace. She felt like crying, realizing how frail she was. She had always made noble resolutions about never using the deaths – yet as soon as a single infant threatened her, all those noble resolutions had evaporated.

She thought about Eric – but there was barely time even for that. The infants returned, and there were more than ever. They no longer feared her silver eyes, or the

incandescence of the eye-chamber. They knew her
defences were beginning to fail. Rachel found herself
shaking. Several of her finest spells rose to inspire her. The
deaths did what they did best: they imagined deaths. They
could devise so many for the inexperienced infants – a
nearly infinite number – and Rachel felt dirty as she
selected amongst them. But she selected nonetheless.

Finally there came a point when Rachel could think of
no other way to hold the infants back except with the
deaths. She stood in the eye-tower, surrounded by
Griddas. Some had started to rake her thighs. Her deaths
clamoured to be set free. Rachel withheld them with
difficulty.

Give me another choice, she demanded.

Her magic had never failed her before, not when her life
was threatened. It looked out into the night and snow and
cold and knew what to do. Rachel forced her way to a
corner of the chamber. She initiated the spell.

The infants had not witnessed anything like this before.
Rachel raised her arms, warning them back. Then a new
light shot from her eyes, raising its blaze from the walls,
from the floor, from the shards of glass, from the air itself,
sucking out everything a Gridda could breathe. The
chamber flickered orange the remainder of the night.

For the first time in its long history, a fire burned in
Heebra's eye.

Eric sagged against a stone wall. The prapsies were either
side of his face. He could feel their eyes on him, and the
racy pitter-patter of their hearts.

His prison cell was a rough circular hole gouged from
the rock beneath Thûn. No magic held him there. The

rock was enough; none of the sophisticated spells needed to contain Yemi or Rachel were needed for Eric.

For a long time he had been sitting against the wall, trying to stay awake. He didn't dare fall asleep. This was the first break in the night Gultrathaca had given him. Why? To tease him? To lull him before the next attack? He wanted to sleep. He wanted more than anything to blank out everything that had happened to him here, but how could he forget all those Witches he had hurt?

Gultrathaca's experiments had started the moment Eric entered the cell.

The first test involved a native magical animal he had never seen before – some kind of dog. Gultrathaca herself let it in. By the time it saw Eric the animal had been deliberately whipped into a frenzy. As soon as Gultrathaca opened the door, the dog attacked.

Eric had no time to think. Without considering the consequences of his actions, he turned the entire scope of his anti-magic on the dog. He had not done this before. He had never even thought to do it. Normally he only cancelled single spells. This time, in his panic, he went much further. The dog was a simple predator – using spells only to increase its bite.

It was no match for Eric.

In his terror he reached for all the spells. He stripped away the sum of the dog's magic. He took everything. What occurred next shocked him and intrigued Gultrathaca. The dog's body, in mid-lunge, seemed to lose all potency. It flopped to the floor, no longer able to lift its head. Without magic, the dog lay panting in weak confusion.

Next came other magical animals, too many to count.

Then Gultrathaca sent against him something altogether grander: a Witch; a High Witch, one of those imprisoned. Eric had no idea what made that first one fly at him with such recklessness. The prapsies were ready, and tried their usual distractions.

'Come after us!' one squealed, flying around the cell.

'Come for us, beast!'

'*Come for us!*'

Against animals, this tactic sometimes worked. They became uncertain about the target, giving Eric enough time to disable their magic without harming them too much.

Against a High Witch it could never work.

She ignored the prapsies and went straight for Eric.

Like all High Witches, this one abounded with magic. Magic suffused her body. It riddled her mind and ensnared her heart. It was the dazzling foundation of her strength and the catalyst for her formidable intellect. The one who flew at Eric had been alive seven centuries. All that time she had lived intimately with her spells. She had used them for so long that she could do nothing without their affections.

Eric shuddered, recalling what happened next. Why had she flown at him with such insane energy? Why couldn't she have paused, just for a moment? There had been no time to argue or think. In self-preservation Eric reached deep inside her and scooped out all of her magic. In dismay he watched as her powerful body slowly unravelled in front of him.

More High Witches had followed, often several at a time, as Gultrathaca attempted to discover Eric's limitations. All the Witches came flying wildly into his cell, but after his initial panic Eric adjusted to what Gultrathaca threw his way. He stopped needing to kill the Highs. He found adroit ways of selecting certain spells to disarm them without serious injury.

For over an hour there had been a stalemate, while Gultrathaca wondered what to try next.

Eric lay down, his face against the stone floor. It was cold, but not so cold that he shivered – clearly Gultrathaca wanted him alive.

The prapsies pressed close to Eric's heart, consoling themselves in its beat. The contact was wonderful for Eric, too, but he wouldn't tell them so. He wanted them to leave. He wanted them to escape. It would have been easy enough. The roof of the cell was open, ten feet or so away. Eric could not climb the sheer walls, but the prapsies could be out and past any number of guards in a second. It was only their love for him that kept them in the cell.

Eric lay quietly, feeling their little hearts thud against his chest. Another hour passed and their rhythmic beat lulled him.

'We'll keep lookout,' one prapsy whispered. 'You sleep, boys.'

'You need to sleep as well,' Eric murmured.

'We will. We are. Each at a time.' One of the prapsies lay on Eric's chest and closed its eyes; the other walked in circles around him.

'All right,' Eric said. 'We'll take turns. One hour, that's enough. Then wake me and I'll keep watch.'

'Yes.'

Eric fell into an exhausted slumber almost at once. When he was breathing deeply, the prapsy pretending to sleep on him rose and stared at the doorway. For the remainder of the night both prapsies stayed silent and vigilant, leaving Eric to rest.

While Eric slept and the prapsies kept watch, the snow-like Essa brooded in the south of Ool. What had happened today, what wonderful thing? They had intercepted the most extraordinary beings. Not Griddas, not those bony spider-lovers. Not even the uncatchable High Witches, long gone from the skies. New things. Unfurred, small, lithe things. Without armour! Frail, keen to love, yet... travellers with Griddas. What were they? Friend or enemy? Friend! Friend! The Essa thought so, but they were always hopeful. How could they find out more?

Poor Detaclyver – so old and tired, so beaten back. So loving. If they asked him he would not let them go to the strangers. He would say they are too expectant. He would say they do not heed their own lives enough. 'Send us out! Send us out!' they would beg. 'It is too far,' he would say. 'You cannot make the distance to Thûn.' He would withhold his mighty breath and not let them go. 'We can! We can!' they would say. He would say – 'No!'

But how long had it been since there was any hope at all for Detaclyver?

No one else could make such a long trip. The Essa shivered in the summits of the Detaclyver, convincing themselves. They did not know if they could travel so far and still have the strength to return. But still – the strangers!

One whole night away. A terrible journey. Could they do it?

Without the breath of the Detaclyver, the Essa left.

They floated northwards, in small bunches so that they did not attract attention. The winds were against them, but they were determined. Quietly, hiding in the night snow, they passed by the storm-whirls. They travelled high over the Prag Sea and the cold plains beyond. As they neared Thûn many of the Essa were too tired to carry on, and returned home to the Detaclyver, but others continued their journey.

They passed over millions of infant Griddas bedded down together in the tunnels under Thûn. They passed over the imprisoned High Witches, where Calen lay in the filth of her cell, wondering about the choices she had made. They passed over Fola and Yemi. Griddas were in constant attendance at the Assessment Chamber – even now, in the night, casting and recasting their spells to keep him from escaping.

Yemi was held too deep for the Essa to help, so they rode the winds instead over Heebra's tower. They could not miss it, that orange lustre in the night. As the Essa approached they saw the taller stranger with long hair standing her ground, wide-eyed, guarding herself against the infants. Many of the Essa were almost frozen when they hurried towards the fire. The first to arrive nearly flew into the flames. Just in time they held back and stared into that wonder, warming their tiny wings. To be so close, yet unable to help! The Essa could not wait to tell the Detaclyver, but aspired to greater things first.

They searched for the second stranger.

Where was he? No way to tell, since he had no magical scent. So the Essa crept into all the Gridda caves, passing the sleepy tunnel sentries. A few Essa became lost and could not find their way out at all. Even fewer found the hole where the boy sat guarded by two strange flighted creatures. They drifted warily next to the prapsies.

The prapsies hopped from foot to foot, wondering what to do.

The Essa touched their baby faces and felt for their minds. 'Can you carry him?' they asked.

'He is too heavy,' whimpered one prapsy.

The Essa landed on Eric and tested his weight. 'Yes, too much,' they said.

It was nearly dawn. Snowflakes so deep down in the world would be seen in the light. They wanted to stay with the second stranger and comfort him, but there was no time. They must get back to tell Detaclyver. He would know what to do.

Were they too tired? Nearly day – and they were so tired. If the wind had changed direction they would never be able to battle back.

Kissing the prapsies, kissing Eric and each other, the Essa rose up the cell walls.

16

Storm-whirls

With the arrival of daybreak the infants surrounding Heebra's tower drifted back to their underground tunnels to rest. Rachel was almost too weary to notice. Left alone in the chamber at last she extinguished the fire, found a place to relieve herself and massaged her aching legs. A few spiders ran about the floor, left to perish by their negligent young owners. Rachel crawled away from them and lay down. Somehow, she slept.

Shortly afterwards, Gultrathaca entered the eye-tower. She watched Rachel for a while, watched her chest rise and fall. Finally she dropped some food on one of her hands. The food was alive: a rodent.

Waking, Rachel swiped it away.

Gultrathaca picked the rodent up by its tail. She offered it again. 'Squeamish? Disgusted? It is the same food my Griddas are eating.'

'I don't want it.'

'But you *need* it. How can you fight effectively if you have no strength?'

Rachel looked at the rodent. She was intensely hungry, but she knew that even if the rat-like animal was dead she could only eat it if she was starving. A Gridda wouldn't hesitate, she realized. She'd eat anything. To have any chance against them, I need to be like that, Rachel thought. I need to be capable of eating this rat-thing.

She reached out her hand – then dropped it. She could not eat the rodent. As soon as she knew for certain, Rachel felt all her precarious courage failing her.

I'm not going to be able to live through this day, she thought. An image of Eric came into her mind and she nearly screamed. What had Gultrathaca said yesterday? Kill yourself, before we discover anything... Rachel asked her spells. She asked for those who would help her end her life. They retreated. Even her deaths retreated. None of the spells were willing; they loved her too much.

Gultrathaca dropped the rodent and let it run off to a corner. 'You survived a night with the infants,' she said. 'Many of the pack-leaders did not expect that. *I* did not expect it.'

A compliment? Rachel ignored her. Standing upright, she straightened her body-suit. She thought of Heiki, of the spectrums, of Mum and Dad and everyone else on Earth whose existence might somehow depend on how she behaved today. She made herself look at Gultrathaca. 'When will the trial start?'

'Immediately. Unless you require a rest first.'

Yes, thought Rachel, that *is* what I need. Instead of that, she said, 'If I survive the trial, what then?'

'I think you know the answer.'

'There'll just be another trial, won't there? And another. Until I'm dead.'

'I'm glad you understand. I will give you a few moments to prepare yourself.' Gultrathaca's spiders followed her out of the eye-chamber.

When the last one skittered out, Rachel collapsed on the floor.

Could she escape? No. Not without being able to shift or fly or shape-change. In that case what should she do? Beg for mercy? How could an appeal to compassion work with Gultrathaca?

The best of Rachel's spells tried to encourage her. They told her how proud they were of her, that they were ready, that they would not fail her. As Rachel listened to their words she wondered how she had ever survived without them, in the time before she knew of her magic.

Her deaths, however, spoke in a different fashion. After all, they said, she *was* being watched. Her trial was an opportunity for the Griddas to judge the capability of all children, not just her. Fight! they argued. There'll probably be only one chance to impress. Call on all our resourcefulness!

Should she? The moment Rachel gave the deaths a fraction of her attention they rose into her mind like the killers they were. Perhaps, they said, if you fight ferociously, with enough flair and imagination and brutal directness, the Griddas might think again about challenging the children of Earth. Or at least they might delay, giving Heiki, the spectrums and sentinels longer to prepare. Isn't that why you're here? they said. Isn't that why Albertus Robertson let you go, when it was the last thing he wanted?

Rachel listened. She wondered how many Griddas she would need to kill to impress Gultrathaca. Could she do it? Should she make friends with her deaths for a day? Rachel pushed hunger and weariness and excuses aside. She probed her heart. She tried to summon mercilessness there.

A group of watchers preceded the reappearance of Gultrathaca. 'Are you ready?'

'Yes.'

'Then follow me.'

As they descended the staircase Gultrathaca said, 'I intend to make your first trial against a youngster.'

'Not an infant,' Rachel replied at once. 'I want to face an adult.'

Gultrathaca nodded appreciatively.

As Rachel emerged from Heebra's tower she saw that Griddas of all ages had assembled to observe the trial. Could Griddas recognize a human expression of fear? Rachel could not entirely hide it, but she did her best. Lifting her chin, holding herself erect, she strode across the snow.

Gultrathaca swept her arms wide. 'Select an opponent.'

Rachel gazed around. To her all the Gridda faces were the same: massive, hard-edged, frightening. 'Any opponent?'

'Any.'

'Then I select *you*, Gultrathaca.'

As soon as Rachel said the name her deaths rose like crude shadows in her eyes. She did not shut them out. She wanted Gultrathaca to see the deaths. She needed everything against this Gridda, the best and worst of her magic.

'Well,' Gultrathaca said. 'An unexpected honour. I see your deaths are ready, even if you are not.'

Making sure as many Griddas heard as possible, Rachel said, 'You have all the advantages, Gultrathaca. I've heard your talk about honour. If it means anything, let me choose the trial. I'll fight you where the Detaclyver lives. I'll fight you there.'

Gultrathaca hesitated, then saw the expectant eyes of the other Gridda pack-leaders on her. They understood the challenge Rachel had set.

'I agree,' Gultrathaca said. 'A private contest, then. But I warn you, Rachel: you may think you have found a friend in the Essa, but they are no match for an experienced Gridda.' Gultrathaca stepped back. A tight, exalted smile spread across her face. Across her jaws, her spiders ran in frenzy.

'Give me my other spells back!' Rachel demanded.

Gultrathaca touched her just under the eye. 'Not everything,' she said. 'You can now fly again, but no shifting is possible, nor any shape-changing. I won't have you escape that way. And if you try to fly anywhere except towards the Detaclyver you will be killed. We will both be escorted, watched.' Gultrathaca chose a dozen adult Griddas to fly with them. Half surrounded Rachel. 'Only one of us will be allowed to leave the Detaclyver alive. If you use any spells before we are within the Detaclyver the escorts will kill you. Are you ready?'

No, Rachel thought.

'Yes!' she shouted.

Gultrathaca sucked in all her spiders and lurched into the brightening sky.

Thrusting their powerful haunches southwards, the Gridda escort led the way. They crossed the city border. Flying in rhythm, they entered the hinterlands of the snow plains of Ool. For a while some infants thrashed behind, trying to keep up, but their immature magic was no match for the older Griddas, and they soon fell behind, their anguished cries piercing the clouds for miles.

After this there was only one sound – the wind pulsing from the thighs of the Gridda escort.

Gultrathaca's motion was assured, her speed dazzling. Not knowing what else to do, Rachel tucked in behind her, saving her strength for what was to come. They headed out over the Prag Sea, and somewhere in that unchanging region Rachel wished with all her heart to feel the touch of real sunshine. Ool's dawn offered little. There was no true warmth, no comfort of colour, nothing to repel the murk of the sky.

She tried not to look at the Griddas. They were a forbidding presence: arms sleekly out in front, brown fur flattened by the wind, their bodies supple and flexed – physiques of daunting strength.

Finally Rachel saw the bulking promontories of the Detaclyver.

And before it, like a bulwark across the world, rotated the mighty storm-whirls.

The Griddas headed straight for them. There was no gap between the whirls. Then Gultrathaca bellowed an order and they moved aside.

As Rachel approached she was merely a jangling speck. Deafening gusts blasted her hair, her clothes, her eyes. Instinctively, she turned her face towards her chest and lifted her hands to protect herself. As she did so, the uproar ceased. It became tranquil, peaceful, without wind, without cold. Rachel glanced around. The Griddas had all passed through the storm-whirls. Only she remained.

The storm-whirls had gently closed together around her.

Rachel gasped, hearing – oh, what was it? She put out her hands, dipped her fingers into the whirls. The sensation was not wind, not like wind at all. The storm-whirls enfolded her. And in that enfoldment Rachel felt their intelligence. She felt their anxiety about injuring her, and their fear of the Griddas whose spells enslaved them. But most of all Rachel felt their love: their magnificent, pounding, grave, reckless love for their ancient partner, the Detaclyver. For all the time they could remember the High Witches and Griddas had kept them apart. Whole families of storm-whirls were rooted to the Earth, forced to hold the Detaclyver back. The endless, painful creeping forward of the Detaclyver was nothing more than a desire to be closer to its companions.

Rachel bathed her face in the storm-whirls, wanting to stay there forever. She turned to gaze upwards, as if human eyes might be gazing back at her.

'Help me,' she said. 'Help me. I'm frightened.'

A terrible sadness groaned through the storm-whirls, and their winds held her head, but they said, 'We cannot. The spell-bonds are too numerous to break. We must pass you on. We cannot hold you.'

Rachel clung to the winds, trying to stay inside – and how the storm-whirls wished for that as well – but the thrall of the spells was too powerful. With a final departing sigh the whirls sent her through. For a few moments Rachel lay beyond, trembling.

Then she saw the Detaclyver.

The Detaclyver had never been mastered by the spells of any creature. It understood exactly what the Griddas had done to its beloved storm-whirls, and as Gultrathaca and the escort approached, its summits elongated into stabbing barbs.

The Griddas reacted at once. Trying to confuse the Detaclyver, they flew in several directions across the sky, giving it many targets. Gultrathaca dropped lower, searching for an entry point in the Detaclyver's skin. Finding one, she dived straight down, bit her way through and squirmed inside.

As soon as she disappeared great swarms rose into the sky: Essa.

In long surges they pushed back the remaining Griddas, keeping them away from Rachel. Another group of Essa surrounded Rachel herself. They carried her towards the Detaclyver, their tiny wings beating in welcome. 'Go in! Go in!' they cried.

'But Gultrathaca, she's –'

'No! No! Believe in us! Go in, up and away!'

When they saw Rachel hesitate, the Essa tried to calm themselves down. Couldn't she understand? Beautiful storm-friend, don't you know Detaclyver will keep you safe? Aren't we full of anxious hopes for you? Go in!

Rachel felt the Essa trying to will her into believing them. She felt their concern for everything: for her, the Detaclyver, for Eric, for the prapsies. Tiny lives, driven by hope, Rachel realized. How could the Essa survive on such a harsh world? Then she explored their magic, and knew at once that no other creatures needed it more. The Essa were held together only by magic. They navigated using magic, found each other with it; in the absolute bleakness and frost of Ool's night there was no other way for beings so frail.

Rachel stopped resisting them. She allowed the Essa to carry her body towards the opening in the Detaclyver.

'Take care! Take care!' the Essa called.

'Aren't you ... aren't you coming with me?'

'No! No!' The Essa placed their bodies across the entrance, blocking the way in to the other Griddas. 'Detaclyver will look after you now. Go! Go to him! Go in!'

Rachel flew cautiously inside. There was no sign of Gultrathaca. Half-expecting to be pushing through skin and gristle, Rachel instead found herself in a kind of tunnel. Fresh air whooshed over her face, almost knocking her down. Then warm, staler air washed into her back.

Not a tunnel, her information spells explained. A capillary: a tube carrying breath around the Detaclyver's body.

Rachel put a foot forward – one step. As she did so, soft light on the capillary floor lit the way ahead. Another step. More light. Another. She walked up the capillary, reaching a fork. Left or right? The light glowed left.

I'm being shown where to go, she realized. The Detaclyver knows I'm here. Can it feel me? What if I run? I'll run!

Rachel picked up her feet and ran. Putting all her trust in the Detaclyver, she would have become completely lost except that the light guided her. Gradually the capillaries widened, until Rachel found herself rushing down broad lanes, all lit brightly. Then, as she turned a corner, a figure blocked her way.

Gultrathaca.

But at first Rachel could not tell. A light shone on

Gultrathaca so brightly that even Rachel could hardly stand it. Gultrathaca's eye-shields were half shut. Several of her watchers floundered blindly about the floor. 'The Detaclyver has done its best to stop me,' Gultrathaca rasped. 'But I see you. I still see you!'

Rachel looked for a way past. She could not go forward – Gultrathaca filled the exit. But there were smaller paths. They led off the main capillary, though none were lit. When Gultrathaca ran at her, Rachel picked the first.

Immediately, beneath her feet, the floor sprouted with spikes.

A trap.

Rachel fell to the ground. When she attempted to stand up her legs only twitched. She looked at her ankles. The spikes were already withdrawing. They left tiny holes. What was happening? Rachel felt no pain. She felt nothing – a lack of sensation.

Her information spells tried to explore her ankles, but for some reason they could not find the way. They felt ill, fatigued, vague. Lacking all clarity, they took an age to tell her:

Poison.

Healing spells drained into Rachel's veins at once, but her mind was hazy and so, therefore, were her spells. They went to the wrong places. With enormous effort Rachel managed to sit up.

Gultrathaca stood above her. 'Goodbye, Rachel,' she said. 'Enjoy the bliss. I left that for you.' She loped away.

For a while Rachel could hear Gultrathaca's heavy tread. Then she forgot about Gultrathaca entirely. A strange sensation suffused her body. It was one of pro-found contentment. Had she ever felt this happy? Her spells understood something was wrong, but they could not remember what. Rachel knew that she must be feeling the effects of the poison, but she had no desire to fight it, not any longer.

The poison entered her heart, and she did not mind.

Finally, she stopped caring altogether. And when that happened her spells also gave in. The finest of them, the spells that all Rachel's life had cared so much for her, even in the time she did not know they existed, stopped caring as well. All their beautiful light left her eyes.

Rachel lay down on her side. She placed her hands under her head. Her eyes wanted to close. She let them. She could no longer move. She didn't question why, not any more. It didn't matter. Her lips parted, falling slack as her jaw muscles relaxed under the final killing influence of the toxins.

She was dying.

Gultrathaca was forgotten. Yemi was forgotten. Mum, Dad, Eric. Everything.

17

the prison world

Eric sat cross-legged on the floor of his cell. The prapsies hadn't spoken for a long time.

'How are you, boys?' he murmured. 'You're very quiet.'

'We are well, Eric,' they said together. 'We are perfect.'

'You should have woken me earlier. I told you to.'

'We weren't tired. We aren't tired. Look.'

The prapsies spread their wings to show him how fit they still were. Not once had they complained while they were in the cell. Eric stroked their nape feathers the way they preferred it, thinking about the Essa. Little flakes. Snow-like beings. He would have thought the prapsies' minds had flipped, if he hadn't seen the Essa himself on the journey to Thûn.

Could he expect help from them?

No, he thought. Don't do that. Stop clinging onto the hope that something or someone else is going to rescue you. He couldn't even depend on Rachel this time. He knew that because he could sense her, a distant magical scent barely clinging to life. What was happening to her? He could also pick out another scent, a life even more precariously in balance than Rachel's. It belonged to Serpantha.

Well? Eric asked himself. What are you going to do about it? What are *you* going to do?

All morning he had been absorbed, thinking about Larpskendya. What had the Wizard meant when he said everything might depend on him now? What am I, after all? Eric thought. Just an ordinary boy, without any magic. I can't even climb out of this pathetically shallow little cell. Any kid nowadays can manage a basic heating spell, but not me. So the prapsies have to put up with being cold...

Could he do anything to affect the Griddas? The scraps of a plan were forming in Eric's mind, but it was too far-fetched for him to take seriously.

At least the experiments had stopped for a while. There had been peace all morning until a severely bruised Gultrathaca returned. Whatever had happened to her, she resumed the experiments again at once. This time, Eric noticed, she used Griddas, though they didn't come close to him. In fact, the opposite; for some reason the Griddas fired their spells at him from ridiculous distances, way beyond Ool.

There were grim shadows under the prapsies' eyes. Despite Eric's protests they had not slept at all, their eyes never leaving the doorway or open roof. 'I'll bet you want to fly, don't you?' he said, trying to cheer them. 'You must be bored, stuck here, not able to fly. Go on! Have a fly round!'

Briefly they flashed around the cell, though clearly only because Eric wanted them to. They quickly returned to him. One watched the cell doorway while the other bent its round head towards Eric.

'You must be hungry,' he said.

'No,' lied the prapsy. 'Are you?'

'Nah, I'm all right.' They both looked away from each other.

'Are you coldish, Eric?'

'No. Not a bit.'

'I could squash next to you if you want.'

'OK, but not because I'm cold, mind.'

The prapsy nuzzled up against Eric's cheek. It kept one eye on him; the other watched the empty ceiling. 'She's coming again,' the prapsy whispered, seeing movement there. 'Gultrathaca.'

'I know,' Eric answered. 'Don't worry. I'm ready for her.'

Gultrathaca approached Eric's cell. No sudden movements. No startling him. She knew how quickly his anti-magic could demolish a body filled with magic.

While she walked healer spiders continued to perform repairs on her. The fury of the Detaclyver! She had been lucky to escape from its body at all, and the Essa had hounded her halfway across the Prag Sea.

She reached the opening above the cell and stood there, leaning down.

Eric! She almost liked the boy. The way he challenged her! Unlike Yemi, Eric did not smile or want to play. He mocked her gloriously. As she gazed at him now, a marvellous anger and bitterness enlivened his features.

'Are you coming down then, you hag!' he bellowed.

'In a moment,' Gultrathaca replied, composing herself.

She thought about Eric's special gift. She had seen it maturing in front of her eyes. Not his ability to destroy magic. That was remarkable enough, but more remarkable still was *how far away* he could detect magic. No Witch or

Wizard could come close to matching it. To fully test him she had unleashed magic from immense range, stretching her Griddas' spell-making in ways she had never asked of them before.

No matter how far-flung the distances, Eric knew each spell was coming.

Gultrathaca's ambitions grew larger with every new test, but how would she obtain his co-operation? Well, perhaps she could. Eric was not like Yemi. Yemi was impossible to manipulate, but Eric could be frightened. Hadn't she already placed him in a world of fear? It was time to free him unexpectedly from that fear. If I offer him hope for his sister, Gultrathaca thought, he'll want to believe it. If I promise him safety, especially for the prapsies, he'll be grateful to accept it.

Even so, at the edge of the cell, Gultrathaca hesitated. It would be so easy to misjudge this situation. It required of her a gentleness that did not come readily.

There would be lies amongst the things she would tell him. Amongst all the other lies would be one important one. Would Eric realize?

Controlling her anxiety, Gultrathaca bent over the lip of the cell and looked down.

Eric looked defiantly back. 'What now?' he sneered. 'Who are you sacrificing this time? Coward! Why don't *you* try attacking me? Do you think you're safe up there, out of my range?'

'I know you can reach me,' Gultrathaca said in the softest voice she could manage. 'But please ... don't. There will be no more things sent to hurt you. I promise. Whether you agree to help me or not, there will be no more attacks of any kind.'

'You *promise,* eh! Guess what? I don't believe you!'

'I am coming down.'

'I'll kill you if you do! I mean it.'

'When you hear my offer you will not want to kill me. I intend to release you, Eric.' Seeing that she had his attention, Gultrathaca floated into a corner of the cell, keeping her watchers in their pits to avoid alarming him.

Eric folded his arms. 'Well?'

'I will set you free,' Gultrathaca said. 'And I will deliver Rachel back to you.'

'Delivered dead, you mean.'

'No. Alive, Eric, and unharmed. I guarantee it.'

'Oh, I'll bet you do!'

Eric's voice was filled with sarcasm, but inside, inside, hope burst wildly through. He fought against it. He knew Gultrathaca was just playing some new game. How dare she! he thought. How dare she! As he gazed at her, he suddenly hated Gultrathaca with more intensity than he had hated anything in his life. Let her throw more Witches against him! That way he could at least stay mad, insulting, half-crazy. But this sudden new kindly version of Gultrathaca – if he listened to it, if he allowed himself even for one second to believe that there might truly be a way out of this, a happy ending – he would not have the nerve to follow through with his own half-plan.

That plan had been the only thing keeping him from falling to pieces already.

'I won't hurt you any longer,' Gultrathaca said. 'I will let you go, Eric. And I will free Yemi and Fola, too. I will free everyone. You can return to Earth. The Griddas will not bother you again. We – I – it is my fault – have made a terrible mistake in the treatment of your entire race. Forgive me.'

Eric nodded as if listening, but actually he was picturing how satisfying it would be see Gultrathaca's body deflate like a bag. He was picturing her as a smear on the floor. And this was no idle image. Eric could do it. Gridda magic was similar to the High Witches'. Gultrathaca had tried to shield her spells from him, but he saw through her.

She had no idea what torment Eric could place her in.

Uncertain how to proceed, Gultrathaca tried complimenting him. 'You never used your full gifts before, Eric, did you? See how deadly you've become! No more primitive finger-jabbing. You don't need to point your fingers any longer to destroy spells.'

Eric realized Gultrathaca was right – and he also realized how much he missed the finger-pointing part of him. It belonged to an older version of himself he wanted back.

'In return for freeing you,' Gultrathaca said, 'I'm not asking you to betray the Wizards or your own species. I'm asking for a simple thing, almost nothing. I want you to help me find the prison world of the Griddas.'

'What?'

Gultrathaca spread her claws over the rock floor. 'I placed you here for a reason. This cell is in one of the original tunnels. The early generations of Griddas lived here. They were just the same as High Witches then, with the same yearning for flight. They were crammed in here, in the dark, to make their eyes grow or wither, while the Highs experimented with them – us – in many ways.'

Eric knew Gultrathaca was telling a version of the truth at least. He could feel the imprint of the ancient Gridda spells. They were graven into the rocks from which they had tried to escape.

'Most Griddas have always lived on the prison world,'

Gultrathaca went on. 'The Highs did not want too many of us spoiling Ool itself.' She lowered her voice, looked away from him in the way she had seen humans do when expressing deep feeling. 'The prison world is a terrible place,' she said. 'Griddas are chained up. A few High Witches used to guard and feed them, but now we have taken over Ool I doubt that is taking place. Our Griddas will be dying there.'

Eric, observing Gultrathaca closely, said nothing.

'I know you can scent magic at considerable distances, Eric. All I ask is that you help us find this prison world. There are spells concealing it. The Highs did that to hide it from the Wizards, but they also kept the planet's location a secret from us. Do you know where it is?'

Gultrathaca asked the question in such a casual, offhand way, that Eric understood its importance at once. He tried to read Gultrathaca's expression. Was that a look of sadness? He couldn't tell if the sadness was real or manufactured for his benefit. But he could see Gultrathaca trembling. There was no doubting that.

He kept her waiting. Then he said, 'Yes, I know where it is.'

Gultrathaca held back her elation with difficulty. She had hoped – but not really believed – his gift could discover a place so distant. It had to be Orin Fen! No other world had such spells guarding it. Could the location of the Wizards' planet actually be in her grasp?

'How far is it … the … the prison world?' she asked, her voice cracking with the effort to keep steady.

'Why should I tell you?'

'Will you … will you not tell me?'

'No. Because if I do that you'll kill me. You'll just send in some animal with no magic to tear me to pieces.'

'No, Eric, I won't do that. I –'

'Shut up!' Eric said. 'Let me think.' He paced up and down the cell floor. He murmured to the prapsies. He lay down, put his hands behind his head, pretended to relax. Then he stood up, walked up to Gultrathaca and shouted at the top of his voice: 'I won't tell you, but I'll *show* you where it is if you absolutely promise to keep your word about Rachel, Yemi, Fola and Serpantha!'

'I will.' Gultrathaca's chest heaved.

Eric glared at her. He could see how much she would give him now, anything he asked for. 'Or maybe I won't show you,' he said. 'I tell you what: I'll agree to think about it, instead. That's all. And while I do I want a better place to stay than this. I want somewhere nicer.'

'Of course … of course, Eric. Whatever you want.'

'I'll tell you what I want, you ugly hag! I want you to warm this place up and give me and the prapsies a decent meal!'

Gultrathaca nodded vigorously. 'Will you help us then?'

'I'll give you my answer when I'm ready. Get out.'

Gultrathaca had never been so insultingly treated. Her jaws ached to kill Eric, but that pleasure would have to be delayed. Not wanting to irritate him or give him any reason to change his mind, she held out her claw awkwardly in the human way of parting.

'Just go away and leave me in peace,' Eric said, turning away.

Burning with rage, Gultrathaca held back her jaws and hurried from the cell.

As soon as she left, Eric started to shake. The way he had spoken! He saw how much she wanted to kill him! How could he have done something so dangerous? But it proved how important he was to her. Eric walked around his cell for a while, his mind distracted, trying to calm down.

The prapsies followed him.

'We'll be fed soon,' Eric told them. 'Good stuff. Get this place warmed up, too.'

'Don't trust Gultrathaca,' one of the prapsies said, running to keep up with him.

'Griddas, don't believe them biters,' the other whispered.

'Shush,' Eric said. 'Shush now. I know.' He stared at the walls, his mind far away. His plan might not be so impossible, after all. Gultrathaca had her own extensive hopes, but Eric's were just as ambitious. He remained still for a considerable time, watched by the agitated prapsies.

'What are you thinking about?' one enquired. 'What are you craftily thinking?'

'Nothing,' Eric said. 'Nothing at all.'

It broke his heart not to tell the prapsies what he was planning, but how could he?

'Eric, don't do anything to make the Griddas angry,' begged one. 'We're better now, better guarders. We will guard you better than before.'

'I know you will,' Eric whispered, gathering them up. 'It's all right. Gultrathaca won't hurt me any more. She won't hurt us at all.'

As he stood there, staring at the walls, not for a moment did Eric believe anything Gultrathaca had said. He knew she wouldn't free Yemi. And even if she freed Rachel, it would just be to murder her when she was no longer useful.

But was Gultrathaca telling the truth about the planet of imprisoned Griddas?

Possibly. As soon as she mentioned it, he had reached out for the magic of that distant world, and found it. There were protections around it, and invisibility spells. The magnificence of those spells! What else could they be concealing except Orin Fen? Eric penetrated the invisibility spells. Knowing that the Wizards had always hidden Orin Fen, he fully expected to find not Griddas but the magic of millions of Wizards on the world beneath. Surprisingly, there were none. Of course, the Wizards would probably hide their scent. But Eric knew with absolute certainty: if there were any Wizards he would be able to detect them – no matter what they did to try to hide themselves.

The planet had no Wizards on it at all.

So perhaps Gultrathaca really intended to take him to a world full of other Griddas.

Eric hoped so. It was exactly what he wanted.

18

tunnels

Wreathed in the final snarl of the poison, Rachel did not notice. Only her information spells, clinging on and listening out for her still, heard the sound. It seemed to well up from the bottom of the world: a warm, scented, fierce wind.

The breath of the Detaclyver.

And on that breath, riding it, came the Essa.

They did not need to beat their wings. The Detaclyver gave them all the speed they needed, boosting their little bodies along the capillaries. Would they be on time? Would they? They had helped before when Griddas tried to hurt the Detaclyver with such poisons, but this new being was far more delicate.

Through the capillaries. Beyond the lungs, up, up, up.

The Essa found Rachel lying on her side, the veins of her face turned black by the poison.

Without considering the danger to themselves, they leaped inside her half-open mouth. 'Quickly! Quickly!

Only the youngest!' Down her throat the smaller Essa flew, squeezing into her arteries. Their absorbent bodies took in the poisons. When they were filled nearly to bursting, the youngsters tottered unsteadily up Rachel's windpipe. Flopping onto her suit, they spewed out the poison – and returned for more. Long waves of them went continuously in and out until the most harmful effects of the toxins were removed.

Then, tired and woozy, and held proudly by their elders, the young Essa hovered a few feet from Rachel. They did not want to startle her.

Gradually Rachel's skin regained a healthier pallor. Her cold face twitched as the nerve-endings came back to life. When she was ready, the Essa helped her eyelids open. She blinked, and the Essa – diffidently – blinked back.

Rachel recognized them. She half-lifted a hand – and that was all the invitation the Essa needed. All their lively voices crowded into her thoughts at once: greeting her, naming themselves, tenderly touching her face, inquisitive and anxious.

'Hey, slow down, slow down!' Rachel said, half-laughing. 'Tell me – tell me what you are. About yourselves.'

The Essa would not do so. They only wanted to speak about the Detaclyver. Rachel learned it had once roamed freely across all the world. Ool had been warmer then, and the Detaclyver had wandered wherever the fancy took him, his edges billowing, accompanied by the majestic storm-whirls and his constant companions, the Essa. The arrival of the High Witches changed all of that. Over centuries, they beat the Detaclyver back to the south of the world. They enslaved the storm-whirls, encased the fish in ice oceans, and set about building the eye-towered cities.

But if the Witches expected the Detaclyver to forsake the storm-whirls, they were mistaken. The Detaclyver fought back. He heaved towards the cities, grappling with the foundations. The Witches tried to starve him. They tried to freeze him, ridding Ool of the warming sun altogether – replacing it with endless winter snow.

Even that did not stop the Detaclyver. Or his wilful Essa. Against his wishes, against all his wishes, they had decided on a way to fight back: to become like the snow themselves. The Essa did so, modified their bodies. For longer than they could remember they had hidden within the snow, defended and loved – defended the Detaclyver where they could, and loved the storm-whirls – whispering words of comfort through the long dark years, so the whirls knew the Detaclyver had never abandoned them.

Briefly, when the Griddas toppled the High Witches, the Essa had hope. But nothing changed. The Griddas simply continued the agonies inflicted by the High Witches.

While Rachel listened to the Essa, she remained still, allowing her healing spells to deal with the last of the poison. As soon as she felt capable she stood up – swaying.

'You are not ready,' the Essa said, holding her arm.

'I have to be. My brother, Eric ... I have to find him.'

'Eric?' The Essa made a shape with their bodies – an outline of Eric lying down, the little heads of the prapsies close by him.

'You know where he is?' Rachel asked. 'You – you can find him?'

'Yes, but not yet, not yet!'

'We can't wait,' Rachel said. 'We've got to find Eric straight away. He hasn't got any magic. He won't survive if –'

'No! No!' The Essa, caught between wanting to reassure Rachel and another purpose, became agitated.

'What is it?' Rachel asked.

The Essa formed a new shape. The darker-hued ones gathered in places where brown would have dusted the wings. A few lined up as antennae: a butterfly.

'Yemi!' she gasped.

The Essa milled excitedly in the air, telling her what they knew.

'We'll find him, of course we will,' Rachel said. 'But if Yemi's survived this long against the Griddas, he can take care of himself. Eric needs –'

'No, Yemi first! Yemi!' the Essa insisted. 'Whispers. We hear them all. Whispers in the tunnels, don't you understand? He won't live. He can't. The Griddas won't let him!'

Rachel thought rapidly. Eric and Yemi were both captives under Thûn. How could she get there? 'I can't change shape, or shift,' she told the Essa. 'But I can fly. If I travel outside, in the air, could you hide me? Surround me, somehow?'

The Essa pondered. 'Yes,' they said. 'For a while.' Several fluttered deep into the Detaclyver to convey their decision. When they returned all the Essa clung to Rachel's body. 'Whoosh!' they told her. 'Detaclyver will start us!'

From the subterranean depths, many miles away, an immense diaphragm clenched and unclenched. Rachel felt her feet lift. Her magic steadied her, resisting. The Essa asked her not to, dancing ecstatically in the new wind.

Rachel let go – and the mighty breath took her.

Sideways she and the Essa travelled, gathering speed,

then up and away, into the summits. A peak shattered and ice particles showered down. Rachel went to cover her face, but the Essa laughed as none of the particles touched her. Up, up, still further up. Finally: the pallid light of sky. Just before the Detaclyver propelled Rachel into it, she had a moment of direct contact with its mind.

It offered her everything: passion, all its ardent wishes.

Then she was in the sky. Trembling with feelings – and hidden by the packed, determined bodies of the Essa – Rachel streamed northwards towards Thûn.

She passed over the storm-whirls. In their great stately way the whirls turned, giving no indication to the Griddas of what was coming. She skirted the edge of the Prag Sea, where fish peered up through the ice. When the breath of the Detaclyver petered out, Rachel's flying spells took over. Enveloped by the Essa, she travelled in the highest skies where enemy eyes were least likely to look. It was not until she entered the clouds over the snow plains leading towards Thûn that the first Griddas started to appear. The wind also veered, so the Essa were flying in a contrary direction to the real snow.

'Not safe to fly any more,' warned the Essa.

'But we're still so far from Thûn! We must get closer than this.'

'There is ...' The Essa stopped. Rachel felt them shiver. 'Go down, go down,' they said. Copying the natural motion of the falling snow, Rachel drifted to the ground. As she landed, she could tell the Essa were striving to lower their voices. They were worried for her. They had braved the tunnels of the huraks many times, but Rachel was too big to hide. The blue cats would surely find her. Their breaths would put her to sleep, like the Griddas' spiders ...

Reluctantly, the Essa told Rachel about the hurak tunnels under the plains. Some of those tunnels led to Thûn itself.

'Is there any other way?' Rachel asked, seeing how anxious the Essa were.

'No, but we will accompany you,' they told her without hesitation.

Rachel wanted to hold them when they said that, but how to hold something so small without injuring it?

Rachel's information spells searched beneath the snow. In one place a tunnel almost broke the surface. She hurried over the top. 'Stay close to me,' she said, using her magic to delve under the snow and grind through the rock beneath.

When the first chink of tunnel-light struck her eyes, Rachel drew back. The tunnel was a dazzling ultramarine blue. 'Why is it so bright?'

'Griddas don't like it,' the Essa explained. 'That is why.' They floated in little bunches ahead of Rachel, to meet the dangers first.

'No, you don't,' Rachel said. 'Get behind me. I'll use my spells.'

Determined to look ahead, a few clambered onto her forehead. The remaining Essa guarded her back, or positioned themselves on her arms to see what might be coming from any side tunnels. Rachel's body-suit felt strangely silky to them. They dug into the stitches, testing that their minute legs could pivot and turn on the material. When they were satisfied, Rachel used a spell to hush her footfall – and took her first step.

She travelled roughly northwards, but the hurak tunnels never kept a single direction for long. They were full of traps intended for Griddas: snares, blind spots, innumerable pitfalls, kinks, silences. Sometimes there were dark patches – perfect places to lie in ambush. Rachel's information spells guided her through. At every twist the Essa expected her to be put to sleep by sneaky hurak breaths, but there was no sign of the blue cats.

Rachel crept forward, occasionally flying in straighter parts where she could see ahead. The Essa became increasingly perplexed as they approached the perimeter of the city. Where were the huraks? They never left their tunnels so unprotected! A group of the Essa flitted down a tributary connecting to the tunnels of the Griddas. 'Empty! Empty, too!' they reported back. 'No Griddas!'

They left the hurak tunnels behind and entered new spaces, the residential networks of the Griddas. There were wide tunnels here, and spacious caves. All of them were vacant. Rachel flew at will through cave after cave. Recent Gridda tracks led from them. All the tracks – hundreds of thousands of claw marks – headed in one direction, towards the heart of Thûn.

'Listen,' said an Essa. Rachel heard nothing. 'Food traps,' the Essa explained. 'We should be able to hear them. Never silent, never quiet, always snapping creatures up for the infants. What does it mean?'

Rachel sent out her information spells. For miles ahead and all around there was no living creature of any kind. 'All the animals are gone, too,' she said. 'Everything.'

'Many have no feet or wings,' the Essa told her. 'How can they be gone?'

'Where do all these tracks lead?'

'Deep, into the deep,' the Essa said. 'The Assessment Levels. Yemi is there!'

'Hold on to me. As tightly as you can.'

'What are you going to do?'

'Trust me.'

The Essa anchored their feet to Rachel's clothes. They crept into her hair. Once they were firmly set, her eyes flashed blue. The colour was so intense it outshone even the hurak tunnels. Almost fearfully, the Essa stared at her.

Giving total freedom to her flying spells, putting all her faith in her magic, Rachel followed the Gridda tracks into the depths.

19

plans

While Gultrathaca awaited Eric's decision, she paid a visit to a former pack-member: the disowned and disgraced, the tainted Jarius.

What had happened to her in that brief time alone with Yemi? At first, when Jarius was dragged from the Assessment Chamber, Gultrathaca thought that Yemi must have passed on some kind of human infection. In fact, Jarius had never been healthier. The old Jarius had been a wreck of fears. The latest version was more poised; she unsettled the guards; a few had even started to listen to her talk of concord and an end to war.

As Gultrathaca arrived at her isolated cell, Jarius emerged with all her new-found serenity from the shadows.

'Welcome, sister,' she said.

'You are no sister of mine.' Gultrathaca circled her in frustration, humiliated by her continued existence.

Naturally she had tried several times to kill Jarius, but it was impossible. Yemi – even from the distance of the Assessment Chamber – shielded her with the same fervour as Fola.

Jarius shook her head sadly. 'The mighty Gultrathaca! I see it shames you to see me standing here, defying you, companion to a boy whose happiness you cannot even dent. But think differently: I am not your enemy, sister.'

'Oh, you are.'

'No. Look around you. There's open talk amongst the guards. Too many infants. The tunnels are overflowing. Skirmishes breaking out everywhere. Pack against pack scrambling for room. It's unbearable. I've heard the infants myself. They fly about the tunnels, restless, jeering at the adults, trying to provoke a reaction. What happens when you lose control, Gultrathaca? What then?'

Gultrathaca smiled. 'Do not concern yourself for me. I still have control.'

'Do you? You can hardly even control yourself. I know what you feel, Gultrathaca. It is the need for combat, for the violence of blood. You've been inactive too long. Like the rest of the Griddas, you can't wait to fight. That is what is driving your ambitions against the Wizards and the children, nothing else. I understand, because I feel it, too. It was bred into us by the High Witches, after all, this longing. But we can escape its pull. Yemi has shown me another way to live.'

'Don't prattle your peace to me,' Gultrathaca said. 'Fight me instead! Without the boy's assistance! I will remove the guards.'

'Why can't you understand?' Jarius said. 'Stop thinking continually in terms of conflict – you against me, the packs against Yemi, Griddas versus children. See beyond the tunnels! It is not merely the Wizards set against the Griddas. The whole simmering anger of Ool is turning on us. The Detaclyver has never been so active. There are Essa in the deeps. Huraks menace the home tunnels. While there is still time, find Rachel. Do everything you can to find her.'

'Rachel is dead.'

'No, she is alive, sister, alive.'

Gultrathaca tried to hide her shock.

'Yemi knows more than your own scouts,' Jarius said. 'Find Rachel. Free her, and make a truce with Earth's children and the Wizards. They want it, genuinely. There is no other way.'

'I would rather die,' Gultrathaca hissed.

'I know. That is what is so terrible.'

'No.' Gultrathaca approached closer. 'What is terrible, Jarius, is that you have forgotten the gloriousness of war. I have already sent an invasion force to Earth. It will kill all the children and adults on that world.'

'Kill them to what end? War for what purpose? And even if you succeed, what will be next for the Griddas? Will they simply go on finding new enemies, killing forever? Is that the great destiny Gultrathaca offers the packs?'

'A lifetime of fighting is all any Gridda seeks,' Gultrathaca replied. 'There is no higher honour. Once you understood that.'

'Do you think the Wizards will allow it? They will never do so. All Griddas may be killed. Are you prepared to be the cause of that? What gives you the right to make such a decision?'

Gultrathaca stared at Jarius, saw her concern to convince her, her anxiety for everyone and everything. It was the same expression Gultrathaca had seen in Fola, Rachel and the other children of Earth. It disgusted her. 'Even if we are all killed, there will be a magnificent fight first,' she said to Jarius. 'Following that, what does it matter? Why look beyond the next battle?'

'Those are not your own thoughts. That is what the Highs taught us.'

'In that regard they taught us well.' As Gultrathaca prepared to leave, Jarius beseeched her, 'Don't lead the packs against Earth. It will be a horrible slaughter.'

'Horrible? Horrible! Oh, Jarius, I pity you. Are you so sterilized that you no longer tremble with joy at the prospect of battle? War is what I want, what we all want. And not only war against the Earth. You're right about the infants: they *are* restless. To occupy them, I'll need to offer something special, and I intend to. I'll give them the Wizards as well. I'll give them the world of Orin Fen.'

'You won't find it. The Highs never did.'

'The Highs didn't have Eric.'

At last – at last! – Gultrathaca saw a quiver of uncertainty cross Jarius's face.

Eric lay back on his new bed, deciding.

His second cell was nicer than the old one had been, much nicer. Gultrathaca had fashioned him comfy chairs and warm blankets. Eric had no doubt she would have given him a cuddly toy if he'd asked. He even had pillows, frilly ones. He couldn't get over it. Did Gultrathaca really think he would be impressed with frilly pillows? Yes, he thought, she did. She didn't understand him at all.

Good. It meant his plan had a chance.

His hands rested lightly on the prapsies. They each had a little cushion of their own on the bed. At home, they would probably have been bickering over who got which cushion, but not here. They weren't even interested in the cushions. They just wanted to stay close to him. Normally they followed him everywhere, but in recent hours they had become inseparable. If Eric got up to stretch in the cell, they stretched with him. If he paced, they paced. If he decided to settle back on the bed, as now, they lay alongside, silent, never taking their blue eyes off him.

'You all right, boys?' he said, wedged between them.

'Yes, Eric,' replied one prapsy. 'But you are not. You are not all right, are you?'

'Oh, I'm fine.'

'No Eric, you are not fine.'

'That's enough. Be quiet now,' Eric murmured – and they were.

'Is there anything you want, Eric?' one asked, after a while.

'Just your company. Get some rest, now. I keep telling you that. Don't you two listen to a single word I say any more?'

The prapsies stayed silent. Eventually one said, 'We will do what you want.'

'Yes, we'll do anything for you, Eric,' the other said.

'I know. I know you will, boys,' Eric replied, his voice almost breaking. And he thought: you will have to; I'm going to have to ask everything of you now.

His fingers curling and uncurling in the prapsies' feathers, Eric forced himself to go over the plan again. As he did so fear pounded through him. He tried to ignore it. He tried, instead, to cultivate his hatred of the Griddas. He was able think more clearly when he shut out everything except that hatred.

Could he carry out the plan? Every time Eric thought about it, his mind moved sideways in terror. To reassure himself, he sent his spell-detecting talents out again. There it was: that big strange world so tantalizing to Gultrathaca. Was it truly a prison planet, full of Griddas? Maybe. Mixed signals like Griddas and High Witches leaked from it, but no Wizards; not once did he detect a Wizard.

The plan, the plan. He practised over and over what he must do.

Griddas lived beneath Thûn. They also lived beneath the other two immense cities of Ool, spread over a wide distance. Eric didn't know anything about those other places, but that didn't stop him reaching out to the Griddas who lived there, into every sinew of their magic. Gultrathaca thought they were safe. She thought that if the Griddas kept their distance from Eric he could not harm them. When he was in his old cell that had been the hardest part of all – waiting until the last possible moment to act against each attack, waiting until they reached his cell. His range was actually far greater than Gultrathaca knew. If she hadn't tested him from such distances, he would never have discovered it. His reach was vast. He could wrap his destruction around every Gridda on Ool. Now, lying here, on this bed, with his head resting on the pillow, he could kill them all.

It intoxicated and repelled him to think of it!

But while destroying all the Griddas on Ool was something, Eric's plan was more enterprising than that. He planned to destroy all those on the prison world, too. He would persuade Gultrathaca to bring as many Griddas as possible, and when they were close enough to the prison world, he would bring all the additional Griddas into his range as well. And, he thought, even if I can't kill them all, at least I'll damage them, hurt them badly. They'll be a long way from home, too far to make it back to Ool.

He realized how terrible these thoughts were. They were outrageous. He knew that. It was an awful thing he planned to do but, Eric reminded himself, he *had* to think like this. Hadn't Larpskendya said it might all depend on him now? Who else was going to deal with these appalling Griddas? There was nobody else. The Essa had not returned; Serpantha was only a wisp of life in a far-off dungeon. As for Rachel – Eric felt her racing towards Thûn, and no one knew better than he what she could do – but against a world of Griddas what chance did she have?

Better to act himself, before she died trying to save him.

There is no one else, he told himself. You have to do it. You.

What upset him most of all was that there was no chance of saving the prapsies. If his plan succeeded, if he killed all the Griddas, he and the prapsies would have to die in space with them. Eric didn't share this information with the prapsies. He didn't want to scare them any more than he had already done. There they were beside him – he never had to look for them – twitching, still in look-out mode, watching the door. How often had their vigilance already kept him safe? How often had their simple belief in him kept him from losing his spirit?

'It doesn't matter,' he said, with tears in his eyes. 'I *can* do it. I must.' He had spoken out loud, without meaning to. Gazing down at the prapsies, he found them gazing back at him with tremulous eyes.

'Do what? Eric, will you tell us?'

'I can't.'

'Eric, tell us!'

'Oh, I can't. I can't!' Unable to stand it any longer, Eric jumped off the bed. 'I'm ready!' he shouted. 'I've made my decision. Tell Gultrathaca I want to speak to her!'

The message was conveyed. When Gultrathaca entered his cell, she appeared as kind and considerate and thoughtful as he'd ever seen her before.

'We still haven't been able to find Rachel,' she started apologetically.

Eric cut her off. 'I assume you'll keep your word. I can't stand being here any more. If we're going to go to this prison world, let's do it now.'

'The Griddas are ready,' Gultrathaca said. 'I will protect you myself. Nothing will happen to you, I promise.'

Eric did not even look at her. 'I hope you have a large army.'

'I will be bringing most of the Griddas. How far is it?'

'A long way.'

Gultrathaca nodded. 'It is a good thing you are doing, Eric.'

'Yes,' Eric replied thickly. 'I know.'

Gultrathaca left Eric, trembling with excitement and apprehension. Had she succeeded? She hardly dared ask herself. After instructing the pack-leaders to make final preparations to depart, she retired to the solitude of her own tunnel for a while. One army was already dispatched, on its way towards Earth. It would menace the children, and occupy the attention of at least some of the Wizards.

But could she control the remaining packs? Would they really follow her all the way to Orin Fen?

While she waited for the main army to gather itself, Gultrathaca went to see Yemi one last time. To reach the Assessment Chamber, she had to thrust her way past hundreds of tunnel creatures. The trickle of animals that had always found their way to him now clogged nearly all the entrances. Amongst them, increasingly, were the lethal huraks. It seemed that all the blue cats for many miles around must be haunting the tunnels.

Dozens of tired Griddas met her eyes as Gultrathaca entered the doorway. Just keeping Yemi inside the Chamber was exhausting work. No Gridda pack could last longer than a few hours if he really wanted to test them. They always left dispirited, the containment spells they had spent years perfecting lying in pieces.

As this shift trudged out, Yemi followed the Griddas to the doorway, chatting good-naturedly. When he saw Gultrathaca he sauntered across the floor, offering her his usual guileless smile.

That infuriating smile! How Gultrathaca had come to detest it!

'*Sere*,' he said.

'No,' she replied. 'No more games.' You've won them all, she thought. We've nothing left to attack you with.

Yemi called over one of his ever-present hurak companions. Hopping onto its back, he used its ears as steering handles. The towering beast, all meekness, swayed dreamily at his touch.

Gultrathaca hated everything about Yemi now. She was

afraid of him, too. Only a fool did not fear what it could not threaten. She gazed at his delicate, frail skull, wanting to bite it – except, of course, the huraks would prevent her. Or, if they failed, his magic would prevent her.

And Yemi's magic *never* failed him.

Gultrathaca had already given up any hope of using Yemi as a weapon. It was only a matter of time, she knew, before he escaped. Then what would happen? No doubt he would return to Earth. Eventually the children or Wizards would find a way to tap into his immeasurable power. That could not be allowed. The only choice left was to kill him – before he prevented the possibility of even doing that.

Could she do it? The resources of the Assessment Chamber itself were formidable. To that she could add a combined assault by her most proficient Griddas. Based on her observations of Yemi, and all she had learned in a lifetime of fighting, Gultrathaca calculated that if a huge number attacked him at once even Yemi could not survive. She had already given the packs an advantage against him. Yemi could no longer shift. She had secretly used his own contact with Jarius to limit him. Did he even realize yet? Probably not. But he would soon. Fresh packs were waiting for him outside the Chamber.

Fola was near Yemi, watching over her brother as always. She picked him up. 'Why you no let us go? Why?' she said angrily to Gultrathaca. 'I wish Yemi would hurt you! I told him, but he no understand what you are!'

'I think he may soon,' Gultrathaca said. 'When he sees how many Griddas I am gathering against him.'

'What do you mean?'

Fola glanced at Yemi. His usual smile had faded. With

quick gestures, he motioned to his animals. All those within the Chamber rushed to surround him.

With immense satisfaction, Gultrathaca stared at Yemi. To wipe the smile finally from his face! His animals were frantic. As Gultrathaca left the Chamber, and saw Yemi's faltering expression, she no longer felt afraid of him at all.

In the afternoon the packs started to assemble at the designated departure points. An orange-brown haze suffused the skies over Tamretis and Gaffilex as the Griddas left in their millions. To watch the Thûn packs go, Gultrathaca flew to the top of Heebra's eye-tower. For hour after hour the packs emerged from the tunnels and swept into the clouds. It made Gultrathaca's heart leap to see the infants. They were taking orders again. Now that they faced the prospect of space, and had a reason to be frightened, they stayed without complaint next to the older Griddas. Real discipline had returned at last to the packs.

With great pride Gultrathaca raised her claws. A passing group acknowledged her with a harsh cry. Other Griddas joined in with them, their uncertainty forgotten, turning in majestic arcs to honour Gultrathaca before they left. She would join them, but not immediately. There was one thing to do first.

Gultrathaca forced her way through the animals to the Assessment Chamber. As she entered, Yemi looked up at her, no longer smiling.

Thousands of Griddas had encircled the Chamber, all with one purpose.

'As soon as the packs are gone,' Gultrathaca said to them, 'kill him.'

20

FREEDOM

Rachel flew at tremendous speed, barely staying in control as she navigated along the Gridda tunnels deep under Thûn.

Some of the tunnels were so cramped she had to flip her body on its side to pass through; others, those reserved for high-ranking pack-leaders, were like caverns. All were empty. More than empty. Rachel sensed events she needed to understand taking place above her – an enormous departure of lives and magic.

As she flew over a hole in one tunnel floor, she halted.

'No!' the Essa told her. 'Ycmi is further.'

'Wait.' Rachel knelt down. A familiar scent wafted up from the hole. Normally her information spells would have picked it up much earlier. But it was weak, terribly diminished. 'Serpantha,' she whispered.

The Essa all fell silent. When Serpantha had first secretly arrived in Ool's skies they had wanted to follow the winds to him, but he moved too swiftly to keep up. They looked over Rachel's shoulder, blinking into the gloom.

'I know Yemi needs us,' she said, 'but I won't leave Serpantha. We have to go to him.'

The Essa briefly consulted, fluttering part-way down the hole. 'He is not alone. There are Griddas, too.'

'I know.' Rachel peered down the hole. It dropped vertically for over a mile. Moist smells drifted up.

'Newborns,' the Essa said. 'That is their smell, the smell of birthing levels. Why is Serpantha with them?'

'I don't know,' Rachel said. 'We'll go down.' She shimmied to the edge of the hole, letting her feet dangle while she calmed herself. 'Feet first,' she said. The Essa took stances on her shoelaces, or leaned forward on the toe caps, ready to confront whatever was out there. Once they were set, they squeezed her tightly. 'Go ahead, go ahead,' they said.

'Don't let go of me.'

'We won't,' they promised her.

Slowly – using her magic as a brake – Rachel slid down the hole. After a long descent a chute dumped them out. The Essa sprang from her at once, fanning out protectively. Before them lay the humid levels of the birthing chambers.

Rachel threw the entrances open.

Normally there would have been thousands of boisterous young Griddas to greet her, all the unrestrained cries of new life. Instead, there were only a small number of newborns. These gazed up with open curiosity when they saw the strangers, too young to know any fear. A few were actually biting a path out of their eggs, or, freshly hatched, tottering uncertainly about on the slippery floor. In a corner a tangle of sisters appeared to be playing a game.

Not a game, Rachel suddenly realized. The scent of Serpantha was on these infants.

She rushed over with the Essa. The closest newborn hissed – and another, liking that sound, copied her.

With fury, Rachel screamed, 'Get away from him!' She raised about herself a sheath of power even the newborns could not mistake, and they fled into a tributary tunnel.

Rachel and the Essa were alone with Serpantha.

The lips of the Wizard were bound with spell-thread. The Essa helped Rachel remove it. They did so delicately, to avoid cutting into him any more than the thread had already done. Inside his mouth there was more thread. As the last thread was removed from his tongue, Rachel felt all Serpantha's ancient spells sigh with relief.

Alive, Rachel realized. Alive!

The Essa flew joyfully around Serpantha, wanting to go into his body, but afraid that he was so fragile they might hurt him in doing so.

All the lovely inner radiance had left Serpantha's features. His face, petrified by the poisons and spells of the Griddas, was grey. His eyes were shut; his hands were clenched, the fingers bound many times over with spell-thread. As Rachel removed the thread, she caught the scent of the latest attacks on the Wizard. They came from the infants she had just chased off. In the end, Gultrathaca had simply laid Serpantha out on a platform of stone for the newborns to practise on.

Rachel wondered: did she dare lift him? She placed her ear against his chest, against his heart. Slow and uneven, it still murmured. And something else was alive within him – as soon as they felt Rachel's touch, Serpantha's spells knew she was there. In their elation, they called out, 'Heal him! Help us! Help us!'

The Essa did not wait for Rachel. They fluttered inside Serpantha's mouth. There was so much damage they had no idea where to start. Quietly, listening, they started work, letting Serpantha's spells advise them. Eventually they re-emerged. 'He can be moved now,' they told Rachel. 'But carefully.'

Serpantha's aquamarine robe was covered in filth. Rachel placed her left arm under his body, preparing to lift him. She gasped as she felt how light he was – virtually no weight at all. It was as if the only thing that had held the Wizard together all this time was the grandeur of his magic.

How should she carry him? It seemed wrong to do anything except hold him in both her arms, but Rachel needed to be more practical. In the end, she pulled him to her waist, clasping him there easily with one hand.

'You need both arms,' the Essa said. 'We will carry him. Allow us!'

Rachel started to hand Serpantha to them. The Essa stopped her. They started jerking in the air, holding each other up. 'What is it? What is it?' they cried.

Never in her life had Rachel felt anything like this: spells; thousands of them; spells everywhere, a deadly Gridda assault. She staggered, barely able to take in the scope. This was not an attack by one Gridda on another, or pack against pack. It was a concentration of spells on an unimaginable scale.

All the spells were focused on a single being.

Yemi.

Rachel felt him. The greatness of his magic, brought to sudden desperateness, pulsed like a generator amid the lesser scents of the Griddas. But there were thousands of Griddas; there were too many. Rachel pulled Serpantha close and flew out of the birthing caves. She did not need to use her magic to trace Yemi; the battle-cries of the Griddas were enough. They led her upwards – Yemi was trying to escape.

'Hold onto me!' Rachel told the Essa.

Her flying spells gave her all their speed up the winding tunnels. As she rose, she swerved past Griddas aching to get to the land above. Higher still, the tunnels breaching the surface were so full of Griddas that even Rachel's magic could not plot a way around. She had to slow down – enough for the Griddas to sense her, and turn.

'Don't try to fly past them,' her information spells advised. 'The quickest way is not through the tunnels.'

'Which way, then?'

'Directly up.'

The rock overhead was hard, but not hard enough to withstand Rachel's magic. She smashed through. Shielding Serpantha's head with her hands, she broke out to the surface. The Essa followed. For a few moments they shut their eyes against the suddenness of light.

Then they saw the number of Griddas.

'Quickly! Quickly!' Some of the Essa hammered at Rachel's lips. They wanted to be inside her now, where they could assist her best if she became injured. Rachel let them in her mouth, hardly noticing the light tickles on her throat. The remaining Essa formed a defence in front of her, calling out fierce words of encouragement.

At a lower pitch, Rachel heard another voice. It was faint, muffled, a human voice: Yemi's.

The Essa looked frantically for him. Rachel knew where

he was. High up in the metal-grey sky. Yemi could not be seen because he was engulfed by Griddas. Hundreds of them, in well-organized packs, were attacking him.

There were noises from the ground. When Rachel stared down she could not believe what she was seeing. Wherever a Gridda tried to leave a tunnel, it was under siege. Animals that were feline and immense had taken up positions around each tunnel exit: the huraks. Wherever Griddas emerged, the blue cats fought them, cutting great swathes through their ranks.

Then a separate movement caught Rachel's eye, and another.

She shook her head, striving to understand.

It was not only the huraks who had come to Yemi's aid. Standing alongside them were rodents. Biting the clawed feet of the Griddas were insects. Trying to confuse them were burrowers. Even the slime mosses had dragged themselves from the depths. These shy creatures, who never normally left the darkness of the tunnels, in their devotion to Yemi came now. Facing the agony of the light, they threw their little bodies at the Griddas. The creatures of Ool wriggled through cracks; they slid from the snows; and they came from the air. From the south, Essa had arrived, fanned by the breath of the Detaclyver.

Despite this punishment, the Griddas continued to harry Yemi. With Essa clinging to their jaws, time after time they smashed into him, varying their spells, attacking in long persistent waves without respite.

Rachel soared towards them. When the Griddas detected her, two packs – over a hundred Griddas – detached themselves from the main group to confront her.

Understanding at once what they must do, the Essa took Serpantha from Rachel – and carried him to safety across the sky.

Rachel did not stop to think. As soon as Serpantha was out of her arms she dived towards the main group surrounding Yemi. She struck with unwavering force and all the capability of her magic. She could not break through – but she caused a moment of uncertainty.

And that was enough. Yemi took his chance. He broke free.

Magnificently, he rose above the Griddas.

Rachel's heart leapt as first she saw his head, then his bright orange T-shirt and baggy shorts. With a bent arm he fended off several infants; with the other he held onto Fola. The Griddas dwarfed Yemi, following him up, trying to separate him from his sister. At first Rachel thought Yemi might get away. The next moment her information spells reported back how little strength he had left. After so many attacks, even Yemi's extraordinary magic was faltering.

'Yemi, shift! Why don't you shift?' she shouted. Then she understood – he couldn't. 'Come to me!' she called out, racing towards him. 'Oh, Yemi, come towards me!'

He heard her. Even amidst the shrieking Griddas, Yemi heard her voice. He turned his imperturbable eyes towards her, and as he did so Rachel sensed new spells. Protection spells. Yemi was sending them. Thinking that Rachel needed his assistance, he was using the last of his strength to guard her.

'No! No!' Rachel screamed at him. 'I didn't... stop it! I didn't mean that!'

Yemi was confused. Rachel was coming too close to the

Griddas. Why? Why didn't she fly away? He held her back, while continuing to send out magic to shield her.

'No, don't do this! Don't!' Rachel wailed. 'Yemi!' A pack of Griddas launched a massive combination of spells against her. Rachel was thrown back, and would never have survived without Yemi's assistance.

But the attack drained him. Yemi could not sustain his shield. Finally he had to choose between protecting Rachel or Fola. He could not make this choice. It was too much.

He wavered – and the Griddas broke him.

Roaring in triumph, they tugged and jarred Yemi across the sky. Two infants took their chance. They snatched Fola, dragging her to the Griddas on the surface.

Yemi cried out – a feeble, lost voice. In disbelief he stared at the hand that had held Fola. Then he came after his sister. Still keeping his protections around Rachel, he entered the Gridda packs on the ground. The huraks tried to reach him, but could not. Rachel was held back by the Griddas. It took all her strength to simply survive their attacks. On the horizon the tiring Essa who carried Serpantha had almost been caught by a group of infants.

Then Yemi re-emerged. Clutching Fola, Griddas scraping at his legs, he rose into the sky. But it had cost him everything to retrieve his sister. One more ripple of attacks, a minor one, was all it took to shatter his last defence. And when that happened the protection around Rachel crumbled. Yemi gazed forlornly at her. He whispered an apology. He stared at Fola, letting out a moan. He kissed her, slow despair creeping over his face.

And then Yemi's features suddenly hardened. Facing the Griddas, he thundered: '*Iro!*'

He turned. He looked southwards. He looked in the direction of the Detaclyver.

And a sound came from there. No Gridda living under the cities of Ool had ever heard it before.

In Yemi's final desperation he had called the storm-whirls.

And they came. First they were a shadow on the southern horizon; then a great scouring of wind that obliterated all in its path. Freed at last from their long servitude, the whirls burst the ice over the Prag Sea. Snow plains became turmoil; defences were shattered; Griddas ran and could not escape; the last shards of the eye-towers were annihilated. Nothing could slow the storm-whirls down. A group of infant Griddas, urged on by their pack-leader, flew to confront them, and were swallowed like scraps.

As the storm-whirls approached the heart of Thûn, the disarrayed Griddas broke off their attacks on Rachel and Yemi. Where it was possible, they fled to tunnels.

A single immense storm-whirl was the first to reach Yemi. As it neared him it slowed down. Its winds calmed. Yemi put out his arms, and he and Fola were drawn inside. Once they saw he was safe, the remaining storm-whirls took up new positions to hunt down any Griddas they could find. Yemi, without a word, drew their attention to him. He shook his head, no.

The storm-whirls stopped.

Yemi's concerned gaze took in everything. He understood the danger. He knew that in his damaged condition, with thousands of Griddas still wanting to kill him, he could not risk staying. But that meant leaving all his friends behind. Tearfully he glanced over them: the majestic storm-whirls, the timid rodents, the magicless insects,

the slime mosses no one else cared about at all. He thought
of Jarius, and wondered what more he might have done
for her. On the ground, his loyal and bloodied huraks
raised their muzzles. Wreathed in frost, they bayed at him,
over and over.

Wanting to let him know she was not badly harmed,
Rachel lifted a hand. He smiled, waved to her. Fola took
her brother's other hand. She raised it for them all to see.
A silence followed as every creature knew what would
happen next.

With a long sob, Yemi pressed his face against Fola's
dress. His storm-whirl ascended, thrusting beyond the
outer rust-tinted clouds. At the edge of space it could go
no further. It waited. Yemi blinked at the darkness beyond
Ool. The anti-shifting spell of Gultrathaca still lay on him.
He did not know how to conquer it yet, but he would
soon. Until then he could fly. No one understood how fast
Yemi could fly. Even he did not fully understand. Holding
Fola's hand, he pushed out into the coldness of stars.

For a while everyone watched the mighty storm-whirl as it
returned to the ground. Then the Essa, who had kept
Serpantha safe, asked Rachel to take him while they
tended to their own battered companions.

'Is there still hope for us? For Detaclyver?' they
questioned timidly.

'Yes. While Yemi's alive, there will always be hope,'
Rachel said.

She turned to look out over the world. In the aftermath
of the battle, Thûn lay desolate. The last standing eye-
tower, Heebra's, had been atomized by the storm-whirls.
Uncanny winds stirred the skies. So much snow had been

lifted into the air by the passage of the storm-whirls that clouds of Essa wheeled in great aimless swarms, having difficulty finding their way back over the Prag Sea. On the surface, huraks roamed in small groups; they pawed the snow longingly. The storm-whirl that had transported Yemi to the refuge of space turned solemnly on one spot, not wishing to leave.

Griddas were scattered everywhere. Still stunned by the impact of the storm-whirls, they flew raggedly about the sky or wandered in a daze amongst the snows, searching for missing pack-members.

Gazing at them, Rachel sensed something was wrong. She sent her information spells beyond Thûn, to the cities of Gaffilex and Tamretis. 'They've left,' she said. 'All the Griddas have gone. That feeling I had earlier...the Griddas here are the only ones still on Ool.' Eric? She trembled, searching for his scent, not a magical one, but his real human scent, or the tell-tale rhythm of his heart. They were missing. Without her needing to ask them, Rachel's information spells sought with all their skilful brilliance for any trace of the magical signals of the prapsies. Nothing. They tried to disguise this knowledge from Rachel, but she knew them too well. Tears poured down her face, wetting the Essa.

'Where...where have the Griddas gone?' she murmured.

'Your world,' the Essa said, catching the tears. 'We think so. A few Essa heard in the tunnels. The Griddas spoke of it.'

Rachel stared at the sky. 'I've got to get back home,' she said. 'I've got to warn them what's coming.'

'We will accompany you,' the Essa said. 'Detaclyver has asked us, and we wish it even if he did not. We are resolute.'

'No,' Rachel said. 'You've done enough already. I –'

'It is not enough! Not enough!' The Essa's voices were fierce. 'Take us!' They dug themselves into her clothes, and feeling their conviction Rachel did not argue.

The Griddas had begun to reconvene their packs. Rachel wasted no more time. She flew with the Essa into the clouds. But before she left her breath caught in her throat, for a beautiful thing was taking place in the south: the storm-whirls were on the move. Travelling at great speed Rachel saw the first ones reach the Detaclyver and wander in half-crazed joy across its body.

Whatever happens, Rachel realized, Ool will never be the same again. She turned away, tears of happiness mingled with sorrow in her eyes and heart.

'Oh Eric,' she whispered. 'Where are you?'

21

Departure

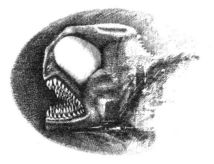

With Eric indicating the way, Gultrathaca led the main army towards Orin Fen. It was the largest force of Griddas ever assembled. Gultrathaca could not see the extent of it: wave after wave, pack upon pack, millions of Griddas making their way across the permanent nightfall of space.

Only a limited number of Griddas could shift, so Gultrathaca had to be content with the lesser speed of flight spells. But the pace was not too slow, because the weakest flyers who could not keep up were left behind. There were Griddas who lost their minds amid the maze of stars. These were also abandoned. Such minor losses meant nothing given the size of the army.

And it showed all the packs there was no going back to Ool – no slinking back to the comfort of tunnels.

There was constant friction between the younger and older Griddas. As soon as they became familiar with the peculiarities of space, the infants again started flouting the authority of the pack-leaders. They were loud, excitable, full of aggression. Gultrathaca tolerated such indiscipline, knowing that she would need all their energy to have any chance of defeating the Wizards. The pack-leaders kept a rough order. Often it was the adult Griddas who needed most support. Many had never learned to enjoy flight. And the flight demanded of them now was without respite, into emptiness.

One Gridda, however, seemed calm enough: a guest who had invited herself – Jarius. At first Gultrathaca had refused her last-minute request, but just before they set off she changed her mind. There was no more unforgivable crime amongst Griddas than to turn against your own pack-members. Gultrathaca wanted Jarius in the first line of assault troops. If she refused to fight, or fought ineffec-tually, her pack-sisters would kill her. It was fitting. Gultrathaca noticed that Jarius did not seem concerned for her own welfare. She paid no attention to the nearest Griddas, even when they bit her. She appeared more con-cerned about someone else: her eyes were always on Eric.

Eric! The enigmatic Eric!

What, Gultrathaca wondered, was she to make of him? He showed the way to Orin Fen without complaint, yet he gave her as little information as possible. On the journey she kept up the lie about the Gridda prison world, and Eric seemed satisfied, but he asked no more questions about it. Perhaps he did not really believe her. Gultrathaca was troubled about that, though she had little enough time to worry about it. Keeping the army on the move required all of her effort. There were no rests, no rocky places to hide in. The Griddas fed on the move. By threatening and coaxing the pack-leaders somehow kept them in motion between the constellations.

Finally, Eric said, 'We're getting close.'

'How much further?' Gultrathaca asked.

He looked up at her. 'You can't tell yet?'

'No. I do not have your gifts, Eric.'

His gaze held her for a moment; then he turned back to the prapsies, resuming his customary silence.

Gultrathaca passed the new information to the pack-leaders. Her heart pounded as she thought about the great train of events she had started. What opposition would they find on the Wizards' world? Larpskendya was awesomely powerful, and there were others of similar strength, such as Serpantha. It was remarkable how that Wizard had held out for so long against her; no Gridda could have done it.

How many more like Serpantha would there be on Orin Fen?

Yet there was no choice other than to go on. Nothing less than a quest of this greatness would keep the fragmenting Gridda packs together. And there was a personal reason, too. Jarius was right about her; Gultrathaca felt born for this time. All her instincts drove her towards blood and the clarity of battle.

But everything, everything depended on Eric.

How best to make him comfortable? Gultrathaca encircled him in her arms, in the same odd way she had seen Fola encircle Yemi. She let him rest. He did not seem to want to talk at all, so she rarely spoke, either. She could not properly imitate the parent-figures of Earth, but occasionally she whispered nonsense into Eric's ear in that private way she had seen Fola do with Yemi.

The journey was a long one, and during it Gultrathaca tried to make Eric feel safe. She let him lean against her body. She made no threats. She spoke kindly. Sometimes she ruffled his blond hair. It was a peculiar gesture, difficult to achieve without injuring his scalp, but Eric seemed to like it – or, anyway, he did not tell her to stop. She even tolerated the prapsies. Each time their small round faces popped out of Eric's shirt, she wanted to bite them. She restrained herself. When they spat at her, she laughed.

Eric's eating habits required special attention. When she fed him it was not with the live or raw food her Griddas consumed, but prepared the way he preferred: heated and stripped into nondescript pieces, so he could not tell what animals it came from.

How much that alone said about these humans!

Even so, as the army swerved to avoid the massive gravitational pull of a red giant sun, Gultrathaca wished she could enter Eric's mind and read his thoughts. He did not appear to have any special worries. He asked about his sister from time to time, understandably anxious. Otherwise, he just pointed the way. Such behaviour was co-operative enough, but could she trust him? No. Because he hid things from her. He would not explain the way, only lead her. He also tried to stop the prapsies' insults. That showed he did not really trust her not to harm them. None of this mattered. She would continue to raise his spirits and keep him close. He could not breathe without her knowing.

'How far now?' she questioned from time to time as they flew.

'Nearly there,' was his usual reply.

She tried to smile as if she cared for him.

Possibly, Gultrathaca realized, Eric had a plan of his own – something simple. She did not underestimate him. She knew just how devastating his power could be at close range. When they reached Orin Fen, and he discovered that it was the Wizard world, who knew what he might try? Perhaps he would try to kill her. As long as the Wizards were destroyed and part of her pack survived, Gultrathaca could accept that – though it would be a pity to miss the battle. However, she did not intend to hand her life away easily. If he planned to give her any trouble, she was ready. When the army arrived at their destination, she had her own plan to deal with little Eric.

Eric nestled against Gultrathaca, pretending he could stand her touch.

She cradled him with all the subtlety of a mechanical press. So what: he endured it. He endured the spiky way she ran her claws over his head. He leant close against her, pretending that was nice, and in a way it was because it meant he could withdraw from the hideous spectacle of the Gridda army. He moaned a little about the journey – not too much, just enough to prove he wasn't hiding his feelings. He sometimes even asked her questions about Rachel. It was painful, but surely it would seem weird if he didn't ask. He did it to show Gultrathaca that he was still clinging to her promises, like a scared kid.

Am I a scared kid? he asked himself.

Yes, he thought. I am. And that was all right, as well. It was all right to be frightened as long as he didn't become too frightened to do what he must do.

As he passed another cluster of stars, one of the prapsies said, 'Eric, your face is wrong. It's twisted. What's the matter?'

'Nothing,' Eric said, holding them both to his chest. 'Nothing at all.'

'Are you cold, Eric?'

'I thought I told you both not to talk to me. You know I'm busy. I'm thinking hard, boys. Don't interrupt me.'

'We know, but are you cold, Eric?'

'No.' They were silent again.

'Are *you*?' Eric asked.

'Yes, we are.'

Eric bent towards them, and realized that neither prapsy was cold. They had only said that to get him to look at them.

'What are you imagining in your brain?' one whispered.

'Nothing at all,' Eric said. 'Don't ask any more questions, now.'

'Why, Eric? Why can't we?'

'Shush. Just be quiet, boys. I'm thinking.'

'What are you thinking?'

I wish I could tell you, Eric thought. Oh, I wish I could share it all with you! The prapsies could be trusted with his secret, of course, but if Gultrathaca overheard or suspected, who knew what she would do to them.

Finding it impossible to look at the prapsies without it making him crazy, Eric did not look at them. Instead, he tried to harden his heart. When the time came to act, he had to be able to do it clinically. So he practised ignoring the prapsies. The silent anxiousness that followed only made things worse. All he could feel was their puzzled eyes eternally focused on him. Once, after a particularly long stretch of quietness, he couldn't bear it any longer.

'That was a stupid thing the two of you did,' he said.

'What, Eric? What was stupid?'

'Back in the cell. Trying to get all those animals and Witches to attack you instead of me. And staying there.

Staying there instead of flying off, when you had the chance. I told you to go. Stupid, really stupid. You could be free now, hiding somewhere safe with the Essa.'

'We did it for you, Eric.'

'It was stupid, that's all. You could have escaped, you know.'

'We didn't want to. Not without you.'

Eric said nothing for a while. Then, in the softest of voices, he said, 'I'm so proud of you both.' Both childbirds nuzzled him and Eric found himself adding something he didn't mean to say. He had to keep his distance from them, because of what he must do soon. 'Don't ever leave me again,' he said.

'We won't, Eric. We'll stay with you always.'

Eric turned away from them. He closed his eyes, attempting unsuccessfully to put the prapsies from his mind. To help with that, he focused again on Gultrathaca. She was obviously suspicious about his behaviour. What if she became too suspicious and decided not to go with him all the way? What if she decided to kill him before they arrived?

The madness of it! Trying to fathom what would keep Gultrathaca satisfied!

However, Gultrathaca became easier to deal with the longer the journey continued. It gradually became clear to Eric that his good-boy act was wasted on her. All she really cared about was getting to the new world. So he kept her happy about that, showing the way, more and more certain he was safe at least until they got there.

No mistakes now, he thought, not this close. They had almost reached the prison world, or whatever it was. The same odd traces like those of Griddas and High Witches seeped from it, but nothing distinctive. He didn't tell Gultrathaca. To anyone except him the traces would have been entirely hidden. Sometimes he sent his deft detections towards the Earth. He knew all about the second Gridda army heading that way, of course – how could he miss such a stench of magic! But there was another scent as well, a marvellous surprise, one he knew well: the scent of Yemi, heading home at some kind of miraculous speed.

Eric felt better, knowing that.

When he could no longer endure to lie against Gultrathaca, or look at the prapsies, or think about what lay ahead, Eric would gaze out over the Gridda army. Strangely, he seemed to have a friend amongst this wilderness of bodies. He did not know who she was, but whenever he glanced over in the direction of one Gridda, she glanced back. As he studied her now, he saw a curious expression. If what there was of a Gridda's face was capable of showing affection, he might have been seeing it.

Eric turned away from her. It was probably not an expression of affection at all – just his own wishful thinking! Anyway, he had to put this perplexing Gridda out of his mind as well. When he launched his anti-magic spell on all the Griddas, he could not exclude her. As a Gridda, she would have to suffer the same fate as all the others.

In his mind, Eric encompassed the entire Gridda army with his destruction.

The destroyer of spells, he said to himself. That's what I am. The spell-destroyer. He tried to feel at ease with that. He couldn't, but this didn't stop him rehearsing over and over what he would do.

At some point Gultrathaca broke into his thoughts. 'Are we nearly there?' she asked again.

'Nearly,' Eric told her.

'Then we can free our Griddas,' she said. 'It has been many generations since we spoke with them. I will ask nothing more of you, Eric. And I will keep my other promises. I will deliver Rachel safely, if I can. I'll take you back to Earth. You will have a place of honour in our memories, and there will be no fighting with the children of your world. There will be an end to fighting.' She paused. 'I am grateful for everything you are doing. We all are.'

'Thank you,' Eric rasped.

22

the preparation of the sentinels

With Serpantha secure in her arms, Rachel set out to catch the Griddas heading towards Earth. Already weary after the battle for Yemi, she had never needed to put so much faith in her flying spells. Gradually she closed on the Gridda army. Taking a long arc around, she overtook them, and for a while pulled far enough ahead to imagine that she, Serpantha and the Essa were the only ones soaring through the bleakness between stars. At last, however, her flying spells began to falter. Transporting Serpantha had drained them more than they were willing to admit.

'Nearly home,' Rachel murmured, urging them on.

'Yes,' they said, offering her what they did not have.

While Rachel laboured, Serpantha lay quietly in her arms. None of the Wizard's great strength had returned, but the Essa had worked tirelessly inside him, and he could think again. He thought about Rachel. Sensing her exhaustion, he secretly questioned the Essa, and judged the distance to Earth.

Too far. The Griddas would catch Rachel before she could make it back – unless he helped her.

The Wizard opened his many-coloured eyes. 'Hello, courageous one.'

A huge happiness spread through Rachel. 'You're... you're awake!' she cried, hugging him, then loosened her grip in case it hurt. 'Oh, Serpantha!'

His gaze held her tenderly. 'How ungracious of me to have held you back,' he said. 'With nothing to offer in return.'

'That doesn't matter!' Rachel said. 'Don't be silly! Of course it doesn't! All that matters is that you're getting well again! Do you want anything? Do you need something?'

'You've already given so much,' Serpantha answered. 'Yet I do have one more request to ask of you.'

'Anything!'

'I need you to let go, Rachel. You cannot make it back to Earth in time unless you leave me behind.'

'What? No, that's not right,' Rachel said.

'It's true, Rachel. You know it is. Your own spells have been saying so for some time. You have been ignoring them.'

Steadfastly Rachel stared ahead, aside, anywhere except at Serpantha. She could feel his eyes burying into her. 'I can't!' she wailed. 'I can't leave you! I won't!'

'You must!' This time, at the top of his voice, Serpantha bellowed it. 'Rachel, everything might depend on you reaching Earth in time to give a warning. Do you want the Griddas arriving at your house to kill your mother and father? Because that will happen! Is that what you want? Is it?'

'The spectrums will realize we're coming,' Rachel said, convincing herself instantly. 'Of course they will. Heiki will know. They'll be prepared.'

'We can't be certain of that,' Serpantha said. 'You can't risk everything for me, Rachel. I won't allow it.'

Rachel twisted her head away, flying at renewed speed away from the Gridda army. 'I still can't shift!' she said, over and over. 'Why can't I shift, why can't I!'

'Please, Rachel,' Serpantha said. 'You can come back for me.'

Rachel knew there would be no going back for Serpantha. He knew it, too. The Griddas would tear him to pieces as soon as they found him. It would be better to kill him swiftly, now.

Rachel looked at him, and felt her death spells rise up.

Serpantha sensed it too – and he did not object.

'Use them,' he said.

Rachel thought of Mum and Dad. She thought of everyone else on the vulnerable Earth. She knew that unless she was to put the balance of all their lives in danger there was only one thing to do.

It was the right thing to do. Serpantha knew it, and so did she.

'It's all right,' Serpantha whispered. 'You can do it. It's all right, Rachel. It's all right.'

Rachel's deaths were like savages, banging on her mind.

She looked at Serpantha. 'I have an answer for you and my deaths.' Tightening her grip on Serpantha, she continued flying towards home.

'Rachel, let me go!'

'No,' she said lightly, stroking his face. 'Not that way.' She ignored her deaths. She held Serpantha even more tightly. He tried to fight her, but she fought him back. Putting all her trust in her flying spells, she headed for the Earth.

Gradually the army of Griddas closed on them. The vanguard became visible, and they saw her. Rachel no longer had the strength to outrun them.

'Help me!' she cried to the Essa.

'We are! We are! Fly on, Rachel! Fly on!' Without Rachel noticing it, the Essa had long been bolstering her magic, plundering all their strength to give her a little more.

Rachel continued to stay barely ahead of the Griddas. An hour went by, more. The rim of the solar system swam in view. Rachel passed Pluto. She crossed the orbit of Neptune. Were her flying spells still carrying her, or was she dragging them half-dead between the worlds? Jupiter fell behind. Saturn's rings. Mars.

There. Earth was a beautiful creamy-blue, though she could not make it in time.

The Essa realized that. All the journey they had stayed quiet, their efforts put into supporting her magic. Now, encouraging each other, they swivelled to face the leading Griddas. If this was the end for Rachel, they would be with her as she exhaled her last breath, whispering their devotion into her ears still.

It was the end, but then a low voice said that it was not.

Rachel felt new spells fortifying her own.

'I'm here,' the voice said. 'I'm here. Rachel, I'm here.'

Rachel felt a shift, followed by the sun on her back – a warm sun. Real breezes tugged at her, the scents of children on them. And clasping her waist, her fine white hair tossed by the breeze, was a girl her own age.

'Heiki!' Rachel whispered.

For a while Rachel leaned against her friend while still clinging onto Serpantha. Finally Heiki managed to prize one of her hands away. 'I've got him,' she said. 'Rachel, it's OK. Let go. Open your fingers. You can let go.'

Rachel had held Serpantha for so long that it felt wrong not having his life in her arms. She allowed Heiki to take him, crying with relief.

'Yemi has returned,' Heiki told her. 'Now you're back, too! I think we really have a chance. Oh, we must have! We must!'

'The Griddas –' Rachel began.

'I know. They'll be here soon. Albertus and the other spectrums have been following them.'

Rachel tried to get her bearings. Heiki had shifted her and Serpantha to a foreign sky over rolling fields. A team of sentinel children was on guard above them, bathed in late afternoon sunshine. Frightened by the brightness, the Essa clustered under Rachel's ears. She swept her hair over them to give them time to adjust.

'Hey!' Heiki said, jerking back. 'What are *those*?'

Rachel had become so used to the Essa that she hardly noticed their touch against her skin. 'They're my guards,' she said. 'And my advisors, and extra eyes.' She laughed. 'A sort of hospital. And my companions. My friends.'

Heiki studied them in fascination, but when she reached out the Essa shrank back.

'You'll have to earn their respect first,' Rachel said.

'With the Griddas coming, it looks like I'll have a chance to do that,' Heiki answered.

Serpantha had regained enough strength to hold his own position in the sky without needing assistance. 'Larpskendya?' he asked.

Heiki shook her head. 'We've heard nothing. And ... Eric?'

'We're not sure. We believe he's with an even larger army,' Serpantha said. 'The number of Griddas arriving on Earth is alarming, but if Gultrathaca truly wanted to destroy you all, the numbers would be greater still. It must be a decoy. She must have loftier ambitions elsewhere.' He paused. 'In fact, if Gultrathaca has taken Eric I can only think of one place the remaining Griddas would have gone.'

'Where?'

'Orin Fen.'

A boy was carried down to them: Albertus Robertson. His face broke with relief when he saw Rachel, but only for a moment. 'Griddas are deploying in orbit over all the world's major populations,' he reported. His head quivered as the spectrums updated him. 'Beijing, Cairo, New York, Calcutta, São Paulo...As anticipated, the Griddas intend to catch as many children as possible in a single overwhelming attack.'

'Wherever they are, we'll meet them and fight,' Heiki said.

Rachel stared at her. 'What? You can't send children against Griddas.'

'We're not just going to let the Griddas tear us to pieces, Rachel. We have to defend ourselves! What else can we do?'

'Heiki, you haven't seen how many are coming.'

'Well, they haven't seen all of us, either,' Heiki said. 'Take a look for yourself.'

Children were approaching from all directions. The elite teams, Rachel realized: the sentinels, all expert flyers. Several units of them aligned in formation, awaiting new orders.

'These won't be enough,' Rachel said. 'Surely you realize –'

'There are more,' Heiki told her.

Behind the sentinels other children had started to arrive. Thievers flew alongside lightning-finders. Ocean-diving deepers approached, still dripping from the seas. Rival gangs from the cities came together. There were avalanchers and other daredevils. Toddlers tagged along in their larger groups. Some had been caught unexpectedly, and were still rubbing sleep out of their eyes, or helping each other pull on coats or other clothes.

And behind these children were more breathless bunches: brothers and sisters, small family parties, clutching each other. From all the towns and villages across this part of the world they came. None were such slick flyers as the sentinels, but that didn't stop them. If they could make it into the air at all, one way or another they did so.

One type of child seemed less fearful than the others – or perhaps they only masked it better. These children were far too precious to be together. The largest sentinel units had one attached if they were lucky – a spectrum.

Rachel watched them all arrive, and noticed something: whenever the children saw her or Serpantha their frightened faces lit up, transformed.

'They think ... they think *we're* going to make all the difference,' she said.

'They're wrong,' Serpantha told her. 'Only one person can make a decisive difference now. We must get to Yemi as swiftly as we can. Rachel – fly me there. I am still not strong enough.'

'Wait!' Heiki held Rachel back. 'We've tried that! Yemi won't listen. He's acting weird, ignoring everyone, just hovering in the sky surrounded by animals. Don't leave, Rachel – please! We need to know what you've managed to find out about the Griddas. Tactics. Deployment. How do they battle? What kinds of spell do they favour? What –'

'Don't you understand?' Rachel gripped Heiki's arm. 'Children can't defeat these Griddas! Even their infants never stop fighting. I've seen them. They don't give up, and they won't care how many they lose to the sentinels!'

'We have to try at least!' Heiki said. 'Won't they kill us anyway? Should we make it easy for them? I won't just sit back and let them! Rachel, I'm depending on you. If you could join that team over there, they need –'

'No,' interrupted Albertus Robertson. 'The spectrums agree with Rachel. We've now been able to scan the Griddas at close range. A few of the sentinels will hold their own for a while. All other children will be immediately overwhelmed. Wait...' His head twitched. 'The first Griddas have entered our atmosphere.'

'Where?' Heiki asked.

'Everywhere.'

The sentinel units above Heiki wanted clear instructions, having been told the same news by their own spectrums.

'The largest concentration is over the Asian peninsula,' Albertus said. 'Over the Huang Hai, the Yellow Sea between eastern China and Korea. The same place,' he added, 'where Yemi is located.'

'The Griddas realize that Yemi is still their greatest threat,' Serpantha said.

Rachel picked Serpantha up, her information spells plotting the fastest path to Yemi.

'One moment,' Albertus said to her. 'Since we cannot win this battle, we should negotiate. We have many materials to bargain with: animals and other foodstuffs; base and refined metals; our loyalty, or at least a pretence of that, and –'

'The Griddas won't be interested in any of those things,' Rachel said. 'They'll only want to fight.'

Albertus Robertson blinked, seeking alternatives from the other spectrums. 'There is no better option at present,' he said. 'Therefore, we *will* attempt to negotiate.'

'It won't work, Albertus. Don't go. These Griddas haven't come to talk!'

'Even so, we could distract them briefly. That may delay the main assault, giving you and Serpantha time to devise a new strategy with Yemi.' Albertus smiled, his lips brushing hers. Then, before Rachel could say anything, his thrill-seekers carried him skyward to meet the Griddas. Seeing those two girls so unflinchingly take him up, Rachel at last understood why, of all children, the spectrums chose the thrill-seekers as their companions – only the most fearless children could ever have flown without question into those clouds.

The Essa had stayed quiet all this time. Now they braved the light and tugged Rachel forward. 'Find Yemi!' they burst out. 'Take us to him! Take us!'

Serpantha held Rachel's hand. With their combined strength they flew across the world.

23

the three layers

Gultrathaca slowed the army down as they neared Orin Fen.

To report on the disposition of Wizard sentries she deployed stealth teams, holding the bulk of the Griddas well back. 'We need to make sure there are no High Witches keeping watch,' she told Eric, to allay his suspicions. 'We don't want them knowing we're here.'

Eric half-nodded, barely hearing her.

Gultrathaca ached for combat. Her pack-sisters had already started inflating their muscles, readying themselves. She wanted more than anything to join them, but still needed to be mindful of Eric. What would he make of the battle-wail of the infants when it started?

As for the Wizards, no doubt they would be prepared. Such a large Gridda army could not have gone unnoticed. Even so, Gultrathaca could not wait for the conflict to begin. Win or lose, she thought, win or lose, did it really matter? Her Griddas were not empire builders. Unlike the Highs, they had no patience for the gradual accumulations of power and status. What Griddas demanded was war, or the prospect of war, or the promise. They were built for its mayhem, designed for its fulfilment. What else could have carried the Gridda packs so far across the insanity of space?

For all those centuries, Gultrathaca thought, Heebra lived in the heights of her eye-tower, fantasizing about this special moment. But the Griddas, not the Highs, would enjoy it. Feeling her heart race, Gultrathaca calmed herself. She quietened her soldier spiders. She told the healers busy dropping painkillers into her veins to wait a while longer. She kept the watchers focused on Eric. This is a glorious day for all spiders, too, she realized; everywhere around her, they were alert and active.

All, that is, except the spiders of Jarius.

Gultrathaca hardly recognized her any longer. There was the same expression on Jarius's face she had seen linger on Fola's so many times in the Assessment Chamber: fear. Only the dumbest animals were without fear entirely, but humans and those they affect are full of fear, Gultrathaca thought. It hovers about their eyes, like a trap. What was wrong with them? What were they afraid of?

She gazed at Jarius, suddenly pitying her.

When Eric and Gultrathaca stopped, the pack-leaders could no longer contain the infants. 'Orin Fen! Orin Fen!' they hissed amongst themselves.

Everyone sensed the planet now. It was so near that Gultrathaca could almost reach out for it. She sniffed, testing the quality of the invisibility spells. They were beyond her understanding. And under the invisibility layer were fortification spells. Gultrathaca probed them, realizing at once that they were virtually impregnable. It would take her Griddas centuries to smash through, or forever.

How long would it take Eric?

Gultrathaca squeezed him lightly. Had she miscalculated? If Eric could not break through the Wizards' protections, most of the Griddas would perish – the infants were too weary to make the return trip to Ool unless they could recuperate on the world below.

Gradually the stealth teams brought in their news. There was nothing to report, no sign of Wizards. Where were they? Snug behind their protections? Waiting for the Griddas to wear themselves out before showing themselves?

'Eric,' she asked. 'Can you ... can you deal with the spells around this world?'

'I'll see.'

Eric stared at the empty space where he knew the planet to be. Its protections were intricate, labyrinthine, marvellously engineered; too sturdy for any number of Griddas to breach – and that shocked him. This was Wizard magic; Eric had no doubt. But where were the Wizards? A couple of old trails marked that they had been here, nothing more. What was going on? Why would Wizards so carefully shield a world of imprisoned Griddas?

There could be many reasons, he thought. He didn't have time now to worry about those reasons. The important thing was that there were Witches on this world. Now that he was closer, Eric realized the leaking scent traces were more similar to High Witches than Griddas, and that made sense. If High Witches supervised this world, he would expect them to be flashing around in the skies below.

He gripped the feathers of the prapsies, deciding.

Beneath the invisibility spells, there were three layers of protection. He had to act as soon as he cut through the last one. Gultrathaca would only keep him alive for as long as she needed him. He might only have moments to wrap his destruction around all the Griddas and Highs on the planet.

Good, he thought. Less time to think about it, to think about what I'm doing.

The prapsies were entirely quiet beside him. They had stopped asking questions, stopped insulting Gultrathaca, stopped fidgeting. They no longer even talked to each other. They simply pressed against him. He didn't dare look at them, not now.

Eric felt, suddenly, like a Gridda himself, or what they represented: the consummate murder weapon. It chilled him, this destructiveness. He felt as if he had become a skilful rolling into one of all death spells, like Rachel's deaths improved on, with no nobler spells to hold them back. All the journey he had been perfecting this deadliness. He knew exactly how to unstitch Gridda bodies. It was a terrible task, and inhuman, not human at all, but he was capable of it. He had to be.

All around him the infants were screaming to each other, almost hysterical. Eric made himself watch. He let the horror of them settle in his mind. He reminded himself what these same Griddas had done to Rachel and Larpskendya, to Serpantha, to Yemi.

To carry out his plan Eric needed to distract Gultrathaca. She was not behaving with the same abandon as the others. 'The planet has several different protective layers,' he told her.

'Can you break through them?'

'If I get help. The defences are too strong for me on my own.'

'What do you need?'

'I'll get rid of the invisibility mask. When I've done that all the Griddas should fire their spells into the protection layers. That will weaken them enough, I think, for me to finish the job. We'll have to rest between layers.'

'Rest?'

'There are several to get through.'

Gultrathaca looked quizzically at Eric. His expression was blank. Was he plotting something? Did he already know what lay beneath? It didn't matter. As long as he ruptured the defences, nothing else mattered. Her claw was waiting for him after that.

She gave the orders to deploy the Griddas around Orin Fen. 'Eric, please hurry,' she said, once they were positioned. 'The Griddas below must be suffering terribly.'

'I'm ready,' Eric said – and he was. All the Gridda army and Witches on the planet were within his range. He also had a surprise. To keep Gultrathaca off guard, he had prepared all the anti-magic he needed. With one silky motion of his mind he would remove *all* three protection layers at the same time.

'Are you afraid, Eric?' Gultrathaca asked, seeing him shake.

He ignored her. He removed the invisibility mask. A huge yellow-brown world was revealed. Gultrathaca signalled for the Griddas to set about breaching the protections. They barely scratched the first layer.

Eric steadied himself. He clutched the prapsies. 'I'm sorry, boys,' he whispered. Encompassing the first protection-layer girdling the planet, he destroyed it. Immediately he smashed the second layer – so rapidly that even Gultrathaca did not have time to notice. Before Eric tackled the third layer he could not help himself. He stared at the prapsies. And they stared back. On the entire voyage, had they ever stopped watching him?

'We don't understand, Eric,' one murmured.

'Oh boys,' he said. 'Forgive me.'

'Forgive what?' Gultrathaca glanced sharply at Eric. She realized that serious damage had been done to the protections without any need for rest. Eric had not required the Griddas.

He was lying.

Eric felt her claw on his spine, and knew he had delayed too long. He should already have broken through the third layer! What are you delaying for? he asked himself.

But he knew, he knew. He was frightened of dying. Now the moment had come, he clung to Gultrathaca, as if *she* would save him. He was afraid of dying and he was afraid of killing. He was afraid of everything.

He couldn't do it – but he had to.

He raised his hands. They were primitive directors of anti-magic, but they had never let him down. He pointed one of them. He pointed the index finger of his right hand at the southern rim of the planet below, and began to trace the tip around the edge.

No more delays. He cancelled the third layer of protection. He closed his eyes.

He was ready.

And so was Gultrathaca. She sensed a dreadful undoing start to work on her, but there was still time. Her nail lay over Eric's heart.

But she did not use it. She wavered. Eric also wavered.

He held back. Gultrathaca had expected to see legions of Wizards pouring from Orin Fen. Eric had expected a flood of Griddas and Highs.

The creatures actually rising up from that world were ones neither of them could believe.

24

huang hai

Rachel, Serpantha and the Essa flew across four seas and two continents, following Yemi's scent.

Finally, where the grey waters of the Huang Hai lap up against Shindao, on the Chinese shore, they found him. Yemi was surrounded by birds. They circled him in protective silence: flock after flock, local birds and birds that had never been seen before over Chinese skies.

And, beneath them, on the shore, there was an even more remarkable sight: animals, pressed up against the surf. The scale of the gathering was so great that even Rachel's information spells could not count the number. All the animals were quiet. Predators stood alongside prey and there was none of the usual noise or panic that occurs when animals are crowded tightly together. Each animal stood motionless, with shut eyes. Their mouths were open, as if inhaling something blissful. Their heads were inclined contemplatively to one place in the sky.

In that place, slightly above them, was a boy in a bright orange T-shirt.

'Yemi!' cried the Essa. There was no path to him, except through the birds. As the Essa tried to make a pathway to Yemi, the flocks turned their beaks on them. Then Yemi's yellow butterflies pushed between the birds. They made a gap for the Essa, guiding them. Rachel and Serpantha followed.

As the Camberwell Beauties led Rachel towards Yemi, she could hear her own heart booming over the quietude of the scene. Yemi's eyes were closed. He appeared to be asleep, his chin pointing towards the animals.

'Have you ... have you ever seen anything like this?' she asked Serpantha.

'No, nor any Wizard,' he whispered.

'What are they doing?'

'I do not know, but can you feel the magic linking Yemi and the animals together? Can you feel the tranquillity of their minds?'

Rachel felt it: the calmness. And it was not merely the minds of the animals and Yemi that were calm. The sea itself was calm. The winds had gentled. A shark, straying under the waters below, beat its fins away again. Even the sunshine, as it filtered through the clouds, cast the same pallid light evenly across Yemi and the animals on the shore. There was no dappling; there was no place where the sun was brighter or darker against his face or that of the animals – as though the natural differences of shade and light should not be allowed to intrude on their meditation.

Rachel felt as if any words would be an interruption of whatever was taking place here, but she had to speak. The peacefulness of this scene would soon be shattered by the Griddas.

Fola hung wide-awake and suspended in mid-air next to Yemi.

'What's – what's happening?' Rachel asked her.

'I can't tell,' Fola said. 'Yemi came here, I don't know why. The animals followed him. They have been just like this for so long.' She shook Yemi. 'I tried to wake him. It's not possible!'

'It is some kind of trance-state,' Serpantha said. 'All the animals are with Yemi inside it. I can't tell if they are aware of the Gridda threat.'

The Essa pulled at Yemi's eyelids, trying to rouse him. Rachel united her magic with Serpantha, attempting every kind of waking spell.

'What can we do?' the Essa cried. 'Make him listen!'

Above them, a shriek levelled across the sky. The noise was not human. It came from the lungs of a Gridda pack. If anything could have broken the quiet reflection of Yemi, this would have done so. His expression did not alter.

High in the clouds overhead, one sentinel unit waited. As in so many other skies across Earth, it stood alone guarding an enormous area. The leader of the unit, a boy Rachel did not know, flew amongst his team, shouting instructions. His voice was hoarse. A small girl with long red hair was by his side, following him wherever he went: a spectrum.

Seeing their courage, Rachel felt anger welling up inside her. Gultrathaca had lied about most things, but what about her accusations concerning Larpskendya? Rachel had not wanted to consider these before. She faced Serpantha.

'Where are the other Wizards?' she demanded.

Serpantha's expression was anguished. 'Whoever could come, has done so.'

'What does that mean?' Rachel said angrily. 'Don't you have a whole world of Wizards? Larpskendya told me that often enough. Even he's not here this time. If I hadn't risked my life to save you, there would be no Wizard on Earth at all. What are we supposed to think of that?'

'There is no time for this, Rachel.'

'Is it because your own precious world's threatened? Is that why no one's here?'

'I will explain, but not now. You must help me to reach Yemi.'

'Help *you*!' Rachel shouted the words, pointing up. 'These children are offering everything because of Larpskendya, because of things he's told them! Where are the other Wizards?'

'I offer myself,' Serpantha said, his gaze steadily on her. 'I have nothing more to give than that.'

Rachel felt like screaming. 'Is this all we're worth to you? The life of one Wizard? After all that's happened, is that all we were ever worth to you?'

'No. You deserve far more.'

'Yes. We do!' Rachel turned her back on Serpantha. 'We do!'

The pack of Griddas had appeared overhead, their angular heads lowered. The mere sight of them appalled the sentinels, but they somehow kept their discipline, spreading out to shield Yemi on all sides. Rachel felt sharp nips on her flesh. It was the Essa: agitated, wondering what to do. They pulled at her cheeks. 'Look!' they cried.

The spectrum girl with red hair had left the sentinel unit. Carried by her thrill-seeker, she had set off to confront the Griddas.

'She's gone to negotiate,' Rachel said hollowly. 'That was Albertus Robertson's last instruction to the spectrums. It must be happening everywhere.'

The girl rose into the clouds. The Griddas did not slow down. They headed straight for her. Rachel shook with the effort to control her anger, barely able to choke out the words. 'See what that girl's prepared to do!' she yelled at Serpantha. 'Where are the Wizards? Gultrathaca said you couldn't care less about us. Have you just been using us all this time? Using us to expose the High Witches, then lure the Griddas to Orin Fen? I suppose the Wizards have set a trap there, so you can get rid of your last enemy.'

Serpantha looked intently at her. 'Do you really believe that, Rachel?'

'What else can I believe?'

'There is no trap,' Serpantha said. 'The Griddas won't find any Wizards on Orin Fen, or perhaps one, if my brother made it back. There have never been many Wizards, Rachel. Of those few born most died during the endless war against the Highs. The remainder were killed when Heebra unleashed the Griddas. Larpskendya hid that from you. I hid it from you. We had to. Only fear of us kept the Witches in check. If they had ever discovered the truth about how few Wizards there are, no world would have been safe.' He put his hand against Rachel's hot cheek. 'That is why Larpskendya has been absent so often from Earth. Do you think he would ever have left your world exposed if he had any choice? Do you think I would have done? Rachel, the reason we are the only two who have visited your world is that there are no others. Larpskendya and I are the last of the Wizards.'

In the sky above, the red-haired girl waited for the Griddas. While she did so, she attempted to hold the nerve of her thrill-seeker by looking into his eyes. Finally, however, even he turned and fled. He knew that only by doing so could he save her life. He fled to the only place there was a chance of keeping her safe – back to the sentinel unit.

As the Gridda pack closed in they divided, approaching from several directions, choosing specific targets among the children. The sentinel unit's leader flew along the line, keeping them steady.

Serpantha, with a sweep of his mind, tried to take in everyone. Rachel felt the start of an immense spell to shield the children – but the Wizard was still too weak to sustain it. Even if Serpantha possessed all his strength, Rachel realized, he could not have held back so many Griddas single-handedly. She prepared to use her own spells, knowing they were not adequate, either.

An initial ripple of attack spells came from the Griddas. The sentinels hastily erected a barrier, withstanding it – just.

'Awake! Awake!' murmured the Essa.

Yemi was rubbing his eyes, wiping away the sleepiness. The animals on the shore were also shaking themselves, stretching, flexing their limbs. Then, with a great clamour of wings, the bird flocks scattered.

Rachel gathered Yemi up in her arms. 'Can you understand what's happening?' She tilted his face toward the Griddas.

Yemi saw them, gazed back at Rachel, showing no concern.

Fola shook his arm hard. 'Stupid boy! *Odé!* Don't you see?' She peered up. 'Look at the monsters there!'

Yemi smiled at his sister, kissed her.

'We need to protect the children everywhere,' Rachel said. 'Yemi, try to understand. Please.'

The Essa raced over to a nearby seagull. They surrounded the bird and brought it back to Yemi. Rachel spread her hands to show they meant to protect everything. How could she make him understand?

'Yemi,' she said. 'I can't shift us. But we have to get everyone away from here.'

Overhead there was a groan – the sentinel unit's defence had been breached.

Then more children arrived. From the west they came, firing spells: three more sentinel units, led by Heiki. The flank of the Gridda pack recoiled. They drew back, trying to recover. But Heiki had no intention of giving the Griddas time to recover. At her signal, the eyes of the sentinel children all turned black. Simultaneously they launched their death spells.

Rachel had never felt anything like the power of the combined deaths. Even the Gridda pack-leader quavered when she felt what was seeking her out. Just before the deaths reached the Griddas, Yemi glanced up. He placed a cordon around the Griddas. He protected them. The deaths struck uselessly against it.

'What are you doing?' Rachel screamed. 'Yemi! Yemi! The children! Protect the children, not the Griddas!'

Yemi looked at her: an indescribable look. He closed his eyes. The animals on the shore did the same. And suddenly everyone – even the Griddas – felt themselves seized.

Yemi chuckled. He threw out his arms.

25

the touch
of witches

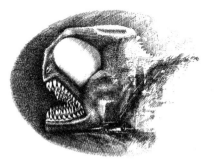

Witches. Skies of Witches. Witches everywhere. Millions upon millions, rising through the lucid air of Orin Fen.

As Eric cancelled the final layer of protection, that was what he saw.

But not High Witches – and not Griddas.

He squinted at the brightness of the planet, trying to understand. Beyond the Witches he saw oceans; he saw radiant cities; he saw mountains without snow.

Was this some kind of trick of Gultrathaca's?

One glance at her shocked face showed otherwise. Eric probed into the magic of the new Witches. He realized they were related to the Highs. The fearsome Griddas were in some way also their more distant descendants.

How could that be?

As the Witches arrived, Eric tried to understand what

faced him. The first thing he noticed was that the Witches were beautiful. They were beautiful in the same way that Larpskendya and Serpantha were beautiful. It was the colours. Eric thought he had seen all the shades of a Wizard's eyes, but he was wrong. It took the light of a wilder sun to bring out every hue. Looking at these Witches, Eric saw them all.

It was a warm sun, an old sun, but these Witches seemed older. Eric could hardly bear to look at them, or to look away.

The Orin Fen Witches shared the same height and proportions as High Witches, though they were more slender, and clawless, with human faces – a single, modest jaw.

The true Witches, Eric realized. When a group of the females left all those millions of years ago, not all had left. The original Witches – these Witches – had stayed with the Wizards.

Slowly the Witches took up a position until they girdled the planet. They confronted the Gridda army. Then, together, they opened their arms.

An invitation? Gultrathaca reeled, baffled. She had expected a battering of Wizards, not this. Confused questions were being raised by her commanders. Where were the Wizards? Disguised? Had the Wizards sneaked behind somehow, while these creatures provided a distraction?

The Witches did nothing to alarm the Griddas. They were patient, waiting until the Griddas overcame their surprise. They made no sudden movements. They merely held out their arms.

Those imploring arms!

Gultrathaca shook herself, feeling an unaccountable urge. Part of her wanted to accept those arms, to be led towards the surface – away from the horror of the sun. Was a spell at work? No. It was something else, something extraordinary about the Witches themselves.

Gultrathaca fought a yearning to go towards them.

All around her, the Gridda army felt similar emotions. The packs were primed for Wizards and death, not this welcome! Should they attack the strangers? Their bodies were ready to fight, but there was no aggression in the Witches to set them off. On the contrary, the Witches were all anxiousness of gaze – and not for themselves. They gazed at the Griddas, as if seeing torture and mutilation beyond belief in their features.

The infant Griddas responded first. For all their noisy bravado, the journey had been long, and they were tired; they wanted the refuge of a tunnel; they wanted these Witches. They started to drift towards them. Touching seemed the most natural thing. The infants touched, breathlessly exploring. Seeing the infants were discomforted by the light, the Witches diminished it. They darkened their own skies, until the cities fell into shade and the big eyes of the infants opened fully.

Pack-leaders restrained some of the infants, but they could not stop them all. Then a few of the maturer Griddas joined them. They slipped tentatively across the divide between themselves and the Witches. The lines began to merge. A leader glanced desperately at Gultrathaca for assistance as her entire pack deserted her. Witches and Griddas intermingled, touching and not touching, curious about their physical differences, repelled and attracted.

But not fighting! Not fighting! All around Gultrathaca could see the blood-lust of her Griddas cracking. Warlike instincts were being replaced by something she could not understand.

'No! No!' she raged. 'It is a trick!' She raced along the lines of her Griddas. 'The Wizards are hiding! They are cowards! Find them on the world below! Find them!'

A few Griddas followed her order, but as soon as they reached the Witches their resolve faded. They slowed, came to a stop, joined the infants.

Gultrathaca saw that even her staunchest pack-leaders would no longer obey her.

She had almost forgotten Eric. He lay in her arms, staring with open mouth at what was happening. The prapsies stood on Eric's shoulders, twitching excitedly.

Gultrathaca stared out over her forces. They were no longer an army. Griddas and Witches were flying openly together. Gultrathaca heard talk between them. She heard laughter. Even her own pack-sisters had left their defensive posts.

This was not a Wizard trick; Gultrathaca knew that. The Witches meant no harm. Indeed, Gultrathaca wanted nothing more than to be amongst them. How she wanted to! But the sight of something held her back. Jarius was no longer guarded. She flew freely with her sisters, her dishonour forgotten.

Gultrathaca could not allow that.

She summoned a death spell. Like all deaths, it gave her simple advice. It made choices easier. One of the Orin Fen Witches hovered close to her. Her smile was concerned, shy even.

Gultrathaca looked at her and loosed the death. It killed the Witch instantly. Seeing this, for the first time the nearest Witches raised their defences.

And that was enough. The Griddas reacted instinctively. More than instinctively: they reacted the way the High Witches had bred them to react. Their bodies pumped with blood; their claws enlarged. Gultrathaca rushed between the packs, instilling confidence. Contact between Griddas and Witches was broken.

Gultrathaca launched another death spell – or tried.

Eric prevented it – and Gultrathaca knew she had lost that favourite killer forever. It hardly mattered. Other Griddas had begun firing death spells. The Witches fell back, defending themselves. They started to fly away – towards the surface.

A chase!

It was a mistake. Gridda pursuit reflexes flickered alive at once. Suddenly pack on pack were descending the skies to get at the Witches.

'Please don't,' whispered Eric. 'Gultrathaca, you can still stop this.'

'I could,' Gultrathaca agreed.

She kicked him away.

Eric fell gasping, in explosive pain. There was no chance to collect his thoughts for any kind of anti-spell. The prapsies tumbled beside him, trying to stop his fall.

Jarius came for Eric. Griddas from her own pack tried to stop her, but she fought through them. Sweeping Eric and the prapsies up, she breathed life-giving oxygen back inside their lungs. They lay in her claws, only half-conscious.

The Orin Fen Witches were retreating to their cities. The Griddas followed. Now that a true fight had started, Jarius could tell that the Witches were not able to adequately defend themselves. They were more magical than the Griddas, but inferior fighters.

Jarius fled with all her speed, but there was no escaping the packs. Carrying Eric and the prapsies made her easy to catch, and several members of her own pack went after her.

Jarius had no choice any longer. With a final gasp of effort, wriggling from the grasp of an infant, she flew towards the planet. Where else could she go now? Where else?

Larpskendya watched it all, concealed by the corona of Orin Fen's sun.

His spells were still recovering. For weeks he had been hounded across all space, never able to get away from the Gridda packs for long. Finally, his shifting spells had made a last great effort. They brought him home.

As Larpskendya saw what was taking place, he almost wished they had not.

He had deliberately hidden, knowing that if the Griddas glimpsed him they would attack without question.

And then he had seen the beautiful, open-souled Witches of Orin Fen try. Those arms! How could it work? Against the violence of the Griddas, it could never work – but it nearly had.

Larpskendya felt tears on his face. What use were they? What use were tears now? Over the centuries all the efforts of the last Wizards had gone into shrouding Orin Fen. Had they been wrong? How could they have anticipated Eric's extraordinary talent? There had never been anything like him. If we had allowed the Witches to join in the endless war, Larpskendya realized, they might now be better prepared. The Witches had wished it. Always they had asked for it. We loved them too much, Larpskendya thought. We kept them apart from war – a terrible mistake.

And then Larpskendya had seen Jarius, and for a moment he had hope again. Here was a Gridda, defending Eric with all her heart.

When Jarius failed as well, rushing with Eric towards Orin Fen, Larpskendya knew it was time to show himself. There was no way to save the Witches, not against so many Griddas. Well, he would do what he could. He would at least give the Witches a chance to reach the cities, where they could defend themselves more effectively.

He flew towards the Griddas.

Gultrathaca recognized him before she saw him: how could she mistake that singular, awesome scent! She approached with the rest of her pack. As she did so, Larpskendya gave her a signal she thought only the Griddas knew.

'No,' she said, laughing. 'Not a personal challenge. I won't give you the satisfaction of that. I will decide the method of your death, Wizard.'

She ordered three packs forward.

On Orin Fen thousands of Witches turned around and started despairingly flying towards Larpskendya. The Griddas held them back.

'There will be no help for you, Wizard,' Gultrathaca said.

Larpskendya raised his defences. Even the three large Gridda packs sent against him wavered when they felt the authority of the spells. But not for long. The Wizard was alone, and they were many, and the battle-blood the Highs had bred in the Griddas would have driven them on now even if they had no chance of victory. Gultrathaca knew Larpskendya might slay all three packs. He could not, however, slay all the packs. Even the great Larpskendya lacked that strength.

As the packs closed in, Larpskendya was a solitary figure against the backdrop of space.

But the Griddas stopped before they reached him.

They stopped to look in amazement at butterflies and children.

26

the fatal gift

Every child of Earth was over Orin Fen.

Yemi had brought them all: the deepers, the thievers, the gangs; the gifted and ungifted; flyers, and those who could never fly; everyone. Many sentinels had been shifted in mid-battle. Spectrums joined them, held by their thrill-seekers. Yellow butterflies flapped, their wings in sunlight.

The youngest children congregated near Yemi. Their eyes followed his, wherever he gazed. Everywhere children were blinking, adjusting to the glory of Orin Fen's sun.

'What's happening? What's happening?' the Essa asked, clutching Rachel. The dazzling world of Orin Fen beckoned to them, and Rachel felt it, too. Like them, for reasons she could not explain, she was transfixed. She wanted to fly towards the surface.

'I've got to find Eric,' she told Serpantha.

'I know,' he said. 'And I must find my brother.'

Eric was not far. Jarius still held him. Rachel approached her warily.

'I'm all right,' Eric said. 'Don't be afraid of this Gridda, Rach. I don't know her name, but she kept me and the prapsies safe. She kept us alive.'

Rachel gazed at Jarius's harsh face. The Essa did so too, not trusting it. Jarius understood and turned instead to Rachel. 'I will take care of Eric,' she said. 'It is Yemi you must go to. He may ... he may try to do too much.'

'Go on, Rach,' Eric said. 'Get to Yemi, but stay away from Gultrathaca. Watch out for her.'

Gultrathaca stared in disbelief at the reunion of Serpantha and Larpskendya taking place nearby. What had happened here? A Wizard who should be dead; children who could never have made such a journey; even the presence of Griddas, the ones sent to invade Earth. Surprised, jolted out of the glow of battle, those Griddas could not wait to continue – but who should they attack now?

Gultrathaca reassessed the balance of power. It had altered. She no longer had numerical superiority, not with all the children to aid the Orin Fen Witches.

If the Griddas fought, she realized, they would lose everything.

Floating close to Yemi, she expected the old infuriating smile. This time, however, Yemi had no smile for her – as if realizing at last that she could not stand it. As she turned away, Larpskendya and Serpantha approached.

'End it here,' Larpskendya said to her. 'You can stop it now, Gultrathaca. A simple command to the packs.'

'What?' Gultrathaca said. 'Before the fight has even begun?'

'How many Griddas would you have die first?' This time it was Serpantha who had spoken.

Gultrathaca stared at him. 'Are you still alive? What do I have to do to kill you?'

'You should be asking a different question,' Serpantha said. 'How can you hold the Griddas back? They will fight, unless you order otherwise.'

'Why should I?'

'There is no way you can win a battle. All the Griddas will be killed.'

'Do you really think a Gridda values life more than battle, whatever the outcome? I'll kill you, Serpantha, before I die. I swear that.'

Larpskendya assessed her. 'We offer an alternative.'

'Let me guess,' Gultrathaca said. 'Some sort of peace. How meek that sounds. Do you believe the Griddas will settle for co-operation with anyone? We'll have war instead, Wizard. It is all we know.'

'That is not true.' Larpskendya's view took in all the packs. 'Most of the Griddas have only known peace. The majority here are infants. I doubt any of them have experienced battle outside the playfulness of the birthing tunnels. If you made them fight, this would be their first battle.'

'I remember my first battle as the best.'

'Do you have the courage to lead them in another way?'

Gultrathaca smiled thinly. 'What would you have us do, Wizard? Relinquish our death spells to play with the children of Earth?'

'What do you think is happening here?' Larpskendya said earnestly. 'You sound like a High Witch, seeing enemies in all places. There *are* no enemies. The children

235

have no quarrel with the Griddas. Nor the Wizards. Only the Highs wanted the endless war. And look at what they did to all Griddas, Gultrathaca, while they waged that war. They put you underground, mutilated you, despised you, denied you everything.'

'We revenged that,' Gultrathaca said. 'This is our fight now, our choice to fight.'

'No,' Larpskendya said. 'You are still following the aims of the High Witches. They manufactured the Griddas for war, but you deserve more than they made you for.'

Gultrathaca glanced at the distant Jarius. 'I have seen the alternative to war. I would rather be dead than like her.'

'Are you sure?' Larpskendya came closer. 'War is not all the Griddas want. I think you know that. You felt it as well. I saw the reaction the Griddas had when they first saw the Witches. Even you felt something, Gultrathaca. I watched you.'

'It was not what I *wanted*!'

'It can be.' Larpskendya paused, seeking a way to make her understand. 'The High Witches constructed you, but the call of blood is just a reflex, nothing more. If Heebra could be here now, see from her grave, she would expect you to fight, Gultrathaca. But she was wrong about the Griddas. You can be more than her machines. You already chose a different destiny when you left the tunnels. And you can again.'

Gultrathaca hesitated. Were her instincts mistaken? Everything inside her shrieked for battle. The pack-leaders were ready, of course. Like her they had trained for it all their lives. She glared at Yemi, aching to see that smile again so that she could smash it. His face remained stony.

She studied the Gridda infants. If she raised a battle-cry, no doubt they would respond. But if they spent more time with the Witches, would they still go with her so lightly into battle? Would they?

Yet to accept terms from a Wizard – any terms – how was that acceptable? Anything but war now was not a victory at all. Not *her* victory anyway, or that of the Griddas. Instead, it would be the victory of Larpskendya and Serpantha. It would be the victory of the Orin Fen Witches. In some way it would also be the victory of Eric and Yemi – and perhaps even Jarius.

Gultrathaca could not bear that thought.

She prepared a death spell, one of her favourites. Not for Yemi. That would have been her preferred target, but a waste. She aimed it at Serpantha.

'Do not do this!' Larpskendya roared.

Gultrathaca raised the battle-cry. It had the intended effect. The infants instantly lost any uncertainty. Ordering her own pack forward, Gultrathaca signalled towards Serpantha. She expected Larpskendya to protect his brother, but he did not do so. Instead, he moved aside. He left Serpantha alone.

Eric called out, 'What are you doing?'

'Don't interfere,' Larpskendya told him.

'You've no idea what skills I've got now,' Eric said.

'I do know, Eric. Stay back.'

Rachel glanced nervously towards Serpantha. 'Don't you want any help at all? We'll all help. You know that, don't you?'

Serpantha smiled at her. 'Yes, I do. Stay a safe distance.' Serpantha said nothing more. He waited.

The Griddas could not understand. They glanced at

Gultrathaca. At her gesture, the entire pack initiated their death spells at once against Serpantha.

Yemi immediately shifted in front of the Wizard.

The deaths withered against his shield.

As Gultrathaca ordered the packs to fire more spells, Heiki exchanged a frightened look with Albertus Robertson. 'Shouldn't we do something?' she asked. 'We have to!'

'No,' Albertus answered. 'This war has gone on an eternity. Let the Wizards and Griddas play it out between themselves, if we can.'

'But I can't stand doing nothing!'

'Can't you?' Albertus turned to her. 'Neither can the Griddas. They have to fight. Part of them can't accept anything else. The Wizards realize that.'

Gultrathaca brought more of the Griddas into the assault, until immense numbers of packs were discharging every kind of spell at Serpantha. None affected him. He did not even have to defend himself. Yemi held the attacks off.

'The boy's power is not infinite,' Gultrathaca told the packs.

'You can't reach me,' Serpantha told her. 'Don't you understand? Even if you overpower Yemi, every child here will defend me – or any other target you choose.'

Like a procession, the packs continued to send their finest spells against Serpantha without any impact. Eventually, the heart went out of them. Gultrathaca gave no order, but the attacks gradually petered out. Then they ceased altogether.

Serpantha was unharmed. Yemi was unharmed. Many Griddas were exhausted.

'You think it is over?' Gultrathaca said to Larpskendya. Scarcely moving her claw, she sent a quiet assault Eric's way. It was so unexpected that he did not destroy it in time. One of the prapsies jumped in front of him. The spell struck the edge of its wing, breaking it. 'Oh, Eric,' the prapsy said. 'Oh.' It flapped the useless wing. The other prapsy ran across Eric's shoulder to hold the wing in place.

'Well?' Gultrathaca screamed at Eric, seeing his fury. 'If you have the power, use it! Finish me!' She looked at her army, and knew it was already defeated. 'Finish us all off!'

Eric listened to the prapsy's mild whimpers of pain.

'Don't!' Rachel snapped, flying towards him.

'Stay out of this!' Eric said – though he wavered, hearing her voice.

Seeing his indecision, Gultrathaca fired another spell, this time aimed directly at the prapsies. Yemi stopped it, but the intention was obvious.

'How dare you! How *dare* you!' Eric did not even need to think. He had long ago perfected his killing technique for the Griddas. He knew how to unravel their magic. He could kill them at once, or he could play out their ruination forever.

Yemi threw a shield around the Griddas. He looked at Eric. Rachel had never seen the look of fear on Yemi's face she saw now.

'Get away, Yemi!' Eric warned. 'I've made my decision.'

Yemi shook his head.

Eric probed the shield. It contained an almost limitless number of spells to guard the Griddas, but Eric had more ways to penetrate it. He started the dismantlement. As Yemi felt the shield failing, he squealed. He called on his butterflies. They surrounded him. They gave him all their strength. It was not enough.

And then Yemi put his little fingers over his eyes and spoke through his tears.

'Stop, please!' he begged. 'Eric, stop it! Eric! Eric! Eric!'

Eric heard him. He heard everyone. He heard Larpskendya and Rachel and Serpantha and Albertus, all those who loved him, all shouting, all striving to reach him. No, he thought. I'm going to finish it. He avoided Yemi's defences. Suddenly he realized that he did not even need to destroy Yemi's spells. He could side-step them; he could alter them. He did so. He removed Yemi's shield and gripped the hearts of the Griddas. He was the spell-destroyer. His was the fatal gift. He knew it; finally he knew what had frightened the spectrums so much.

There was no magic in the universe that could stop him.

The Griddas were disintegrating. Some were alone. Others were held by the Orin Fen Witches. Where they could, the Witches had gone to the Griddas, trying to keep them intact. Eric saw Gultrathaca. She shook as all the magic was loosened from her cells. Larpskendya was making his way unsteadily towards her. He reached her. She shuddered in his arms, like a child. He held her, in tears tried to hold her together.

Eric felt warmth near his ear. 'Eric,' the prapsy whose wing had been broken said to him. 'Don't, boys.' It kissed his eyes. It made him look down. Eric looked. Jarius was under him, still clutching him, her face jolting.

Eric gazed at her, and beyond her. He saw Fola, unable to comfort Yemi. He saw Witches crying. He saw Serpantha crying.

He ended it.

The Griddas breathed again.

All except one. She did not want to breathe. Gultrathaca wanted to die, but Larpskendya held her tightly. He held onto her life.

27

the WIZARD's PROMISE

Eric had only just withdrawn his destruction in time.

The Griddas, strewn across space, barely seemed to know where they were. Drifting aimlessly, the infants gathered in small groups, not sure why. Older Griddas felt their bodies; they felt wrong.

The prapsies held tightly to Eric, helping him to recover from what he had almost done. He shook as he peered between the warmth of their feathers. And wherever he peered spiders were on the move. Soldiers were searching for enemies they could not find. Healer spiders called to one another, understanding how ill their owners were, without understanding what to do.

But there was healing of a kind on Orin Fen the spiders had not dreamed of.

In graceful lines, the Witches ascended. Each took a

Gridda into her private care, into her arms. Part of Orin Fen had been put in deep shade. The Witches carried the Griddas there, towards the consolation of the dark.

Gultrathaca was one of the last to be taken. There was a Witch waiting for her as well, but Larpskendya carried her himself. He held her wordlessly, because she was not yet ready for words – and Larpskendya was not ready, either. As they gazed at each other a mystery of feelings made them both weep. Larpskendya found a place where there were other Griddas, ones Gultrathaca knew. Should he leave her now, or should he stay? He did not want to leave her.

Above him, Jarius still held Eric. As one of the Orin Fen Witches embraced her, ready to take her to the surface, Eric said, 'No. Wait. I – what is your name? I don't even know your name.'

'I am Jarius,' she said.

'Thank you,' Eric murmured, touching her face. 'Thank you, Jarius.'

As she gave Eric and the prapsies back to Rachel, and was being led away, Jarius turned to the Witch who held her. 'I wish to be taken to my own pack,' she said. 'They need me now.'

Rachel spent a moment repairing a broken wing. Then she, Eric and the prapsies followed Jarius as she was gradually taken down to the shadowed part of Orin Fen. And then, while Larpskendya stayed below with Gultrathaca, everyone else suddenly seemed to arrive beside them at once. For a few moments no one said anything, but the prapsies soon broke the silence. They were hungry, and sick of being quiet all the time. Eric took an ear-bashing, and knew it was not the only one he would get.

Everyone watched until the last of the Griddas had disappeared below. 'What will happen?' Rachel asked Serpantha at last. 'What will happen to the Griddas now?'

'Until they recover, their needs will be taken care of,' he answered. 'After that, they will have some choices to make. We will all have choices.'

'Will they still want to fight?'

Serpantha smiled. 'Perhaps, but I am hopeful. If anything can persuade them otherwise, the devotion of the Witches will do so.'

'And you?' Rachel stared up into Serpantha's eyes. 'What about the Wizards? If there are only two of you left, when you die, will there...'

'No.' He kissed her. 'Each generation a few Wizards are born. If the endless war is finally over, Larpskendya and I will soon have company. I look forward to that. I look forward to many things.'

Eric started to shake again. The prapsies quietened down at once, steadying him. 'I nearly killed them all,' he whispered, raising his hands. 'How could I have done that? Oh, I nearly did.'

'But you held back,' Serpantha said. 'That was harder. That required more strength.' He lifted Eric's chin. 'There is greatness in you. Don't you know that yet?'

Eric stared at his hands. 'I'm frightened. What...what am I, Serpantha?'

'You are a forerunner, Eric. A beginning of something. There has been nothing like you before. I suspect there will be a different destiny for all of us, because of you – and those you lead.'

'Those I lead?'

'Don't you realize?' said a voice. 'Even now?' It was

Albertus Robertson. He and a few other spectrums were close beside Eric, observing him intently.

'Realize what?' Eric said.

Both of Albertus's girl thrill-seekers laughed. They glanced briefly at each other, held hands, smiled – a parting smile. Then one of the girls held Albertus's face in her hands and kissed him. Afterwards she breathed deeply and turned to Eric. She waited, her expression full of yearning.

'What's happening?' Eric asked.

'I am not the natural leader of the spectrums,' Albertus said.

'You're not?'

'No, Eric. You are.'

'What?' Eric said. 'But the ears …'

Albertus shook his head. 'Are you still measuring those you meet by how they appear? Surely you've learned that lesson by now … besides, the spectrums may soon be altering again. I'm not certain in what way.'

'But – how do you know I'm your leader?'

'We've always known,' Albertus said. 'However something told us not to reveal it to you until now. And there was another reason we did not tell you, Eric. We were frightened of what you can do.'

The thrill-seeker girl who had left Albertus stared at Eric. She wanted to go to him, but she needed his permission first.

'Are you still frightened?' Eric asked Albertus.

'No.' A complex expression crossed Albertus's face, and suddenly Eric could hear thousands of voices. It was the voices of all the spectrums opening up to him. The thoughts were not chaos; he heard each one clearly, personally.

The girl could wait no longer. 'I was always your thrill-seeker,' she said. 'If you wish it, I will be. Say that you do. I have waited so long.'

'I don't need –' Eric began – but she would not let him say no. She took him in her arms and, as soon as he felt her touch, Eric knew it was right. He did not feel embarrassed.

The prapsies watched. They saw the look Eric gave the girl – the same private one he shared with them. Upset, but not wanting to spoil this special moment for him, they stayed still. They tried to pretend they did not exist at all.

'What's up with you two?' Eric said loudly.

'Nothing,' one prapsy said. 'We're fine, boys.'

'Thought I'd forgotten you, eh?' Eric said. 'Get up here, you flipping idiots. Introduce yourselves. She's going to have to get used to you, so help her.' The prapsies sprang from his shoulders, hovering beside the girl. 'Say hello,' Eric ordered them.

While the girl introduced herself, a flash of sunshine lit up Orin Fen.

Drawn by the intricacies of light, and encouraged by the Witches, most of the children had already started heading towards the planet. Deepers plunged into the golden oceans to discover what wondrous life swam there. Others went further out across Orin Fen, to the exalted mountain heights. There was no snow, but surely there would be something else … As for the thrill-seekers, they seemed to have gone completely wild. They whirled and soared across Orin Fen, and for a brief time, as Rachel watched, it appeared that even the spectrums had almost forgotten themselves as they took in the beauty of the yellow-brown skies. Rachel saw other children. Some were escorting more timid youngsters, or those with little magic, helping them to explore the strangeness without fear. Rachel looked for those she knew: Marshall, Paul, more than she could name, brave children.

'I want to go there,' Eric said, pinching her. 'Hey, Rach, you coming?'

She hesitated.

'What's up?' he asked. 'You want to go somewhere else?'

'Home,' she said. 'I want to go home.' Then she laughed. 'But I want to go to Ool as well! I've got to take these ones back' – she squinted at the Essa dancing with happiness around her head – 'and I want to see the storm-whirls, and talk with the Detaclyver. And most of all I want to go to Ithrea. I have to be sure that Morpeth's safe.'

'Well,' Eric said, 'I can't take you to any of those places. But I can do one thing.'

Rachel felt shouts of joy. They came from inside her. Eric had freed her shifting spells. Her eyes turned blue as they crept up to be alongside the flyers and see what they had missed.

'Bright skies! Bright skies!' the Essa cried, staring at the colours.

'Oh, so that's what you like,' Heiki said to the Essa. She made her own eyes dazzling, trying to persuade a few of the Essa to join her.

Serpantha had been peering beyond Orin Fen, into the emptiness of space. Rachel noticed his uncertainty. 'What is it?' she said.

'Oh, many things,' he answered. 'I will not delay your return home, or any of the other places you wish to go, but it would honour me if you could find another reason in your heart to join me on Ool. Calen and the last of the

High Witches are still imprisoned. I would like you to be there with me when they are released.'

'Didn't they...betray the Wizards?' Heiki said. 'Especially you.'

'Betrayed? Yes, I suppose they did. There have been so many betrayals. But whose was the first? Who is to say what set the High Witches down their terrible path? Were the Wizards entirely blameless? In those ancient days, when there was no threat to our supremacy, did the Wizards do everything they could to persuade those first Witches? When they wanted to leave Orin Fen, who asked them to stay? Larpskendya and I made a promise to each other: that no matter what happened, we would never lose faith, not in you, nor in the Witches, wherever their hatred had taken them.' Serpantha smiled sadly. 'In any case, does one betrayal deserve another? Would you have me leave the Highs in their chains?'

'No,' Heiki answered. No. I...I wouldn't.'

'I'll come with you,' Rachel said. 'Of course I will.'

She held Serpantha's robe, for a while lost in its silken feel. Then she looked up. Strangely, while almost all the other children were now on Orin Fen, Yemi had stayed behind. He stared longingly down at the surface, but he did not fly towards it. Instead, he clung to Fola while looking at Rachel, waiting for her.

'What's wrong?' she asked, flying over. 'Yemi, what's the matter?'

'He doesn't want to leave you,' Fola said. 'I told him you no mind, but he never listens to me, you know that.' She half-laughed. 'He says he's always leaving you, and he doesn't want to, but –'

'I know. It's all right.' Rachel brought Yemi into her

arms and held him tightly. Several of the Essa naturally crossed over to him; they couldn't help themselves. 'You've got something you have to do, haven't you?' Rachel whispered to him.

Fola smiled. 'Yes! He tried before, but it was too hard. No more. Oh, no!'

Forests flashed in Yemi's eyes: the plants of a purple-skied world: Trin.

'Yes, go now,' Rachel said. 'Don't wait for me. I'll come when I can. Go to them.'

Yemi's gaze took in the miraculous colours of Orin Fen lighting up the children below him. There was no need for him to say anything. Rachel understood exactly how he felt. He glanced at her one more time. Then, amid a flutter of wings and a giggle of wonder, he, Fola and all the Camberwell Beauty butterflies vanished. They left behind a trail of yellow sparks that faded only slowly.

Rachel's eyes were moist. Below her, Witches beckoned with their elegant arms, inviting her down. 'If we're going to Ool, we should go now,' she said to Serpantha. 'But I wish I knew Morpeth was safe.'

'He is,' murmured a voice. 'He is.'

Larpskendya had returned from the shadows of Orin Fen. 'I heard you planned to leave, and I thought you might do so before saying goodbye. My spells would not allow that!' He held her shoulders, his eyes shining. 'Ithrea is safe, Rachel. The Griddas never discovered it, but even if they had I wonder how they would have conquered it. Trimak, Fenagel, Leifrim, Morpeth – there is a dedication amongst them, as amongst you all, that I cherish.' He stared at her. 'Before you leave for Ool with my brother, may I ask you to accompany me on a short journey? I would like to show you my world. It seems only fair, as I have had the privilege of knowing yours.'

'Orin Fen is ... so beautiful,' Rachel said, gazing down.

'Yes, but no more so than your own world,' Larpskendya replied. 'There is beauty everywhere. On Earth I have seen such wonders, and not only from the most magical. I have never seen tenderness or resolve greater than that shown by the parents of your world. Nor have I seen more courage than that shown by children, or should I say one child: you, Rachel.'

Rachel lowered her face. 'Oh, I ... I didn't do so much,' she said. 'I haven't got as much magic as Yemi. I can't do what Eric can do. They were more important in the end.'

Larpskendya gazed at her. 'No. That is not true. And even if it were, do you think I would love you any the less for it?'

Rachel buried her face in his robe.

Larpskendya lifted her face and kissed her. He laughed. 'Will you follow me, or do you want to lead?'

Before she could answer the prapsies started chasing the Essa. They had wanted to do so ever since they first saw them, and even the Essa could not out-dodge a prapsy. 'Behave, boys,' Eric said, winking at them. He stared down at Orin Fen. 'Where shall we look first, then, Rach? Those cities look good.'

The Essa whispered in Rachel's ear. She laughed.

'Well?' Eric said. 'Decided yet?' He waited. Heiki waited. Serpantha and Larpskendya, all of them.

Grinning, Rachel flew towards Orin Fen, not towards the cities, but the quieter places, higher up, the mountain peaks of that lovely world.

The magic of all children has been released. Throughout the skies of Earth they swoop, crossing continents, changing shape, diving to the ocean depths and playing the deadly new spell-games.

Rachel bides her time, watching the skies for what she knows will happen – the invasion of the Witches. But when it comes, it is not in the way anyone expects, and there is also a new enemy — the huge, terrifying Gridda-breed. To confront them will require all of Rachel and her brother Eric's skill and courage, as they embark on a journey that takes them to Ool, home of the Witches — a world where mountains move and breathe, the sun never pierces the clouds and the snows are alive.

The Wizard's Promise is a story of dazzling excitement, breathtaking action and memorable characters — the child Yemi, too young to understand the vast scope of his powers; Eric, the spell-destroyer, who will discover his true destiny; and the mysterious Wizards, led by Larpskendya, whose influence may decide the fate of everyone on Earth and beyond. Like *The Doomspell* and *The Scent of Magic*, it is compulsive reading.

A Dolphin ★ Paperback

Cover illustrations
by Geoff Taylor

UK £4.99

ISBN 1-85881-844-3

9 781858 818443